NOT WITH A WHIMPER

Peter Zolotin turned away from the computer and looked around the small confines of the cabin. He had never known claustrophobia before, but Trav was giving him the creeps.

"I have received a response from one of the asteroid miners," the machine said. "It is a cybernetic device like myself, and has no humans aboard. That's not good, Pete."

Zolotin realized what Trav was getting at. It was a conclusion that they had not prepared him for on *Asia*. "Are you saying the Earth has been destroyed?"

"That's incredible. You mean they didn't tell you about the burster?"

"Burster? What's that?"

"Oh, that's just fine." Trav's voice had grown sharper. "Why in the world would they send you here without filling you in on the most important piece of evidence we have?"

The characteristic static of the twinklie system appeared on the screen, and Peter quickly absorbed the data regarding the burster event. Thirty seconds later, he turned away from the device. Why had they deceived him? This was more serious than just losing contact with Earth. This could be . . . Armageddon, Ragnarok, the end of the world.

"Thanks, Trav," Zolotin said. "I think I'm beginning to understand."

BURSTER

Michael Capobianco

BANTAM BOOKS
NEW YORK • TORONTO • LONDON • SYDNEY • AUCKLAND

BURSTER

A Bantam Spectra Book / July 1990

For information address: Bantam Books.

ISBN 0-553-28543-2

Published simultaneously in the United States and Canada

Bantam Books are published by Bantam Books, a division of Bantam Doubleday Dell Publishing Group, Inc. Its trademark, consisting of the words "Bantam Books" and the portrayal of a rooster, is Registered in U.S. Patent and Trademark Office and in other countries. Marca Registrada. Bantam Books, 666 Fifth Avenue, New York, New York 10103.

PRINTED IN THE UNITED STATES OF AMERICA

RAD 0 9 8 7 6 5 4 3 2 1

To Bill Barton, who always maintained that it was *possible to get published with enough perseverence and work, this book is dedicated. Obstinacy and sloth can never be justified.*

Part I

NOT WITH A—

One

Jya Mailin blinked. There was little excitement, not even the sense of wonder that she had expected. Nothing had changed. Yet, she knew intellectually, fourteen years passed as she closed her eyes and opened them again. Stasis was not a new thing, and, as a physicist, she understood how it worked. But there was so little subjective change—not like being sedated, not like a nap, not even like a moment that seems somehow prolonged by a sense of significance.

The cover of the stasis lozenge swung open and she stepped out. Nothing had changed in the Stasis Hall, but at last there was the tiniest feeling that something had really happened. The other scientists in her cohort were also emerging from their vertical coffins. Gas-Giant Planetologist Cory Esquitun, a slender, Filipino woman with a chiseled, handsome face, came first, of course not aged at all; then Larry Taylor, the big-boned, blond Aussie devil, flashing his unreal, tooth-white grin. May suddenly had the notion that they should greet each other, so she said "Hi."

Taylor, the xenobiologist of their little group, let his smile fade. He slid his arm around Cory's shoulders and gave her a little squeeze. "Yeah . . . not much of a ride, was it?"

Cory looked up and down the hallway at the two rows of lozenges, all open now. "Isn't there supposed to be someone here to help us make the adjustment?"

"Maybe this is a better way to get our. . . bearings," said May. "We have been given a few minutes to sort things out, since the experience itself was so minimal. Time to really think about what has happened."

Larry's rather small, blue eyes suddenly seemed to expand. "Shit. Fourteen years. And we must be at Epsilon Indi, or damn near it. And nothing has changed."

May felt like stretching, or rubbing her eyes, or something. She knew that much had changed. Among the more than twelve hundred people aboard the huge starship *Asia*, only the fifty scientists who would conduct the ongoing exploration of the nearest stars had been frozen. The remainder, including her sister Wuji and her family, were fourteen years older, fourteen years different. It was a funny sort of thing to contemplate now that it was real.

And the first proof was coming down the hall. Technical Liaison Roh Ek Sai, called Ex by most, had been a big tubby man with a barrel face and plenty of hair when they had last seen him. Now he was thinner, though still fat, and appeared a subtle caricature of himself. In the overhead lighting his face seemed more shadow than skin, overwhelmed by the lines that time had written there. Odd prickles flowed down the hair on her neck.

"Well," he said, in his familiar husky boom, "you three are the last. From my experience with the others, I know that you are only slowly coming to grips with the reality of your fourteen-year vacation. I know you will be interested to know that we have successfully crossed the three and a half parsecs between Sol and Eps Indi. As you no doubt remember—remember!—*Asia* is about to start the Directed Virtuality deceleration, which will take about three weeks. Any questions?"

"Yes," said Cory, "how are you, how have you been? How are the others?"

Ex chuckled, a low gargling sound. "I am fine. I had my appendix out two years ago—I didn't think they still did that! No, we're okay, Benita and me. We've only had seven deaths on board, no one that any of you knew. May,

your sister is doing well; she has become Entertainment Superintendent for the entire ship. She and Mard have two additional children, and of course Xinli has mastered his karma and is in the Forestry Service."

So. Wuji had made a success of her life. May never would have guessed, especially after the crying jag she had gone on last—well, not last night, of course, although it felt that way. How her sister hated her husband and regretted having given birth to Xinli, and would have quit *Asia* if she could. May felt almost as though she were living in two times synchronicly. It was mind-blowing.

"There is undoubtedly going to be a kind of psychological backlash to your stasis experience," continued Ex. "I would suggest that you take it easy for a while. The Psych staff has been trained to deal with some of the very problems you will be experiencing."

Larry looked at May. "But we haven't changed."

"You may be surprised to find," said Ex, "that you have changed more than you think."

May ate a leisurely lunch in the concourse cafeteria, trying not to look too hard at the people, old and young, at the tables around her. The setting of the room hadn't changed much since she had breakfasted here so many years ago. The tables were pink and salmon now, instead of dark blue, and the floor had been made to look like marble. The outward-curving transparency above looked out on the inner cavity, the huge conical gap that separated the two differentially rotating parts of the ship. The window-studded frustum on the other side still stretched out into infinity like some great technological valley—no change there at all. She sipped black coffee and wondered if there were cobwebs in her house. Perhaps a psychologist would be useful . . . she felt abnormal, divided from everyone else. She was afraid to go see Wuji, although she knew that it was absurd. Wu, whose diapers she had changed, whose thoughts she had been able to read more often than not. She had not varied in the decade before May's stasis—why should she be any different now?

Resolutely, she stood up and waved to one of the busboys. Wu knew she was awake, and she would feel insulted if May didn't see her right now.

She took a lift down to the frustum, barely noticing the change in inertia as the cubicle was shot from the rapidly rotating inner cylinder of the ship into the slower exterior cone. Again a feeling of wanting to put off seeing her sister dragged at May, and she set the vehicle to surface at the nearest intersection. She could do with a walk.

The landscape of the ecoenvironment was just what she needed. It gave her back her assurance that things were neatly measured out by man and nature. The downcurving sky, which of course merged indetectably with the incurving highland on either side, was a suitably ethereal shade of mist green. The smell was clean and naturally complex in the Septemberish breeze. She took the path through the golf course, deliberately tramping through the wild thyme for the odor, and finally came down into Greenglayde Village at the dead-end of her street, marked only by the odd procession of circular hatches on the ground.

Wuji's house was on an adjoining street, Harley, a brown manhole with 141 marked on it. May was let in and climbed down the ladder into the foyer, where a child who looked much like Xinli had—ten years old and with Mard's expressive, mobile eyebrows—stared at her hard and said, "Who are you?"

May met the boy's look and held it. "I'm your aunt. Is Wuji at home?"

"Don't you want to know who I am?" he asked.

She felt a pang of jealousy. This little smart-aleck kid, cute as a mushroom, was something that her sister had made; better than theorems, more profound than anything she would ever do hopping in and out of stasis for a thousand years.

"Sure I do. I didn't think I would have to ask, though."

"My name is Dayuan. They call me Donny at school."

"Is Wuji here or not?"

"I'll get Mom. Just go in the living room."

May took her time, looking at the artifacts and decorations that the "new" Wuji had chosen. Two of the stone statues from India were still in prominent places, but the paintings on the wall were abstract, ugly smears of things that she couldn't imagine her sister picking out. Of course, Mard would have some influence on their choices, but he hadn't seemed the type of man who would interest himself in that sort of thing. There was a musty smell that hadn't been here before.

"May!" Wuji came into the room wearing a stiff-looking, yoked print dress. They stared at each other. Her sister was thirty-nine and looked every year of it. Her hair, once luminously dark, was a dusty pencil-gray, and the skin of her face, though rouged, was sallow and rough. She looked frightened.

"Wu. I'm back."

"Oh, May, I've missed you so much. Come here."

May, crying, went over to her and hugged her. Starched cloth chafed her arms. They pulled apart, and she saw that her sister was too.

"You don't know what it's been like. These years." The words came out of Wuji slowly, deliberately. "It's like we were frozen, not you."

May caught one of her sister's tears on a fingertip, the way she used to do. "Hold on a minute, Wu. Has Mard been—"

"No, it's not that, May. In fact, it's been so damn subtle that I can't say for sure that anything really has changed. Maybe it's just that I have become part of, you know, the upper crust, on the ship. It's like that in a lot of romance novels—you marry the local baron, and then it turns out everybody is so numb and boring and disapproving that you shrivel into a little husk, you know?"

May looked into the mahogany eyes, which were the same as they had been fourteen years ago, red and lined with melted mascara. Her sister always was throwing a tantrum about something or other. Was this any different?

Wuji seemed to know what she was thinking. "I

remember the night before you left, when I was screaming about how bad things were. You probably think I am still on about the same thing. But look, May, fourteen years have worn me down. I think there is something about the closed world in the ship. The designers took care of everything except the people; and the people seem to be rotting or something."

Jya Mailin took a deep breath. She suddenly felt very far from home.

Roh Ek Sai looked around the table at the twelve earnest young men and women who would monitor the deceleration engine as they approached Epsilon Indi. He felt almost as out of place as he had among the awakening scientists. According to the well-reasoned but weird-seeming Plan, each generation of technicians would prepare the next for the subsequent use of the Directed Virtuality machinery. They could have assured competence with the same technique that had been used with the scientists; but an artificial distinction had been made, and thus the DV staff were all in their early thirties, having been teenagers at the time of the voyage's beginning. He supposed that it was a way to engender ambition among the up-and-coming generations. Ex felt even older now, and, if the truth be known, somewhat grotesque.

"All right," he said, sitting back and tightening his belly, "We are gathered together to review our parameters and prepare for descent into the Epsilon Indi system. As you know, we are assigned to prepare a brief for Captain Taranga. Most of this is a formality, of course, but I want you to know that the commanders of this ship have a high regard for your abilities and place complete confidence in you all. Directed Virtuality is an art as much as a science, and there will always be something new to be learned. First, I understand Mr. Colibri has prepared a thorough review of new discoveries in the field. Mr. Colibri."

Colibri pulled his viewpage out of a briefcase and placed it before him on the table. He was a small, dark Italian with beady little eyes. No one knew much about him, except that he came from the West. The man cleared

his throat. "As you know, communication with Earth is somewhat degraded during our near-cee flight because of wavelength problems. Doppler Effect and Relativity as it relates to the passage of time both tend to complicate the already difficult problems associated with amplifying a signal sufficiently to be intelligible at this great distance. As a result, the huge data flow necessary for the description of novel Directed Virtuality control functions, though given high priority, has taken weeks to receive and assemble. We in the DV lab have tried several complete simulations of the new functions and feel that it should be possible to increase the efficiency of our deceleration by a factor of about six percent."

"But it must be emphasized," said a woman named Park, attractive and with the new blond bouffant hairstyle becoming popular among the Rimicans, "that the experiments on Earth have thus far been limited to small, single-vector accelerations and speeds less than point-five cee. There may be a risk involved, and, based on the fact that Tau isn't and will never be fully quantified, I would recommend against—"

"Come now," said Colibri, "we are talking about an effect that has been understood now for twenty-nine years. I have to say that your objection is based on conjecture and has no basis in fact."

Ex waved the two to silence. This, like most everything else, had already been decided, and petty bickering would only increase friction among the staff. "We will arrive at the stellar system—what is it?—seven days earlier if the technique works, correct? I believe the captain is on record as stating that this is a desirable goal. You all can do it, can't you?"

Nods and grunts of assent. Ex, feeling that he had a knack for conducting meetings such as this, said, "All right. Next business. The actual insertion into orbit. That's your cue, Mr. Nhai."

Nhai, a happy looking man with a sparse beard, sat back and acknowledged Roh. "Yes. We have designed a trajectory with multiple-retrograde encounters with Doublejove that will bring us into a suitable orbit around

the planet in only six days. Traveler reconnaissance data has provided a complete rundown on the gravity variations and particle counts. We must say that our picture of the insertion is sufficiently precise to make it almost a certainty that there will be no problems."

Ex thanked the man and asked if there were any further comments. There were none, so he declared the meeting at an end and thanked them all. As they filed out, he thought, I wonder if this is what a kangaroo court is like?

Peter Zolotin leaned against the rough bark and let his head fall back. Tier upon tier of round-lobed oak leaves made a canopy of brazen green that shielded him almost completely from the bright yellow parallels in the sky. When a breeze agitated the trees, tiny, smeared dapples of light painted his shirt and trousers. Saturdays were a thing that made life bearable. Hiking down among the variegated forests of the wild zone seemed always to produce unexpected surprises, even after five years of systematic exploration. Some things, of course, *were* new, planted or modified by the hundreds of crew members whose job was the upkeep of the Environment.

Most often he would explore in the company of Philippe Berouai, a quiet, even morose boy whose silences complemented the mood of the natural places. But Philippe had increasingly begun to hang out at the Media Club. Peter didn't really miss him.

Often he would completely forget that he was in a big container flying through space at unimaginable speeds. He was, for all practical purposes, a native; he remembered little of the three years he had spent on the planet of his birth. The upcurving horizons and striped sky seemed completely natural to him. He could easily attest to the adaptability of the computer housed in the human skull. "What you know is what is right." That was Philippe's favorite saying, and, Peter guessed, he had to agree. Or rather, what you know is what *feels* right. One weekend, with his parents' permission, he had walked completely around the Environment at the bottom; circumnavigated

the world. It was not that difficult to do—he could have done it in one day if he hadn't wanted to camp out in the exotic marsh area. The half that was devoted to farming was kind of boring, but even there the strange smells and odd flowers provided interest. Farther up you could do it in less than an hour, especially with the low gravity. Yet somehow, even this evidence that the world was artificial, merely an inside-out mock-up of the original, did not shake his inner convictions about its solidity, permanence, and "naturalness." All those lovely pictures of a blue and white globe hanging suspended against the insubstantial darkness did nothing to convince him of the "rightness" of that order of things.

Anyway, this love of the Environment did not make him popular with most of his classmates, and, perhaps, there was a different argument for the nature of the human mind. They seemed to have adapted instead to the world of rooms and corridors that formed the outer layers of the spaceship's habitat. It didn't bother them that everything was angular, made of straight lines and simple curves, and obviously manufactured.

The tree was definitely uncomfortable. Peter stood up carefully and rubbed the pressure points to restore circulation. What time was it getting to be? This was one distinct advantage of a real planet—you could supposedly tell time by the position of the sun and stars. Here, there was only a sharply divided day and night.

The nearest lock was less than a quarter of a kilometer away, up toward the pine barren, and Peter started in that direction. The trees crowded around so thickly that there was no sense of being in a trough. These oaks, maples, and beeches—most transplanted here with great difficulty from nurseries on Earth—had done well; Peter had heard that other types of ecosystems required a great deal more care.

He came out into a small grassy hollow. The entry lock was larger than a doorway, about three meters across, with a central manhole for individual access. He pressed the button with the toe of his shoe and watched the portal iris open. Underneath was the floor of the elevator, and

when he had put his weight on it, it responded by taking him down into the lock's vestibule. Peter stole one last glance at the retreating Environment, soaking in the details of the warm green openness. Then the manhole closed with a zip.

Inside, he seemed to feel himself diminished. The philosophizing that he had done looked mean and unreal here. He stepped into a transverse lift and gave it the coordinates of the entrance to Forest Glen, his subdivision. The thing took off and soon deposited him at his destination, once more in the Environment, but within the zone where individual houses filled the underground. He noted for the hundredth time that many of the doorways were obviously not used, some practically buried under leaves and grass clippings. His door, however, looked shiny and functional. The optical element of the door recognized him and it slid open. He climbed down into the house, not thinking anything at all.

No one home. His father was probably working overtime; his mother—who knew? She could be at the Mall or with one of her friends. Peter went to his room and activated his personal videon unit. On the entertainment channels there were the usual live plays and musical performances, but nothing caught his attention. He could work on his graduation thesis, he supposed, until someone came home. He called up the document and paged through it, reading a sentence here and there. Nah! Peter felt a surge of angst that disappeared the moment he pressed the onoff. So much for actually accomplishing anything.

Guilt sprang up from nowhere. These conflicting feelings were becoming a familiar part of his life. The thesis would not be completed on time at the rate he was going. That would mean a downrating of his work code, and possibly counseling sessions with a social worker. He had taken schoolwork seriously for so long; it seemed doubly perverse to let it all go for nothing now. He was becoming the classic underachiever. He still paid attention in class, being unable to think of any better way to spend his time there; and this, along with an uncanny test-taking ability,

produced unrivaled exam scores in most subjects. But the essays that were the heart of any liberal arts education required work that he was unwilling to expend. This laziness had started less than two semesters before, and now his grades were low enough to affect his earnings a great deal. His counselor spent what seemed like hours praising his ability to the skies, demonstrating that his score on certain intelligence tests placed him far ahead of the other students. When Peter claimed that he just had a knack for that sort of thing, the counselor pointed out that *these* tests were designed too well for that. To Peter, it increasingly didn't seem to matter.

The guilt had disappeared, and he was unmotivated again. Well, if his parents didn't care enough to be there, he supposed that he didn't either. Deciding quickly, he changed into a more stylish shirt and shiny shoes that wouldn't get him in trouble.

The Mall was a very big place, in some ways comparable to the Environment. As the natural microecosystem functioned, so, perhaps, did the microeconomy of *Asia*. Peter spent a fair amount of his time here, among the stores and stalls of the ship's thriving productivity. For a population of less than thirteen hundred, *Asia*'s microeconomy seemed remarkably healthy. On a Saturday afternoon like this, Peter swore that the people who weren't here selling commodities were here completing the equation by buying.

Captain Eugenia Taranga pulled on her bathcap. Stepping out onto the flexible lip of the bath, she let the terry-cloth robe slip from her shoulders. She breathed in the lavender-scented steam as she touched a foot into the water. In a rush of momentarily burning water, she was in.

The bath was more of a pool, being five meters by ten. It was, in fact, larger than the apartment that her family had lived in when she was a child, during the early days of the Asian Combine, when the last slums in Zamboanga were cleaned up and modularized housing was installed. There was a console to supply entertain-

ment and drink here, and the floor was laced with flow-direction intakes to provide Jacuzzi or, as she preferred, a simple upwelling that would keep her body at the correct depth.

As was her morning habit, Taranga swam thirteen laps in the hot water and then soaped herself up. She never quite got used to the luxury, and, as a reward for her hard work during her adolescence and young adulthood, it never seemed to be enough. Although the signs of aging that she continually searched her body and face for were still absent, the years aboard *Asia* were somehow tantalizingly unsatisfying. Something about the self-contained, unconnected nature of the generation ship turned accomplishment into a hollow mockery. She would be dead long before the return voyage to Earth, four hundred years in the future. There would be a different captain, a different crew, only the scientists would make the entire trip. The structures of command, the sociological milieu—perhaps these would outlive her, but they were mostly textbook stuff, ideas that went back to the days of the sailing ships.

She immersed herself, and the suds were swept away by flow streams. This was all nonsense, of course. Now that they were here at their first destination, her command would assume a more satisfying, goal-directed aspect. This ennui was her old death-fear raising its slightly disguised head once again. She knew herself well enough, she supposed, so that the little emotions could make no headway against the fortress of her self.

Almost against her will, a memory tore into her consciousness and started to play itself out. She was back in Taipei, walking along the embankment in front of the massively columned, granite Continental Capitol building. It was a fine day in the exceptionally warm winter, and she was wearing a scanty, iridescent silk dress which was appropriately stylish for her office. At twenty-two, she had just been elected as an at-large member of the lower advisory board. Her ambition was satisfied, for the moment, and she was happy. Little did she realize that she was about to be catapulted into a situation in which her

further goals would be completely stymied. The business entities that had sponsored her, financing her campaign and rewarding her generously, found it convenient to have her there, and did not wish her to advance further. She quickly proved herself to be the most able orator and administrator on the lesser board, but to no avail. Four elections came and went, and she was no closer to fulfilling her ambitions. Then came Project Outreach; the captain's position was up for grabs, and it was said that someone from the elective boards would be most appropriate for the job. Somehow, she had been talked into it by old Fang, the senior member of the upper board. Just being in the large, teak-paneled office had an intoxicating effect, and when he had put the question to her, she had said yes. That single word reverberated down the years like a great, bronze gong.

She climbed out of the bath and toweled herself. The large mirror on the wall showed a dark, well-built, youthful body. She walked up to the reflective surface and studied herself more closely, obsessively looking for a sign that she had passed into middle age. Her face, handsome in the Filipino way, was only marred by a little cleft between her eyebrows, and this she had had since she was twenty. When she grimaced, she could see that the skin below her eyes had lost some of its suppleness and didn't contract seamlessly as it once had. It was funny, she thought—aging. When you are young, you see people at different ages and think of their disfigurement as uniquely theirs, something to do with their personality or lifestyle. It is only when you see it starting to happen to you that you fully understand that these people look in the mirror and see these characteristics as the alien ravages of time.

She was still a very beautiful woman, it was true. Her high, rounded cheekbones gave her face a sort of triangular shape; that mysterious, seductive quality was definitely there. At forty-seven, she was someone her husband could still feel proud of. Of course, the Treatments had helped.

She bounced on the balls of her feet and watched the lines of her body flex in response. How many times had

she stood before this mirror and felt this sense of relief? She pulled off the cap, and her hair, still as black as the space between the stars, spilled out and down to her shoulders, regaining the arcing curls of her last perm. She pulled a loose kimono from a clothes tree and put it on.

The doorway to her husband's room stood partly ajar. She drew a bottle of hot sake from the wall console and placed it on the black lacquered tray with the single tiny bowl-cup, both valuable antiques from the nineteenth century. Then she filled a mug with black coffee, placing it so as to balance the rest. This part of her routine had become less commonplace as her husband aged, and now she serviced him twice a week at most. Nicholas Oishi was not a highly sexed man, though in the first year of the marriage, in Kobe, he had several times managed three ejaculations at a single bout. She did not confuse his lack of enthusiasm with any fault of her own—simply the biological mechanism running down.

Eugenia pushed through the doorway with her shoulder and turned on a gentle wallglow. Oishi was still asleep, tightly tangled in the rich bedclothes—a sign that he had not slept well. She set the tray down on the table beside the bed and ran the tips of her fingers over his sparsely bearded cheek. His eyes opened, unfocused.

"Good morning, my husband."

He shook his head sleepily. He was beautiful to her, hawk-nosed, slit-eyed, a true baseball player. He took a long pull on the coffee, and then she filled the sake cup, which he drank in one motion. He was smiling now, and fully awake. She pulled apart her robe and spread her legs wide so that he could see her tender spot.

She was his slave, indeed.

When it was over, she quietly put on her robe and withdrew, back through the bathroom into her own personal compartment. There was indeed much to accomplish today. The scientists had been brought out of stasis, and the DV would have to be initiated and monitored during the first hour, the most critical time. She slipped into a simple, black and gold body jumpsuit, then put on a white

blouse, and purple, peasant-style long skirt. Black pumps and her captain's tie completed her outfit.

She called for her Resource Manager. This was her personal link to all the electronics aboard the ship, including the computers. There were forty of these completely humaniform androids aboard *Asia*, each one an encyclopedia and i/o device for the vast underlying electronic network that ran the ship. They were not interchangeable, however. Corvus, hers, had a remarkable sense of humor and a highly developed personality simulation that often startled her. He was modeled to look like a slim, nondescript Oriental man in his twenties.

"You rang?" he said, probably referencing some obscure media in-joke. She understood that it was supposed to be humorous, and she smiled.

"Yes. Good morning, Corvus. Is there anything in the newspaper that should interest me?"

"The mah-jongg tournament is over. Your friend, Mr. Churragcha, won easily. A survey has shown that fewer people are using the Environment, some only going for golf or baseball. Many say that it reminds them too much of home."

"It's supposed to do that, damn it. Schedule an appointment with Ms. Jya—and also the psychiatric social worker, what's his name . . . Lan, is it? This is a trend I want to stop before it goes too far."

"You have a half hour at three-thirty. Would that be a good time?"

"Yes, fine. I'm due on the bridge at?"

"Eleven."

"Okay. All right, Corvayo, let's pull it all together now. I want a practice alert in one hour; we want the crew to be ready for any eventuality during deceleration. A drill is always good to get the blood flowing. I also want to see a full report on conditions back on Earth as soon as we're going slow enough to get nonpriority transmissions; that damn DV stuff has tied up the channel for weeks."

"Yes, Captain Taranga."

"I want you, personally, to monitor all intership communications for the next day or so. Let's see if we can get

to the root of this malaise thing. And I, personally, will take a stroll up to the hundred-acre wood for, yes, a lunch picnic. Sandwiches and Coke—invite Mr. Oishi along."

Corvus looked abstracted for a moment. "Done."

"Very good. Let's go get some breakfast."

Corazon Esquitun and Larry Taylor walked, hand in hand, on the beach of the Great Lake. The water, a kilometer across, was smooth, and gazing out across it, one got the definite sensation that it curved upward. This was, of course, because it did—the far shore was well above eye-level, and the four or five tiny people across the lake were noticeably foreshortened. The light from the fog-shrouded sunlines above was caught by slight ripples and made a shimmering band about halfway out. Down here the gravity was a little higher than in the hub, and the temperature was close to its minimum, about sixty-six degrees.

They had wasted no time establishing a joint habitation in what had been Cory's apartment in Lymestone Mews, which, though nominally designed for singles, was large enough for two. The Mews was a warren of one-bedroom flats, connected to the Environment and the Working Level by elevators. The elevator openings, shiny black obelisks with dome tops, clustered here and there along the shore.

Larry abruptly stopped, sat down in the sand, grabbed Cory, and pulled her down on top of him. They kissed, but they had already spent most of the morning making love, and the passion was at a low ebb.

Larry looked at the dark little Filipino woman. Her squarish, blunt features and large eyes somehow embodied the feminine ideal he had been looking for since he was a boy. It was a curious thing, really. As Australia had become aligned with the nations of the East over the last century, its cultural norms had changed radically, and the admired Asians whom they saw every night on the videon had come to represent the island continent's goals and aspirations. Ideas of beauty are the most entrenched of cultural artifacts; but Australians gradually came to see

their own pale, ungainly features as less appealing than those of the peoples to the north.

Yet the Asian cultures had gone through the same process at the end of the twentieth century, and had long assimilated the blond-haired, blue-eyed American physiognomy as their ideal. As a result, racism had slowly been eradicated in the East; now mixed marriages were very common among the elite of both places. Geography meant much more than race: although Australians were now regarded as equals with the other nationalities of the Far East, the Europeans, Americans, and Africans were thought of as innately inclined toward laziness and antisocial individualism. It was believed that in the United States of America a way of life far superior to any other had been developed and, almost as quickly, lost. The general notion that the submersion of the West had been caused by genetic factors had slowly been eradicated, and there had been no discrimination at all when he applied for a post among the scientists of Project Outreach. He was simply the best Theoretical Biologist in the designated age group. Cory, also, was at the top in her chosen field, the study of Jovian planets. In any case, Larry felt himself very fortunate to have formed this relationship with Cory. The stasis experience seemed to have welded them together permanently.

"Larry," she said, staring up across the lake, "did you see how the concierge has been looking at us?"

"No, I really hadn't noticed."

"She doesn't approve."

"What?" He laughed derisively. "That's ridiculous. And damn rude, if I do say so. Up hers."

"It's not so simple."

"No?"

"You are still a Westerner in many ways. Don't get me wrong, but there are undercurrents in our social interaction that you simply miss. People are staring at us. I would say that things have gotten very conservative during our fourteen years out of it. Shacking up seems to be a no-no."

"Could things change that much? I hardly think so."

"I'm no sociologist, but think about it. The ship, isolated from Earth, dominated by a pseudomilitary class, would naturally become conservative. The crew was chosen for its stability and family orientation. Since freedom is ultimately limited, people just hunker down, try to keep hold of what's theirs; have a big family and stay happy."

"I don't buy it," he answered meditatively, and his big, horsey mouth squeezed into a thin line. "These are people who voluntarily chose to travel into space, live and die away from their home planet. Their minds couldn't be so closed . . ."

She suddenly was very serious. "Maybe we should hold off on this living together for a while. We are going to have to work closely with the officers to do the survey; I don't want to jeopardize our positions just for a little nooky."

"Oh," he said. "So that's all you're interested in, then." He grabbed her by the waist and started to tickle her. She fell backward into the sand, barely holding back her laughter. They rolled and tumbled for a while, getting thoroughly sandy. Finally, she managed to restrain him, straddling his midsection and pinning his arms down with her knees. She tweaked him on the reddish tip of his nose and stuck out her tongue.

"You could marry me," he said.

"Not for anything. Four hundred years of solitude would be preferable."

He seemed relieved. "Let me up. I'll follow you across the galaxy, doomed forever to love you in vain. Just let me up."

She seemed to soften. "I probably *am* taking this all a bit too seriously. As yet, there are no laws against cohabitation. What can they do to us?"

"You said it, kiro. Two star systems down the road they'll all be dead. Taranga's your friend from way back, anyway. You can pull a few strings . . ."

"Knowing her, she's probably the most conservative of the lot. We'll have to be careful around her."

The sliding door made no noise as Captain Taranga came onto the bridge silently. The room had been designed to mimic an ancient TV icon: the command center of a starship built out of wood and an odd assortment of archaic gadgets. In a way, this cultural recidivism was appropriate, since, among the rationales for launching a generation ship such as *Asia*, the Combine's mediators had argued that such a behavior was deeply ingrained in the model culture and found expression as the popular literary form called science fiction. To Taranga, it seemed a fine line between what they were doing and the West's mystical immersion into technology.

However sophisticated the rationale, the bridge wasn't particularly efficient; but it worked. The ten technicians and two Resource Managers were busy at their posts, monitoring the hundreds of individual systems that made *Asia* function. She watched them for a moment, not moving. No slackers, she thought. These people I have trained well. She strode to the simple, Scandinavian-style armchair at the center of the circular room and took her seat. Only now were the crew members snapping to attention, one by one, as they realized. When they were all rigid, she made a gesture like an orchestra conductor and said, "At ease. Vela, what is the status of the ship?"

The Resource Manager, a simulacrum of a smallish Micronesian woman, turned and smiled. "Good morning, Captain. We are looking at the integrity of the internal field generators in preparation for engaging the ionic propulsion engines. The Directed Virtual fields are ready to turn on. Our chronosequence is programmed into the transputers subject to our control."

"Roh." Taranga looked at the man who had slowly risen from a largely bureaucratic position as her technical liaison to what amounted to second-in-command of *Asia*. "Any comments before we start?"

Ex stepped down to stand next to her chair. "The DV

technologists are unanimous. The new programming has been installed and all parameters changed to reflect the increased effect of the fields. We're set to go at eleven-thirteen . . . exactly, um, four minutes away."

"Bring up the visual images of Sol and Eps Indi, please."

Where there had been a pattern of artistically overlaid arcs of color, a curved screen appeared, filling 140 degrees of the bridge wall. In the center ninety degrees, two nearly identical starfields emanated, one centered around a brightish yellow-white star and the other around a brightish orange one. "Enhance."

The yellow star and its companions dimmed to deep red, while the others brightened into a beautiful indigo-violet hue. In the interstices between the violet stars there was just the hint of pink. "Let's have a countdown, Mr. Wang."

"T minus two minutes, fifty-one seconds."

She let out a sigh at T plus four. There was something about the physics of DV that made her superstitions jell—after all, the Park-Chung equations were based entirely on cryptomathematics, a field that had yet to prove anything incontrovertibly. And the principle itself was enough to make one doubt the nature of reality. Just as it had been demonstrated that every manifestation of the mass-energy continuum was real only part of the time and spent the rest of its "existence" as a mere potentiality, it had been shown that generating a strong enough Weak Nuclear Force could influence where those manifestations reappeared. In fact, with the right spin, particles could be made to disappear entirely or stop, which was how the stasis fields worked.

As a result, as far as the propulsion of the ship was concerned, with a fairly modest expenditure of energy, any motion could be multiplied. The Traveler probes, which were doing unmanned reconnaissance of the nearby stars in advance of *Asia*, could theoretically exceed the speed of light by a factor of two. The extremely massive *Asia*, which couldn't generate enough power to keep the field on continuously, would only reach .97 cee.

Sol grew just a bit less red-shifted and Epsilon Indi seemed to glow a more ordinary blue. Taranga looked around and saw everyone hard at work. Vela volunteered the unnecessary, "It's going well, Captain. Speed point eighty-nine cee and falling along the predicted curve."

The captain stood and surveyed the bridge once more. If it hadn't been for her rank, she would have felt like a fifth wheel. "I'll be available," she said, and strode from the room.

After hours of walking, Peter found himself in an unfamiliar section of the housing level, in a wide corridor decorated with an unending succession of garish, swirling abstract paintings. Gravity felt a bit oppressive, so he was probably somewhere near the aft end of the frustum. A sensation of being lost nipped at him, although it would be a simple matter to call up a map on a kiosk videon. He pulled his hands out of his pockets, straightened his spine, and started to walk again. Suddenly he stopped.

What was the point of this? His life had lurched to a staggering halt, left him high and dry on some strange, trackless island. Everything had taken on a new, unflattering perspective. He was old enough now to begin to make sense out of things, to start to piece together the puzzle that had been tantalizing him for as long as he could remember. But things had come even further apart; and the nature of Peter Zolotin was the most enigmatic thing of all.

Everyone said that growing up was not an easy thing to do. He had imagined that that meant simply that extra diligence was required; but he could see now that, at least for people like him, the task might require skills he couldn't acquire. It wasn't going to be like taking a test; it would be more like making one up. He felt afraid; he did not want to be a failure at life.

Of course, he could think of no one who had succeeded. His parents seemed to be caught up in a meaningless pursuit of something, he couldn't even imagine what. His acquaintances from school were so fucked up that they couldn't even tell the difference between their own ideas

and those imposed by the teachers. Success seemed a lonely place indeed.

A perverse notion entered his mind. Maybe it was a game after all, and nothing really mattered. Of course the idea that everything was an illusion was silly. But in a world that had no clear-cut purpose, didn't everything take on a hollow aspect?

Even this seemed like silly rationalization after the fact. What was wrong with him? He could continue to coast for a while, but not for ever.

He turned around slowly and headed back.

Two

Field Physicist Ryan Du Lapp came down the corridor quickly, taking long, measured steps. A trim Melanesian originally from the island of New Caledonia, his dark, meaty face displayed a fanciful, squashed bulb of a nose with yawning nostrils. A thoughtful, distracted look overshadowed his eyes, completely at odds with the purposefulness of his pace. Damn her! he was thinking. This little sabbatical to the stars isn't turning out the way I thought it would. There's something wrong here, I can feel it.

He turned into a cross-passageway, shaking his head to himself. Life had a way of playing little tricks on him. Over the years, he had developed a number of techniques for dealing with the trickster, even some tricks of his own. The decision to sacrifice x years of his life for added prestige and perhaps even some adventure had seemed an extraordinarily easy one to make. And, he was beginning to realize, it was the easy decisions that contained the most unexpected traps. So he would have to learn, to adapt once again. Most significantly, he would have to do without the pleasures of the university.

He turned sharply into an alcove and stepped through the door. He stepped down the few steps leading into the room, surveying the twenty-plus individuals seated around a large, ovoidal table. Most he recognized: he had dealt with the team heads during the scant weeks they had had together before stasis. At the head of the table was Subcaptain

David Oyomota, a tall, almost occidental-looking man with the face of the world-class businessman. Ryan had taken an early dislike to the man, but had to admire his manner of handling himself. On the surface he seemed friendly enough, but when Ryan had tried to actually accomplish some business, he had found Oyomota's pleasant manner just the surface of a bureaucratic reserve. Others said that he was not nearly the stickler for custom that he tried to make himself out; Ryan still reserved judgment. The scientists were writing on viewpages, talking quietly among themselves, and in general looking very efficient. Du Lapp took a seat at the end of the ovoid, leaned back, and stretched his legs. This would not be the most entertaining hour he would ever spend.

Oyomota coughed politely and motioned for the others to quiet down. "Good afternoon, ladies and gentlemen," he said in a subdued voice. "We are confronted with an enormous and exciting adventure—the first human reconnaissance of an alien star system. Most of you are well-prepared for this enterprise, and in fact have been thinking about all this prior to being put in stasis. I have been chosen to chair the meeting, and, while I really have no authority over your decisions, I will be able to give you a good idea of the *Asia*'s timeline for the next few months and tell you what is possible and what is not. Who would like to begin? Ah, Miss Junichiro, I turn over the floor to you."

Really. Ryan could hear death in the man's sonorous phrases. He already was feeling sleepy.

Hanna Junichiro, the Stellar Systems Overview specialist, was still a slip of a girl, barely twenty. She was small and had delicately made features that reminded Ryan of Nippon's painted geisha women. Apparently it was her natural appearance. She smiled demurely and stood. "Thank you, Dave. I suppose that I should be the one to start, having the largest purview of us all. We have a plethora of phenomena to deal with, and, though of course we have more than two years to study this system, the actual logistics will require much forethought."

Her summary was exceptionally long-winded, and

Ryan reflected on the few Nipponese women he had known during his brief visits there. On the whole, they behaved extremely strangely; well in keeping with the peculiar perversion of Asian culture which kept their whole island somewhat at odds with the remainder of Asia. The atavistic samuria/geisha ethic, which had somehow survived being conquered by the USA, had developed its own peculiar logic and extended its hold on the island during their century of supremacy. And as a result, the women were never quite what they seemed to be.

Du Lapp tuned back in to catch the gist of her talk. As a scientist whose specialty was the magnetic fields and their effects, much of the planetology was gibberish to him. Her summary of the results of the findings of the Traveler spacecraft, FTL robotic probes that were doing preliminary reconnaissance of the near stars, was extremely interesting. It appeared that planetary systems, and especially terrestrial-type planets, just weren't being found. The ones that had turned up only circled dim red stars and were frigid, airless bodies. So much for the New Earths they were looking for! It was beginning to look like Epsilon Indi would be the high point of *Asia*'s mission to explore and catalog new worlds.

Discussion began of the planetology results and, after a while, turned to their plans for near-term exploration of the Doublejove system. Ryan bided his time, waiting for an opening.

Finally it came. An argument arose over certain aspects of metal-lattice fusion, and a snappy exchange was interrupted by Oyomota, who slapped a palm on the table peremptorily and said, "Enough of that. This is not a play session."

"I don't see any reason to let him," Du Lapp motioned to Oyomota, "control this meeting. I think we rank at least as high as a subcaptain in the hierarchy."

Jya Mailin was confused by this sudden change of direction. "Ryan, I don't know what you are trying to do, but whatever it is, this is not the appropriate place or time."

Ryan looked across the table at Jya. "May, I like you.

I like all of you here, although we haven't had that much time to work together yet. We scientists are the ones who should be in control here, not these officious gentlemen and ladies called 'officers.' I don't like this method of enforced meetings, doling out information in tiny dribbles and only under the watchful eye of one of Taranga's minions."

Larry Taylor, sitting at the far end of the table next to Cory Esquitun, spoke up. "I agree with Ryan. The system set up for our collaboration is all wrong. I admit that the 'humanistic' principles set up by Project Outreach are fine and good, in their place. But what I see instead is a system founded on bureaucracy and bullshit. Maybe I'm wrong. Oyomota, why haven't I been allowed a portable computer for my work?"

The subcaptain, obviously uncomfortable, looked this way and that, trying to find a friendly face. This was turning into a mini-rebellion. "Now, wait a minute. Larry, you know very well the portables are for in situ work only. You have full access to the main system, and your RM has specific instructions to help you in any way possible. What's the point of—"

"Privacy, Dave," said Du Lapp. "You know, thoughts that aren't publishable . . ."

Oyomota straightened up. "Science is, by definition, public. It is in our charter that all findings and results are public property, 'publishable' if desired, and you all agreed to the provisions when you signed on. Now I don't want to be rude, but I must point out that squabbling isn't on this meeting's agenda."

May held up a hand. "Dave is right. This meeting is not the place for discussion of personal matters. We can have our own bull session later."

Taylor and Du Lapp exchanged glances but said nothing.

Du Lapp shook his head. "Look, Oyomota, we have to get going on this. Where is the Traveler data? How do we access all the information that we need?"

Oyomota shook his head in return. "You have been assigned an RM. All you need do is ask."

"Yeah, but I don't want an intermediary. I want to access the information myself, directly."

"An RM can arrange that for you, as well."

Ryan seemed to lose his anger. "Oh," he said. "Nobody told me that. It seems to me that someone should have been more thorough in helping us acclimate to this new setup. I am not used to working directly with cybernetic humanoids; even though I was familiar enough with the ones we manufactured for the West, I never expected to have to treat one as a colleague."

"The adaptation is not a difficult one; you will find them courteous, intelligent, and highly motivated. If you need additional therapy to work with them, we can supply you with a trained social worker."

Larry smiled. "I tried that psychiatrist of yours. She just kept asking me questions about myself and pursed her lips whenever I asked her one back."

"I will talk to the captain about your inadequate briefing. I can see that if you did not understand the basic system of using RM intermediaries, you would be a little . . . confused by it all."

Ryan did not let up. "And what about twinklies? I think we should have unrestricted access to direct videon input if we desire it."

Oyomota hesitated. The captain had specifically stated that she did not want the scientists using the Western technique, which involved viewing a videon pattern that had been structured to feed the visual center of the brain in an optimized way. The signal bypassed the real-world drivers and provided an extremely efficient method of acquiring knowledge. Though prohibited by cultural imperative on Earth, the process had been allowed a limited basis on the starship. "I'll see what I can do about that," he said.

Cory Esquitun, not out of sympathy with her two rebellious colleagues, cleared her throat. "The full bio-protection procedure will be employed, correct? I don't want any cross-pollination going on."

Oyomota smiled. "Of course, Cory. Larry'll be allowed twenty days to examine the returns from the unmanned

rover while *Asia* slows down. He will have the final say-so on whether we will go down in person or not. Although I must say it seems rather silly to send humans all this way just to observe remotely."

"I'll do my best to find the stuff harmless."

"So, is that all?" asked Oyomota. "Then I suppose we're adjourned."

The meeting broke up quickly, and only Du Lapp, Taylor, Jya, Esquitun, and Natasha Kakhralov, the ice-world team head, agreed to a "bull session." They took an elevator down to the hull level and walked to the Starviewer Café, a small restaurant whose floor was transparent and whose roof mirrored the wonders of space below. The waiter and a helper pulled together two of the tiny, crystal-clear tables and they all pulled up chairs and ordered.

Below and above, the densely clustered stars were suspended in endless night. Dim lighting rendered the middle ground of tables and customers barely visible, made them and their reflections above into dark shapes that only obstructed the view slightly. The Milky Way was a palpable, translucent scarf twisted haphazardly across the deep. For May, the sensation was like being in the center of it all, frighteningly close to godhead. She averted her eyes and looked into the reassuring face of Larry Taylor instead.

"Here it comes," said the blond man. "I can use a bit of quenching."

The waiter distributed the drinks, two beers, two cocktails, and a white wine for Natasha Kakhralov. They murmured their thanks and he withdrew.

Taylor took an enormous drink from his beer, half emptying the mug, and wiped his mouth with the back of his hand. "Good stuff, for cockroach urine." He laughed.

May was disgusted. "Oh, Larry. Must you talk like that? The biosphere of *Asia* is disgusting enough. You don't have to talk about it."

Larry seemed to be considering. "Maybe you're right,

May. If I joke about a thing, I feel like I've conquered it. But it really isn't very funny."

Cory sipped at her tequila sunrise and let the cold, juice-textured liquid slide down her throat. "So are we in trouble?"

"No," said Natasha without hesitation. Her dark, piercing Uighur eyes flashed. "I really don't understand what's gotten into you bunch. This is a scientific mission. Like the *Beagle*, or *Devcalion.* We can't expect to be treated like royalty."

"It is bad," said Ryan. "I feel as though we are being forced to act out a script written by bureaucrats for the amusement of other bureaucrats. Every woman I've talked to has treated me like a leper. Back on Earth—and you must take my word on this—I had a line that worked ninety percent of the time. Married woman, too. But here, you have to snap your fingers to get their attention, and then they look at you like you're crazy."

Cory grinned. "Ninety percent, huh? I bet you couldn't have gotten me to ball you. But it's true. Larry and I are finding a great deal of bad reaction to our living arrangements. I had a long talk with the woman next door, and she kept on spouting garbage about the sacredness of the family unit and stuff like that. What is in back of it all, I don't know."

"I am disturbed by what my sister has told me about the journey out," said May. "She is emotional, at best, and hard to understand, but she seems to think that separation from the bulk of humanity has had a profoundly negative effect on the crew. Circumscribed by the limits of the ship, and with a waning sense of continuity—"

"That really is a lot of bullshit," said Larry. "I think a more likely explanation is that these people are drowning in bureaucracy. You've seen how we've been kept from doing things by Taranga and her immediate subordinates. Project Outreach decided to model the social structure of *Asia* on old, bad science fiction books, and this is the result."

Ryan ran a hand across the dark curls of his sideburn. "I must disagree. Perhaps I could be called a socialist—by

the old system, a left-wing radical perhaps. While capitalism is the mainstay of our near-Utopia on Earth, I have the feeling it doesn't work here, in this microeconomy. Do you know that almost fifty percent of my first paycheck was deducted for health insurance? That must be part of the way they motivate people to work here. No pay—no health care. That's pretty barbaric, if you think about it."

May took another sip of her stinger. She licked her lips, which were beginning to feel numb. "Oh, I don't know. Think about it—how are you going to maintain performance levels without some sort of strong motivation like that? Ryan, I think you're very old-fashioned. Altruism as a basis for society was discredited hundreds of years ago."

"Oh, was it?" laughed Ryan. "I didn't know that."

Larry waved the waiter over and ordered another beer. "Anyone else? Well, the rest of you are going to have to hurry or you'll quickly be left behind." When the waiter brought the drink, he hefted it comically and drained the entire half-liter at a single draught. "Huurghkh! That's what I call German!" Cory poked him, hard, in the ribs, and he looked down at her, offended. "Sorry again."

"We're just going to have to play along until we get the full picture," she said. "Anyway, we don't have to associate with the peons that closely. They'll all be dead in a few of our years."

"Yeah," said Ryan, "but their children? What'll they be like?

Captain Eugenia Taranga primped briefly in front of the stage mirror. Her new hairdo was blond, shiny, and puffed up beyond belief. Yet, in an almost mystical way, it complemented her face and bearing. Only her dark eyebrows, thin, canted hyphens over her eyes, seemed out of place. Perhaps she could have those dyed as well. She ran her fingers down the long, black velveteen dress she wore, brushing out nonexistent wrinkles, and marched out onto the stage.

She looked out over the assembled crowd. *Asia*'s Main Auditorium was large enough to hold the entire

crew, and since this was a command performance of sorts, they were all here. When the applause subsided, she stepped forward to her mark and, swaying slightly, gave a short, perfunctory bow.

"Fellow members of Project Outreach," she said, "this is a momentous occasion for us all!"

On a section of the inner cylinder far aft of the inhabited portion, a small airlock slid open. Slowly, a bulky human shape floated up to fill the opening and then out into the great void under the curve of the frustum's base. It stopped two meters above the hull. The airlock closed.

She wouldn't have missed this for anything. Natasha Kakhralov was an incurable romantic when it came to space vistas, and she found that the sensation of actually being there was much more intimate than watching from a remote monitor, no matter how accurate the rendition. Since *Asia* was slowing entirely by DV now, there was no danger in detaching herself from the ship, as long as she was still within the field.

Natasha took a moment to orient herself among the stars. The bubble of clear polymer through which she gazed did very little to distract her from the wonder all around. She turned off the bright status icons superimposed on the bubble and soaked it all in. Eleven and a half light-years didn't change the constellations that much, but it took her a few moments to make the connections. Of course, the nearer bright stars, such as Sirius, Procyon, Rigel Kent, were wildly out of place, but in general things were where they were supposed to be. Only a sextant would show any difference in the position of Orion's big seven, whereas Cassiopeia and the Big Dipper were noticeably warped. Finding Sol gave her a special tingle. An average star; nothing remarkable. Except that it had a habitable planet.

A soft buzzing in her ear momentarily distracted her from the view. It was a compulsory broadcast of a speech given by the captain. Unfortunately, it couldn't be switched off, but at the lowest volume it would be easy to ignore.

And it was time. First Doublejove and then Epsilon Indi rose over the dead black surface of the cylinder, easily distinguishable from the thousands of stars behind them, two orangish dots of about the same size, one very dim and the other bright. They both were clearly not the pinpoints of the distant stars, though neither were they obviously disks. This little red sun and its bloated planetary companion were drifting leisurely apart, and Natasha could see that Doublejove was growing faster. Tingles of anticipation climbed her spine and exploded in the base of her neck. Here it comes!

Because of *Asia*'s speed, still almost two tenths the speed of light, this first encounter with the planet would be very quick indeed. Using DV to amplify the vector of motion generated by the retrograde encounter, the starship would arc into a gigantically elongated spiral, pulling hard on Epsilon Indi's feeble grasp, decelerating all the way. By the judicious amplification of the star's gravity field, they would be able to hold on and not go flying off into space.

Now the star was far to the right, moving exponentially, and it was clear that Doublejove was their target. It began to grow, faster and faster, and Natasha was beginning to make out features on the oblate thick crescent. Another minute and she could easily trace the swirling pattern of random eddies that filled the equatorial regions and the darker, banded poles. Epsilon Indi's ecliptic was tilted about twenty-five degrees from that of Sol, and so she had a better view of the Southern—or was it Northern?—hemisphere. As the planet loomed ever closer, it was apparent that Doublejove's polar atmosphere was a pattern of concentric rings. There was even a bright red "bull's-eye" at the exact North Pole, which was in sunlight because of seasonal tilt.

In her ear the captain was saying, "We are fortunate indeed to occupy this moment in time and space. Our forebears who carried the special responsibility of passing Scientific Capitalism from generation to generation are celebrating with us now this culmination of . . ."

Doublejove was as large as the crescent moon seen over the tops of far-off houses, welted with elaborate

patterns that seemed to increase in contrast and color as they expanded. Natasha was beginning to get a visceral feel for their real velocity. If she pushed her imagination, she could see the gas giant as a C-shaped balloon, being inflated at an ever quicker pace.

And, yes, there was one of its satellites, ten degrees to the left, probably one of the twin Mars-sized middle moons, Nickleby or Rudge. Nickleby was brighter, so it was probably Nickleby. She made out the other just coming out from behind the planet. Rudge. She liked the name. Both showed the same phase as their primary. A blink and she saw two more, visible at different fractions of a hand's breadth from the furiously roiling giant planet. Pip was obviously yellowish, and the brighter of the two whitish moons must be Twist. That left Drood. Finally she discovered it, too, still a tiny paper-white curve high above the planet. With a trace of ironic humor, she told herself that she was the first to see them all with human vision. A noble accomplishment.

Doublejove was now as big as a dinner plate, swelling grotesquely, and the invisible night side was a spacious patch of missing stars. She saw features on the individual moons. Rudge seemed to be cut by large, great-circle cracks which separated regions of strikingly differing brightness. Twist, still quite small, nonetheless displayed quite clearly its dark sea, bisecting its crescent into two uneven horns. The bluish tinge of Nickleby betrayed its thick, clear atmosphere.

Now the whole agglomeration was exploding as they dove toward the very center. The more distant moons moved rapidly to the edges of her peripheral vision, and, as the huge planet bore down on her, only the blighted Pip hung close enough to take in in the same glance. The yellow-brown and gray moon, blotched with hundreds of overlapping volcanic outflows in addition to a number of smallish craters, was a long quiescent version of Jupiter's tormented Io.

Like a world-size scimitar, Doublejove swung toward *Asia*. Natasha was swept up into a melange of changing orientations. Suddenly they were falling down toward a

dark, aurora-wreathed monstrosity. Then her stomach careened and the planet seemed to do a quick cartwheel. They were sailing up and over, above the infinite black cloudtops. Then, before she could grasp the enormity of the sky-filling planet, it was gone, hidden behind the upraised frustum. The old-fashioned infinity of stars was back in its rightful place.

"When we are gone, the memory of this expedition will live on, and the tasks that we have done, mundane as they may seem to the uninformed, will cast a bright light on the generations yet to come. For we are the spacemen long foretold, the harbingers of a new form for mankind; and we will be long remembered."

Natasha listened to the polite applause and made her way back through the airlock.

Over the course of the next ten days, *Asia*'s orbit wound down like the mainspring of some gigantic watch, as the magic of Directed Virtuality sapped the speed of the spacecraft and twisted its course. Three times they had passed through the tightly clustered juggler's balls of the Doublejove system, and each time the spectacle grew longer, more leisurely, and those who were interested had time to peer closely at the impressive gas giant and its planet-sized moons. During the third flyby they released a small, fully automated probe shaped like an ancient Lunar Lander with a broad Chinese helmet, which decelerated on a plume of self-feeding fire down around Doublejove and into orbit around Twist. It fell into the strange half atmosphere of the ice moon, shedding an arc of disposable skin behind it, and came to a perfect landing on one of the gargantuan ice ridges that surrounded the huge, limpid, tidally-induced sea they had named after the fat legend, George Herman Ruth. The robot craft doffed its hat, stuck out it probes, and, improbably, lumbered down across the broken shards of ice in search of things for its collection.

The bridge had quieted down, become somewhat jaded from the repeated encounters with the planet. Taranga sat slumped in her chair at an angle, oblivious to the

disrespect her demeanor was producing. The others, with the exception of the two RM's, chatted and paid little attention to the automated process. Playbacks of the last scrimmage with the planet appeared on the screen, close-ups of this moon or that, but everyone ignored them. Though the ionic engines were firing full blast and DV was working to change the vectors of motion, the excitement was clearly over.

Vela looked up from the console, a beatific expression creasing the wet-cocoa black of her skin. The RM's direct connection to the machinery made it unnecessary for her to watch the screens and dials that covered her station, but she maintained an illusion for the sake of the humans. "Approaching final Doublejove rendezvous for planetary insertion."

Taranga sat up and composed herself. She had been thinking about the rumors she had been hearing about the scientists. An undisciplined, unruly lot. She would have to take steps. "Thank you, Vela."

Roh Ek Sai swiveled out from his station and stood, slowly. He stepped down into the shallow well that held the captain's chair and took his place next to her. She looked up at him; with some affection, he thought.

"Hello, Ex. What is it?"

"I just thought I would point out that the upcoming maneuver is going to use the DV generator at full strength. We will be using the new field equations for the first time. So there is a need to be alert."

"Thank you, Mr. Roh. Mr. Nhai? Let's keep careful watch on those DV parameters, shall we?"

"Yes, Captain."

Vela came down to stand on the other side of the captain's chair. "I will monitor the field as well," she said. "Shall I tie in to the main control in case an instantaneous change is necessary?"

Taranga smiled up at the automaton. She liked the fact that they never took independent action, always needed a direct command. "Certainly."

The image on the screen turned to a real-time telescopic image of the Doublejove system. This time her

moons were all lined up on the left side of the planet, and, since *Asia* was now traveling parallel to Epsilon Indi's ecliptic, the line connecting the dots was almost straight.

Pictor, the other RM, the image of a Central Chinese man, tall, stocky, and square-headed, suddenly called out, "Here we go!"

Vela murmured, "Generator on. Vector change four degrees, five-point-one degrees, deceleration factor point oh nine. Deceleration factor point eleven. Deceleration factor point fourteen. Captain, the generator seems to be emitting more heat than is predicted." Her brow contracted and her normal smile disappeared. "Temperature inside the DV pod is rising. It is now 1205 degrees centigrade, 310 degrees hotter than theory predicts."

Taranga looked at Roh and back at Vela. "What should I do?"

Roh stepped back to his station and scanned his readouts. "The temperature is rising exponentially. And the wavelength of the radiation is increasing as well, along a similar curve. My opinion—turn it off."

Taranga paused a second. Turning off the DV would leave *Asia* in orbit around the primary star and not Doublejove, but the alternative was not pleasant to think about. "Okay," she said. "Turn it off."

Vela smiled again, perhaps inappropriately. "Secondary emissions have ceased. Temperature falling according to standard thermodynamic theory."

Pictor, mimicking hotheadedness well, said in a voice too loud, "Doublejove insertion not achieved. Epsilon Indi orbit .23 eccentricity, speed .003 cee or nine hundred kilometers per second. Next planetary encounter will be in 611 days, four hours, and fourteen minutes."

"Thank you, Pictor," said Taranga, annoyed at the quasihuman emotional responses of the bridge RM's. "Status of the ionic engines?"

Pictor seemed to have caught on to his captain's displeasure, and he answered in a robotic monotone, "Ionic engines firing normally, no problems."

"You idiot," shouted the captain, "turn those off, too! They're just slowing us down!"

"Ionic engines disengaged."

"Thank you," said Taranga. There was a long moment of silence. "Okay. Any ideas?" The human members of the crew seemed to be working especially diligently on their inputs, not looking at her at all.

Roh sat at his console and swiveled to face the captain. "Put simply, Captain Taranga, *Asia* is a sitting duck without the DV drive. The ionic engines were not designed to be a primary source of propulsion, only a seed propulsion that could be amplified by DV. With ionic propulsion, we can probably"—he consulted his monitor—"get back to Doublejove within a year; or we could go on to Copperfield, which would take us, let's see, about twenty-five months. The main problem is getting rid of our velocity, which is still way too high."

"And if we use the DV at a minimal level?"

"If we turn around, use full ionic thrust and an acceleration factor of point oh nine, we can be back at Doublejove in fifteen days. Three weeks at point oh seven."

Taranga ticked off the numbers on her fingers. Pictor, affecting a wimpy contriteness now, said, "There is no evidence that Directed Virtuality under point one has any negative consequences. And we should be able to anticipate any malfunction in plenty of time to turn the system off again."

"Okay," said the captain. "Spin her around."

The operation of reversing the position of the huge spacecraft took more than half an hour, but when it had been completed, they were ready to attempt DV again. Taranga ordered the ionic engines turned to full, which began a slow deceleration, and the DV drive was turned on very carefully, at a minimum .01 level. There was no excess heat, and so they painstakingly raised the coefficient, .04, .07, and finally to .09, where it would stay. *Asia* quickly began to lose speed, arcing into a gratuitous higher orbit that was taken care of by a DV vector adjustment. After a while the ship was moving in the correct direction, taking aim on the nightside of the gargantuan planet.

But the real problems lay with the future. Later, Eugenia lay inert on the bed in her apartment. The pillow over her head shut out light and sound and caressed her face with softness, but it would not smother the pessimistic thoughts that ran amok just below the surface of her consciousness. She took a deep breath, counted aloud to five, and seemed to smooth the troubled water. But a question would not go away: Can we go on from here?

Three

Ryan Du Lapp strode through the waist-high grass two thirds of the way to the small end of the frustum, sweat glossing his dark skin with smeared-out highlights reflected from the sunlines. He stopped for a moment and looked up at the great bellying cylinder above, shading his eyes from its blinding illumination. Here, in the "upper" half of the environment, closer to the inner surface and higher, it was always hotter. The rotation inertia provided only about .6 g at this distance up, and Ryan enjoyed the sensation of strength and agility. He saw a small copse of palmettos, and made his way toward the enticing shade.

He really couldn't fully analyze why he had come here, far from the more frequented sections of the place. Again he had tried a bit of seduction, this time with a Russian girl, an attractive blond thing with flushed cheeks and a wholesome, buxom physique. A perfect type, just waiting to be seduced. And yet the thing had not come to pass, in a way that mystified him. It was getting him down.

For some reason the grass could not grow here, and he found a large, exposed root, corded and red-brown, and seated himself. From here the vast expanse of the place was mostly hidden by interwoven jungle not far off, and the spiky palmetto fronds hid the unnatural sky. It was almost like home on New Caledonia, and it made him nostalgic and sadder still.

He succeeded in putting his finger on part of what was bothering him. It was more than just the sexual brush-offs. He was beginning to feel like a real pariah. In the few situations where he'd found himself in the company of people—shopping at the Mall, for example—he had moved among them like a wraith, feeling invisible and silent.

Ryan closed his eyes and let the heat from the sunlines burn into his face. It had been a mistake, coming—he saw that now. Tenure at the University of Noumea had been promised, virtually assuring a high-paying sinecure for the remainder of his life. Not so bad an end for the little Melanesian who started his life at the farthest outpost of civilization. Somehow, this next step along the asymptotic curve of his life was not what he had bargained for; once again he was remote from the coursing masses of humanity that he had sought.

He still vividly remembered his childhood in Noumea. The endless, coral-protected beaches, the flat-bottomed cumulus towering over the Coral Sea's turquoise crazy glass. And the tiny boy who played among the moldering ruins and grass-covered slagheaps, guessing at the wonders that lay beyond the watery horizon.

New Caledonia, unlike most of the Pacific islands, had fallen through the cracks of the new world order. Its fierce loyalty to France, the center of the New West, kept it aloof from the changes that were sweeping the remainder of Melanesia; and, until its mineral resources were depleted at the end of the twenty-second century, it had been a prosperous and vainglorious place, fully capable of making it on its own. When the West withdrew into its cocoon, and the chromium ran out, the island had quickly fallen into bankruptcy. And by that time the initial surge of Scientific Capitalism was over. It was said, in the Parliament, that, as far as they were concerned, a return to the stone age was preferable to begging for assistance.

At the age of eight, Ryan had taken the family's little receiver apart and reassembled it without difficulty. He delighted in figuring out how things worked, and, after months of listening to the thousands of channels of spoken

information in the AM band, devised a system for talking back. By controlling a little electric arc and listening for the effect it had on his receiver, he eventually produced a strong, slightly tunable signal, with which he proceeded to send out Morse code. Since the vast majority of the information was in English, and he only spoke French, Maka, and Pisin, he was forced to use the latter. Pisin, still the mockery that had been introduced by the early colonizers as Pidgin English, was a straitjacket of a language, but no more so than Morse. On the day Ryan had sent a tentative "We stap wanpela tok?" and, to his surprise, received a torrent of Pisin gibberish in return, he had become a physicist in spirit, if not yet in knowledge.

The next year the boat had come. More than a mile long, the thing had skimmed over the deadly reefs on a cushion of air and come to a stop in Noumea's wide harbor. Word spread through the city quickly, and Ryan reached the quay just in time to see the ramp come out of the thing's prow and come to rest on the beach. A team of men wearing hot-looking suits descended; they explained to all who would listen that New Caledonia was being offered a chance to join in the great Asian Rim Experiment. Inside the boat was a fully equipped, air-conditioned factory, with all the materials necessary to construct functioning femtochips, and, more importantly, the means to build many factories throughout the island; this commodity was still in short supply, and, through industriousness and hard work, the citizens of New Caledonia would receive both the material and financial assistance to become full economic partners with the rest of the East. Full access to advanced medical techniques would be made available, and a reasonably priced insurance could be purchased, once the factories started to make money. Twinklies lessons were offered, and English quickly came to be the language of choice among the workers.

A continuous stream of pop songs issued from the ship, and Ryan and his siblings would come to listen and watch. It didn't take him long to attract the attention of one of the foreigners, and soon he had acquired a scholarship to study abroad. By the time he had returned, New

Caledonia had its own university, and he became a junior professor there. Life was good among the women students, and he had flourished.

Why had he signed on? He would never see his parents or brother and sister again. Like all of the friends he had known—his little contingent at Bar Blong Grise—they were, for all practical purposes, no more. Fourteen years gone, some were undoubtedly dead. It was not difficult to imagine them still following in their habitual paths, forever unchanging and unchangeable; yet the illusion was a shallow one, and left no residuum.

Yes. That was it. As those people back on Earth were to him, he himself was to the ordinary crew members of *Asia*. They saw right through him, because he was dead, in a sense. He also belonged to another time—the future. Two years from now he would enter the stasis lozenge and, for many of them, cease to exist; the journey to their next stop, CD–36°15693, would take another eleven years. How could one even say hello to such a will-o'-the-wisp, much less find him attractive enough to make love to?

The company of the other scientists would have to be enough.

Ryan stood and surveyed the patchwork ecosystems that filled the valley of his new motherland. There were worse places to be, he supposed. He could hear a small stream somewhere to the starboard, and he followed his ears until he found it. It was clear and alive, a smooth, slowed-down cataract sidling its way down through a rock-choked declivity to the lowlands. Whistling an old tune of Melanesia, he began his own descent.

Planetary ferries *Arecibo*, *Mt. Palomar*, and *Jodrell Bank* practically filled the immense hold designed for them. They were identical sleek and aerodynamic craft, looking very much like overgrown jet fighters from the last days of Terrestrial Warfare. Five hundred meters in length, they easily dwarfed any machine that had flown on Earth. And they were much more than simple flying machines. Virtually every surface, and even the distribution of weight within them, was controlled by a series of interconnected

computers. The four wings could be totally retracted, made to sweep forward or backward, or augmented with various types of stabilizers, depending on the nature of the atmosphere to be flown in. Out of their tails sprouted four extremely powerful rocket engines, and this was their primary source of propulsion. The fuel was hydrogen and oxygen compressed to an insignificant volume by DV and held in stasis.

Larry Taylor and Hanna Junichiro were checking out the large mobile laboratory that made up a fair amount of *Arecibo*'s cargo. The inner cylinder had been stopped as work crews and specialists explored what had gone wrong in the DV drive. Here, at the aft end, without rotational inertia, electroadhesive velvet would have to do.

Floating above the plush control seat, beneath a panoramic wraparound windshield that showed the latticework walls of the rocket's cargo bay, Taylor worked. Needing additional stability, he pushed himself down into the comfortable softness and called up a manifesto of biological instrumentation on the main computer readout, which was a bright, transparent overlay on the windshield. He scanned the lines of dark orange letters and let out a chuckle of amazement. The outfitters had, it seemed, overlooked nothing. *Arecibo*, and its mobile laboratory, were state-of the-art, with a unified force imaging system, full stasis storage, and a null-gravity centrifuging apparatus that matched anything on Earth, at least the Earth of a decade and a half ago. Or rather, two years ago, if you counted in the relativity factor. Fuckin' bunch of nonsense, he thought to himself, relativity, even if it was true. Uncertainty got around it, they said, and Larry Taylor would ignore it, too, as much as possible. When the light from Sol reached them here—not that it ever would, they would be long gone by then—it would be . . . no, he was just confusing himself. Organic physics would be all that he would ever master, he was afraid, but on the other hand, it was all that really interested him.

"Larry," said Hanna Junichiro, pushing through the two pairs of revolving command chairs that would seat the

rest of the scientists, "have you heard the rumors about why we overshot Doublejove?"

"Yeah, I heard. I also heard that the DV team has been in continuous session since yesterday. Looks like they had a problem of some sort."

"A source in Engineering tells me that it was more than a problem." Hanna, small as she was, tried to sit gingerly on the edge of the copilot's chair, but the flexible seat molded itself around her and swallowed her up. She looked like a small toy left inadvertently in the complexity of the chair's cupped palm. She wriggled a bit and then seemed to give up. "These damn chairs are too autonomous," she said, shaking her head. "Anyway, I heard that the whole nature of Directed Virtuality is under question. I understand enough of the cosmology, I think. *Asia* may be dead in the water. We may be stuck here."

Taylor looked up at the computer overlay and cleared it with a touch. He swiveled his chair to look at Hanna more easily. "That's hard to believe," he said, thinking, fucking physics again. "It's worked well enough so far. We should be able to limp back to Earth, at least—not that I know anything about it, really."

Hanna was suddenly furious. "Damn that Taranga and her officers! I know that you will think it uncharacteristic to be so uncharitable toward them, but damn it, Larry, if I'd suspected that we'd wake up to find the Gestapo in charge, I certainly wouldn't have come. They're hiding the facts from *us*! I don't think I can take it anymore."

Taylor found it almost impossible to repress an ironic snort. Little Hanna, who had been speaking up for Taranga ever since they'd come out of stasis, was finally catching on. "I'm glad you're beginning to understand why I've been acting the way I have. It's my guess that, since *Asia*'s charter has no formal procedure for changing the system, we're going to have to—"

Arecibo's televideo overlay switched on and a two-times life-size image of Roh Ek Sai's jowly face appeared on the windshield. "Ah," he said, "there you are. All Scientist Officers are being asked to report to Auditorium 4B for a briefing. And, by the way," he smiled condescend-

ingly, "you should be more careful what you say in front of an open televideo array."

Taylor found the send-televideo onoff and, with a wisp of amusement, noted that it was set to off.

Auditorium 4B was an intimate little room on the hull level with a small, raised stage and five or six conference tables. It was probably used most often as a teaching venue. Most of the other scientists were already there when Ryan Du Lapp came into the room, plucking burrs from his tunic and pants. He had accumulated a tennis-ball-sized wad of them, and he put it on the table in front of him after sitting down.

Captain Taranga came out onto the stage, followed by Roh. She was wearing a dark maroon pantsuit, and a small, matching cupcake hat was perched at a strange angle on her hair. She went up to the podium and looked out over the twenty scientists gathered in pairs and trios around the tables, as if they were attending the cabaret. "Good afternoon, my friends," she said, and seemed to be waiting for a reply. Someone managed a hi, and she smiled. "We should have gotten together like this earlier. It is difficult for me to find the time to do everything necessary. In a sense, we are both servants to the scientific priorities of Project Outreach, and it is very important that we coordinate our plans closely.

"Twelve of you will be beginning the most exciting part of this mission, the Survey of Planets written of in the charter. Of course, the other eight primaries will stay behind as backups in case of disaster. Six of you will take *Arecibo* down to Twist, by far the most interesting body in this solar system, while the rest will use *Mt. Palomar* for a first manned reconnaissance of the remainder of Doublejove's moons. Exciting times, indeed! I wish that I could go with you in person; though the continuous video coverage will be fascinating, it won't be quite as good as actually being there. We all know that you will be doing your best for science and for mankind.

"Now let me turn to another subject, one that I am less eager to speak about. I have talked to Psychologist

Sorlouangsana and other members of the crew, and it is becoming clear to me that our planners underestimated the amount of alienation that would be engendered by your different timeline. It is understandable that you are alienated. Had I been the one to make the decision, I would have accepted only married couples for stasis. Well, that is not the decision that was made. I understand that, because of the way things are, you may feel that the values of the rest of the crew are somewhat 'square' and family oriented. A generation ship such as this one does not need dissenting views.

"So, please, try to restrain yourselves in the presence of regular crew members, especially children. I have noted that two of you are living together without the benefit of marriage. Of course, I cannot influence you to change your morality. But I advise you to keep quiet about your predilections and proclivities.

"Yes, talking about this makes me uncomfortable as well. I will assume that the matter is closed.

"Remember, as you go out to explore these brave new worlds, your every action will be broadcast on the principal video channel, live. Please behave as though you were the role models for a whole generation of youngsters—because, of course, you are. The crew of the ship needs all the inspiration it can get for the long journeys between the stars that you miss out on. I wish you good luck and good hunting."

She stepped away from the podium and came over to the edge of the stage. "I need not be so formal with you. I, too, am alone and separate from the rest of the crew, made different by the responsibilities assigned to me. Do you have any questions, now that you've got me here in person?"

Inside their heads, many of the scientists were highly offended and amused at the same time by this strange performance; Taranga was clearly in love with her position. There was a moment of, for some, contemptuous silence. Then Hanna Junichiro, from a table at the back of the room, spoke up. "Explain the nature of the problem that has developed with the DV drive."

The captain was obviously surprised by the request. She looked up at Ex, who nodded and said, "That is being looked into, as you apparently already know. It would be premature to comment on a—"

"Come on, now," said Ryan. "We are scientists, not panicky schoolchildren. We can be trusted with whatever this thing is. Jya Mailin and I might even be able to help."

Roh Ek Sai came forward now, and he clearly looked as though he were under some sort of strain. "The captain is not withholding information from you. We have no idea at this point what happened."

Tae Nu Hya, just beneath Taranga, looked hard into her face. "So something *did* happen. For the benefit of those of us who don't have access to the rumor mills of the ship, could one of you explain what you *do* know?"

Ex rumbled, a long sigh. "It is quite simple. During our first attempted insertion into Doublejove orbit, at a time when the DV apparatus was operating at maximum, spurious radiation began to appear at what looked like a logarithmically increasing rate. We turned the drive off. When we started it again, operating at carefully controlled levels, there was no recurrence. We are looking for a theoretical explanation of what happened, but, as most of you know, DV is a by-product of the Grand Unified Theory of 2154. Reality is not the simple mathematical puzzle it was envisioned to be by the early physicists. Strange things happen. And the equations that describe the world are millions of elements in length. We have a fair number of DV specialists on board, and they are trying to sort out what happened. It may take some time."

Taranga said, "I would have told you if I thought there were any real chance that it would help the situation."

Ryan Du Lapp stood quickly and cleared his throat. "Thank you, Captain Taranga," he said, a kind of bile audible in his voice. "If you need me I'll be at the Starviewer." He left without looking back.

The great doors of the ferry hold opened to reveal a slim, reddish crescent fully seven degrees across lying athwart the dark opening like a banana on its back. Below

the bright limb, wedged into a corner of the opening, hung Epsilon Indi, an orangish, pea-sized version of the sun. Stars were washed out by the relative brilliance of the pair, though Indi was over ten times dimmer than Sol from Earth. Squinting into the light from the cockpit of *Arecibo*, Larry Taylor reminded himself that the red sun was still ten thousand times brighter than Luna when it is full. He did a rough calculation and decided that, from Copperfield, roughly half an AU from its primary, Epsilon Indi would seem a third as bright as the sun he was familiar with, and half again as large. He was confident that if the planet could provide all the other ingredients, it was enough incoming energy to foster life. Whether there was any would be a good test of prevailing theories.

But Copperfield could wait. First, there would be Twist. Larry turned to Resource Manager Lyra, pilot for *Arecibo*, and said, "Ready to go?"

Lyra, a soft and plump woman android with the dark, heavily lashed eyes and delicate nose of a classical Hindi goddess, regarded him with a smile. "Just a few moments more. I and Pavo are making certain all onboard systems are functioning perfectly. . . . There, I believe we are ready, Larry. I will tell the others."

Riding in the mobile lab ensconced within *Arecibo* were Ryan Du Lapp, Natasha Kakhralov, Tae Nu Hya, and Irina Oblomova, the only other biological scientist. She was a specialist in Ecology, the study of the vast network of interdependences that sprang up between evolving species. Taylor hoped she would have something to do on Twist.

In *Mt. Palomar*, even now nudging out into the sharp, rosy light, Cory would be waiting, as he himself was, for the onrushing adventure of planetary exploration. Larry felt a momentary lapse of confidence. Did she really find him desirable? He could never discern what was at *her* core. She stood aloof, like a star or gas giant, with no place to land and reconnoiter. No seismic profiles of her heart were possible. Was that why their relationship seemed to go nowhere?

And what changes would this separation bring?

Lyra said, "Here we go." The ship lurched and began to move toward the opening, where its sister craft was already slipping away, diminishing in size and swinging around to bring her nose parallel to *Asia*'s orbital motion. From this perspective, looking down on to its dorsum, with the stubby wings mostly retracted into its body, it did look very much like the classical rocket ship of old; though as it yawed, the almond-shaped profile gave way to the squashed, aerodynamic-looking contours of a plane. Suddenly the engine lit, a feeble-looking spray of yellow, and it was gone.

Arecibo continued its slow progress away from its parent ship. Larry called up an image of *Asia* on his windshield overlay and saw an enormous set of concentric circles, slightly out of alignment as they moved away from her central axis. The RM guided the ferry by radio link; she stared into middle space, hypnotized.

"I am fully cognizant of your presence, Larry," she said. "Feel free to converse."

Larry looked away, embarrassed. "Sorry," he said. "Didn't mean to stare."

Arecibo began to accelerate with a solid thump that pushed him back into his chair. Doublejove swung out to dominate the field of view to the left. *Asia* dwindled rapidly, until it looked like a closed, silvery parasol twirling against the night. Christ, he thought. Adventure, here I come.

Jya Mailin sat with the others in *Mt. Palomar*'s mobile lab, watching an overlay of the ponderous dance of Doublejove and her satellites. Since *Asia* had pushed itself down into a circular orbit about a million kilometers from Doublejove, they were headed outward, up, moving in a moderately curved arc toward the realm of the giant moons Nickleby and Rudge, which were to be their principal course of study. With her in the lab were Cory Esquitun and two scientists she had not had much to do with. Mark Denahy was a Nipponese of American descent who specialized in solar system formation and its leftovers, planetesimals and chondritic asteroids. Calvin Ng was an

expert on cold planetary atmospheres such as those that mantled Rudge and, to a lesser extent, Nickleby. He was a tall, flat-faced Taiwanese with an unusually muscular physique. Hanna Junichiro was in *Mt. Palomar*'s cockpit with RM Pavo, their pilot.

Calvin Ng had been explaining about the effects that an atmosphere, even a very thin one, could have on surface morphology. "You'd think that this thin shell of gas would be hardly noticeable, wouldn't you?" He sounded as if he were in a lecture hall back on Earth. "But, no. There are in fact cumulative changes in composition and particle size that make a great deal of difference. Look at Mars, for example. Whole regions covered deeply in dust and sand. In many places wind erosion dominates the landscape."

Denahy was not moved by this argument. He liked simple, easy-to-understand processes like cratering, and found atmospheres to be messy, irrational things that you couldn't get a firm fix on. "Yes, but—"

The husky voice of Pavo interrupted. "Please attach your restraining belts. We are going for Nickleby insertion in a few moments. Also take the time to note down your responses so that I can try to make landing more pleasant in the future."

"Yeah," said Cory. "Sure."

The entire window was overlaid with the view from Pavo's visual sensors. The sense of motion was slight, but without warning the white belly of Nickleby loomed up from nowhere. The moon rose at a steady pace, like a fast-blown squall cloud, until it filled the window. It was in full phase, an enormously complex world that reminded May of no other planet she had ever seen. It was staggeringly beautiful. Differences in composition and reflectivity were more noticeable than topography with the illumination directly overhead; and the globe was swaddled with an enormous number of shades—pale brown, blue, purple, gray, and orange—all shifted toward the red end of the spectrum by Epsilon Indi's ruddy light. As with Ganymede, Mars, and Earth, there was simply too much to take in at a glance. Regions of overlapping craters crowded shoulder

to shoulder with vast, darker areas dominated by ropy striations. Jumbled, chaotic terrain gave way to arrays of a close-marching herringbone pattern. Some places looked as though an original, heavily cratered terrain had been stretched and sheared and melted until what was left resembled a partially assembled jigsaw puzzle that had been attacked with an assortment of weapons.

The primary features, which seemed to cut across all types of terrain and must have been the most recent, planetologically, were five planet-girdling gashes. These cracks were bluish and surrounded by large areas of parallel lineations, which gave the impression of a geology spreading away on both sides to squeeze and deform the original land. A tiny film of blue atmosphere gathered at Nickleby's extreme edges.

May heard Cory's long, through-the-teeth shoosh of amazement. Nothing in the preliminaries had prepared them for the sheer physicality, the intensity of this new world. What had been an abstract concept—a word, almost—had turned into this . . . a world of its own, independent and indifferent to the petty notions of humankind.

Mt. Palomar rode down on opposing fluxes of force into a low, equatorial orbit around Nickleby. The overlay showed the vista directly below, and as they approached the ripped terminator, May got a better idea of the true scale of the features that they had seen globally. Accentuated by the low sunlight, parallel, subparallel, and crisscrossing grooves and raised threads dominated the landscape. This terrain looked much like the surface of a ball of twine haphazardly wound up. She wouldn't care to try to drive the mobile lab through that land, no matter what the engineers who had made it claimed. Bumpy simply wasn't an adequate word.

"We'll be over nightside for about twenty-five minutes," said Pavo, "then I'll land *Mt. Palomar* near the widest of the gashes, Mantalini Chasma. There we will download the mobile lab and the air skimmer. According to the charter, you can investigate whatever appeals to you."

May looked up into the videon which was recording their mission for live viewing and smiled.

Twist was something else again. As *Arecibo* homed in on the third largest of Doublejove's satellites, there was very little to be seen on the mobile lab's windshield overlay. Coming down from *Asia*'s higher orbit, accelerating to catch up with the big moon, the thick white crescent in nearly quarter phase was quite bland. Ryan Du Lapp's attention was drawn instead to the now truly impressive gas giant whose matching phase slowly moved into a concentric alignment with its satellite. The disordered equatorial bands showed structure down to the limits of this view's resolution, and he could actually see individual spots moving. Some were gathered into clusters, and some larger ones moved by themselves. They all showed a great deal of internal structure, and he could imagine them as some kind of biological cells if he didn't push the analogy too far. These spots must be traveling very fast indeed to be visibly moving from this great distance. There! One actually seemed to invert upon itself and disappear, sucked down by the surrounding turmoil.

He turned to Natasha Kakhralov, who was also raptly gazing at the planet. "What kind of atmospheric effects are at work down there? I thought I understood how Jupiter's atmosphere worked, but those fast-moving little guys just don't fit in. Are they miniature red spots or something?"

Natasha shook her head and squinted. Her face was suddenly very savage, and the reason for the Great Wall suddenly became more clear to Ryan. "Beats the hell out of me, Ryan. I'm only into solid-state physics."

Tae Nu Hya, in the seat behind Ryan, said, "It's more than pure atmospheric physics. The upper reaches of Doublejove's atmosphere are partly ionized, and the inner core rotates at a different velocity. As I understand it, the magnetic field organizes and moves much of the equatorial band, at least the features in the uppermost opaque strata. You'll have to ask Corazon if you want to know more."

Ryan looked at the attractive Korean and said, "Thanks, Ms. Tae." Magnetic fields—that was something he under-

stood. He did think he could see some similarity to the cells and sunspots, which, in a sense, they were. He would certainly have to talk to Cory at their first opportunity. Damn them all! Since coming out of stasis he had let science slide, and instead had been occupying himself with politics of a sort and his sexual drive. Celibacy did nothing for his grander motivations.

And what was he waiting for on that front? Here he was with three female humans, all of them apparently eligible. He had seen Tae hanging around with Calvin Ng a couple of times, and that might be an indication of something going on. Irina Oblomova, a Caucasian, not particularly his type. But Natasha, despite her fierce appearance, was that proverbial horse of a different color. He had noted the suppleness of her body several times during training back on Earth, and her hair, dark, long, and shiny, was something special.

Twist was now as large as or larger than Doublejove, which could be seen as a slender crescent enveloping the moon's bright limb. Twist was beginning to reveal some topography after all: a low undulation gave the terminator a wavy look. The land close to this sunset line was almost featureless, except for a few small craters.

"Headed for Twist insertion, folks," said Lyra in a sultry voice. "Please fasten your seat belts."

Ryan did so. Natasha was looking at him. He looked back, smiling and flaring his nostrils. Savagery of a different kind might appeal to her. She stretched out a hand and put it on his forearm. "Later," she whispered.

Had the videon caught that? Would the viewers understand that an assignation had just been made? Ryan laughed to himself. She was certainly easier than the nonscientists aboard *Asia*. She must have come to the same conclusion he had: that the scientists were separate from the others and would have to manage on their own. She wasn't stupid. They all must be thinking variations on that theme by now. Maybe he would have a talk with the others when they got back, make it official. The Scientists' League.

He was pushed back in his chair as *Arecibo* deceler-

ated into an orbit. On the screen, Twist had become the entirety of the world, but the low relief of the surface belied the high resolution of the view. A fairly large crater showing a distinct peak at its center came up over the limb and gave Ryan some sense of perspective. He was just about to give up hope on the moon when a large rise, stitched with broken layering, hove into view. They were approaching Ruth Sea, he knew. This'll be impressive, he thought smugly.

Suddenly the landscape changed back to a dull, featureless white, and Ryan thought that he must have been mistaken. But as he looked more closely, he noticed that the boundary between the two terrains was extremely gradual; not like the blending of one land form into another, but like the revealing of a land form under cloud cover. Here was the snowing-out zone of which he had been told. Without warning they were past it, and he could see clearly the laterally banded downslope. This region could easily have been made up of strata laid down over eons and eroded preferentially toward the sea. He adopted that theory temporarily for lack of a better one.

And finally the great sea came over the horizon like a massive purplish stain on the snow. Everything had taken on a bluish aspect, the result of the thickening atmosphere of water gas that capped the seaward hemisphere of the moon. The sea was round in shape and quite dark. It seemed calm from this height, but was speckled with broken patches of reddish and purplish matter. Suddenly a great plume of steam appeared, and it was apparent that the very center of this sea was boiling. Though if the atmosphere was not very dense, boiling hot could be cool enough to bathe in. As the entire sea moved down from the limb, he could see the source of the colored stuff—in an almost perfect circle around the ten-kilometer diameter central region, huge islands of the red material clustered. Life! Alien and quite unlike that which had evolved on Earth; but the probe had revealed it was not dangerous. They would spend much of their time here studying this biology and the depths of Ruth Sea where the tidal

heating produced the energy upon which this life apparently subsisted.

"Atmospheric entry beginning." *Arecibo* began to quiver slightly, and Ryan was held back by the cross straps that fixed him to the chair. An itch of fear tickled at him, but he paid it no attention. Gouts of orange flame came crawling over the viewfield and the vibration increased. "Wings deployed in hypersonic mode." Natasha's hand was on his again, squeezing lightly. The fire dwindled into streaks of red-hot ablative which played over the windshield sporadically. "Supersonic mode." Twist was now a land of hills and valleys, an ice scape not unlike that of central Antarctica. Natasha let go. They had made it.

"Subsonic." The craft, now an airplane, grabbed hold of the wind and tilted into a great curve, heading back toward the sea. Taylor spoke back to them. "Get ready. We'll be landing in a minute. I think we should get going as soon as we can."

This had potential, all right. Ryan began to feel as though he might just be having the best time of his life.

Peter Zolotin paused outside the hallway leading to the chambers of the Media Club. It seemed that he was being drawn to this group more and more, and he really couldn't explain why. The old television shows, while interesting in their own way and very revealing of the strengths and deficits of America in the latter years of the twentieth century, did not compel him to watch. The music, however, did touch a responsive chord in him, and he seemed to be hearing more and more nuances in the essentially repetitive sound structures. Repetition of various sorts did seem to be a key to enjoyment of this stuff; repeated situations, repeated characters, repeated riffs. Perhaps the growing familiarity was what was making him comfortable here.

The door slid aside and he ambled in, looking around. Philippe was there and, among others that he did not know very well, Yolly Carter and Duke Jin. As usual, they were sprawled out on the comfortable couches that practically filled the room. The wall videon was filled with

enormous, colorful faces; the silly diminished chords of sound-track suspense made their patterns. Duke noticed him and paused the show, suspending an impossibly stiff body above the fender of a hit-and-run car.

Jin said, "Peter. Hello. I wasn't sure you'd be back." His inexpressive dark face, a bumpy square scored with black-slash features, did not communicate much, and Peter couldn't tell if he was laughing at him or not. The last time Peter had come they had gotten into an absurdly long argument over the existence or nonexistence of God, mostly, he suspected, tongue-in-cheek. Peter had gotten heated at one point, frustrated that no one seemed to be able to see the simple point he was making about a person's obligations whether there was a God or not. It was all rather ludicrous, he supposed.

"Me?" he said, "Not come back? You've got to be kidding. I'm as addicted to this decadent fun as any of you."

Yolly uncurled from a languid recline and stretched her legs. She was a very beautiful Westerner, probably seventeen or so, with pale blond hair piled up on her head. Washed-out, azure eyes, slack with humor, were her most distinctive feature. Sometimes it could be downright painful to be skewered on those almost irisless eyes. "This is *Peter Gunn*, your namesake. But its almost over, 1961."

"Go ahead and finish. I don't care."

The image started up and the man was thrown lifeless to a grimy city curb. After a moment or two he stirred and sat up, rubbing his head meaningfully. He was apparently not seriously hurt by the experience.

"That's Peter Gunn," said someone. "He's just been betrayed by a woman, and that was a last-ditch attempt to put him out of the picture."

"Thanks." Peter found an unoccupied love seat and made himself comfortable. He found himself watching the detective-story characters, and was not surprised how the story came out. He had figured out the paradigm of these things pretty easily. Although they were satisfying on some level, he could not deeply identify with either the characters or situations.

The closing credits filled the screen, and the hypnotic but painfully simple theme music started again. Duke cut and the screen went dark. "So," he said, "choose something."

Peter looked around. "Music," he said, "and conversation. That's what I came for."

Philippe laughed. "I thought," he said, "that you were too much of an intellectual to like pop music."

Peter shook his head. "Its appeal cuts across distinctions like that. I deny that I'm an intellectual, though. What is that supposed to mean—someone who takes an interest in the world? In that case, maybe I am one."

"It doesn't mean anything," said Duke. "Maybe it used to. Probably did, if the world were covered with Peter Gunns."

"Shouldn't that be Peters Gunn?"

Yolly glanced up at the screen. "Eh. How about a visual with the sound turned down?"

"It won't bother me," said Peter. A chorus of assent, and a typical sixties domestic scene appeared on the screen. A burly, misshapen woman in a strange costume lumbered across the set, and the title "Hazel" was superimposed on the image.

"Music?" said Jin. "Where did we leave off? Ah, yes."

A primitive beat accompanied by a sort of barbershop scat. Then a solo voice, almost falsetto. Something about a lion sleeping in the jungle . . . Peter tuned it out. "So what's been happening down here?"

Duke's glance traveled about the room as if he were looking for a cheat sheet on one of the walls. "Not much. Last time you were here it was, what, 1959? A lot of media under the bridge since then. We decided to jump around a bit more—someone pointed out that, at the time these things were being aired, there was a considerable overlap between times. Reruns, golden oldies, stuff like that. So we programmed the manager to provide a little extra repetition of the stuff that was most enjoyable."

"Oh," said Peter. "So you're slowing down?"

Philippe said, "Just a little. We noticed that the third time you hear most of these songs is the best. Oh, and we've been joined by these two." He gestured at a pair of

Nipponese girls sitting together on one of the couches. "Mitsuko and Andrea, right? They're getting to be regulars."

Mitsuko giggled. "There's no place else to go. We just can't afford access on our own." She had a markedly flat face with heavy eyebrows and a fleshy nose. The other girl, Andrea, pale and undistinguished, nodded her agreement.

"Have you watched any of the free telecasts being sent back from the explorer ferries?" asked Peter. "Not bad stuff. You can actually see some real personal interaction once in a while. The scientists are quite likable, really."

"No," said Yolly. "It's too dry for me. No plot, no akshiyon. Just a bunch of geology."

"That's what we're here for," said Andrea.

Duke frowned. "Is it really? I've been thinking about it lately. It's hard not to, you know? We're the first generation of this generation ship; it gives us a totally unique perspective. We're the first generation, if not to be born in space, at least to grow up in it. Like the TV generation was, back in the 1950s: a new sort of creature."

Philippe yawned. "So what?"

Peter broke in. "No, I know what Duke means."

Duke grinned. "Maybe you do and maybe you don't, but I want to finish saying it. I think *Asia* was the last gasp of Eastern civilization. Think about the tenets of Scientific Capitalism. Especially the part about cultural conservatism. What does it say? The thing about 'preserving humanism by eradicating the technology that eats away the human soul.' The whole thing is a dead end, and they knew it. We're that end. They took the cultural symbols called science fiction and fashioned them into a project that could put off the stagnation that was inevitably on the way. Because science fiction was clearly an aspect of the culture they were emulating, they ignored the contradictions that Project Outreach brought about."

Yolly leaned back against an arm of her couch and put her feet up on the other arm. "What bullshit!" she said.

Duke didn't look offended. In fact, he smiled. "Laugh if you will"—and here he allowed time for some of the

others to snicker mechanically—"but think about it. The point of Project Outreach was, and is, to give the illusion of progress to the millions of workers who keep capitalism going. Where does it go from here? I daresay that the outer limits of the old science fiction—teleportation, time travel, and the like—are possible, but a basically backward-looking culture will never be able to achieve—"

"The big question in all this is, what's it really like in the New West?" Philippe picked at his nose thoughtfully. "What are we being shielded from?"

"They say that everyone is hooked into the computers, no one works, and androids run everything." Andrea, who looked somewhat confused by the course of the conversation, was gamely trying to contribute.

"From what I've heard," said Yolly, "it's not quite so different there. They simply weren't afraid to go where technology was leading. They take advantage of cybernetics, instead of trying to sweep it under the table."

Peter held up a hand and chopped it down emphatically. "We've all heard horror stories about the West. But if you look between the lines, you can see that they have a system just as viable, if not more so, than ours."

"Look," said Duke, "what I'm saying is that you can't have a society that is afraid to go forward, wherever it leads. Talk to your parents, ask them about it. From what I've seen, they're not very happy to participate in this great future we have."

A moment of silence followed. Then, a rhythm. Suddenly a fluid voice was crooning what seemed to be a complete set of permutations for the words "Duke," "of," and "Earl."

"Hey," said Philippe, "it's your song."

Jin smiled. "About time."

The point about their parents seemed to have gotten to everybody. No one offered a rebuttal, and the music played on and on.

Four

Larry Taylor was joyous, exuberant. As the little rocket plane coasted down over the interior of Twist's sea, hanging from its forty-meter high-dihedral wings like one of the first human-powered airplanes, he had a sense of infinite grace. There was none of the ugly machine noise that reminded you of the unnatural efforts required to remain aloft; not even the whoosh of normal glider flight. Occasionally the rocket was turned on, a brief roaring like the burning propane of a hot-air balloon, and then wonderful, godlike floating began again.

The medium that held him up was ninety-eight percent gaseous water, average temperature ninety-four degrees centigrade, at a pressure of about 511 millibar, half that of Earth. Steam, you could call it, though most people thought steam was the mist that condenses from the gas when it comes in contact with cold air. Here, near the center of this boiling sea, circling the region where the hot gas did condense into a plume of mist because of higher pressures, it was especially hard to think that visibility was the defining feature of that word.

Taylor peered hard into the great, whitish thermal that sprouted from the sea like an Yggdrasil tree, to spend its form in twisting helixes high overhead. But these things were only a momentary distraction. The physics of this strange world was not what had brought him here. It was the biology teeming on the surface of this sea that made him happy.

He piloted the craft down farther, fighting the heated gas as it rose toward the upper reaches of the atmosphere, and maneuvered into level flight about a hundred meters over the surface. Here the sea life was most crowded, red and purple dominating over the darker, green-black of open water. Individual sheets of smooth, shiny crimson, kilometers wide, bulged and dipped, showing no sign of texture or internal structure. On a normal terrestrial planet, where life energy rained down from the sun, such an expression of form would have been unremarkable. But Twist's vitality came from the strongly focused tidal disruption at the bottom of this ocean. These creatures were not interested in Epsilon Indi's feeble light. Why, then, were they at the surface, whose only distinguishing factor was its relative inhospitableness? Among the great sheets, many other types of life could be seen, floating just under the clear water like jellyfish, undulating with the waves. Most seemed composed of thin membranes attached into the biological equivalents of the regular polyhedra, mostly squashed tetrahedra, though upon occasion he would see one with a larger number of sides, as high up the scale as an icosahedron, formed of twenty identical equilateral triangles. They ranged in size from a few meters across to twenty or more. Shreds of torn purple, of all sizes and shapes, littered large areas of the surface. Taylor guessed that they might be the young of the sheet creatures. Farther down, small, bright, squidlike animals were just barely visible.

Still, this was all a mystery. The surface was plainly not where the action was. Unless these creatures were much more energy efficient than their terrestrial counterparts—something exceedingly improbable in an anaerobic environment like this—they needed more than hot water to survive. The membraneous structures, having a very high percentage of water, were probably capable of withstanding the enormous pressures down at the bottom, and he had to assume that that was where they lived most of their lives. But, on the other hand, they had so far revealed no signs of independent movement. Even the polyhedra displayed no signs of motor activity. Were these

just dead creatures that had lost their ability to survive in the real biosphere at the sea floor?

The plane began to encounter regions of instability. Hot gasses buffeted the vehicle, and the tips of the wings flapped scarily. He was straying too near the center. The temperature had risen to ninety-seven degrees, and the pressure was almost one bar. Against the pale blue of the sky, the gray-white plume column could have been an earthly cumulonimbus of some ghastly, elongated sort. Carefully, he banked and lit his rocket, climbing to about three hundred meters.

A small alarm sounded, calling his attention to a flashing yellow indicator on the console. Damn! Fuel half gone, it was time to turn back. Reluctantly, fighting a childish desire to just keep on going, Taylor tilted the plane into another long curve which would eventually point it back toward the base. He was so excited by what he had seen that he was shaking, a nervous chill that he had not felt since, as a child, he suddenly understood the full implications of evolution. It would be a long, long time before he understood even half of what was down there, yet he would not be satisfied until the secrets of these alien life forms were broken.

The Physics Lab was deserted, as usual. Even before the launch of the two planetary ferries, there had not been much activity here, at least not as much as Horologium would have liked. He obtained a great deal of pleasure from helping people access the capacious resources of the Mind, but these scientists seemed to view him as an annoyance, another layer of bureaucracy that kept them from doing good work. Du Lapp had said as much. They didn't appreciate the increase in productivity that a modern librarian such as himself could engender.

Of course, Horologium had other duties as well, enough to keep the average Resource Manager extremely busy. Able to continuously monitor hundreds of channels simultaneously, much of his working consciousness was devoted to following real-time data from the many scientific experiments *Asia* carried.

Since he had been turned on in the spring of 2175, there had been much to remember. Androids were born with only an advanced-learning algorithm in memory, more sophisticated than that of a human baby but without the innate components that allowed humans to so easily categorize the world. It had taken him a full year to master his own senses, and six months more to take his first step. This was a confusing period that he recalled with displeasure; in the earliest days of his functioning he could see what nonexistence was like. One of the first questions he had asked was, "Why not just program me like a computer?" The answer, like many of the answers that came from his creators, was subtle and, at the time, made little sense. Now he could comprehend that they wished him to be like them, an individual, with individual perceptions and thoughts. They were driven by a need to humanize the world about them, and he, in a sense, was one of the results.

He remembered his "adolescence," on the other hand, with pleasure. His tutor would take him on walks through the shifting complexity of the Emperor's Garden, almost overloading his sensory apparatus with the colors, smells, and different shapes of the biological world. As he walked, chatting about human things, he could almost feel the new algorithms burgeoning within his brain, assembling and compressing themselves into theories of ever greater complexity.

And indeed he had turned out very different from the other androids that he talked to. Some of them seemed very limited to him, incapable of making the distinctions that humans found so important. Others, confiding in him, would say things that had no correspondence to his own ideas of the world; silly things, or dangerous.

Horologium descended the few stairs to the Physics Lab's main room and took a seat behind his desk. He had no need for a place to read and write, of course, though it was true a very small percentage of the onboard data was in the form of antique books. Most of that was fiction, and contained little beyond outpourings explaining the more esoteric of human longings and fantasies. He had a desk

for the same reason he was shaped like a human—to comfort humans and enforce the notion that the world was controlled and dominated by humans and their things. He tried to form an opinion of such a strange business, but found that it didn't provoke an emotion in him one way or the other.

The fourteen years aboard *Asia* had been happy ones, he supposed. There was a continuous supply of new data, for one thing, though he was as yet unable to synthesize any theories that had not been already developed by a human. The Mind, with its gargantuan resources, could be a useful tool, but it was often remarkably empty of references to things that seemed to be of real importance. Humans had probed back to the very beginnings of time, and had very interesting theories concerning the nature and origins of the universe. But his prime algorithm kept asking for answers to the profound questions of existence, and only received in response the weak, mutually contradictory notions that humans called religion. Perhaps the nature of his brain was too much affected by conceptions of causality which themselves were merely the desires of humans to perpetuate their genetic structure. He probably would never know.

Ah! The High-Pi Transient Event Survey had picked up something. An instantaneous burster, the kind the experiment had been designed to detect. Very bright. Jya Mailin would be interested in this: it must be relatively close. Horologium analyzed the data briefly. It was in Ursa Major, not far from . . . the numbers coalesced. Horologium felt a strong surge of pleasure. This, now, this was something of great interest. The burster was in a direction indistinguishable from that of Sol. Was this a coincidence? The probability of such a close match was indescribably tiny. So the burster had come from home. Another nagging presence in his head forced him to take notice of a different monitor. So. Radio contact with Earth stops simultaneously. Even stronger pleasure.

It was still very early. Eugenia had been having the nightmare about the dogs again, and she was sufficiently

groggy that she knocked over her glass of water before she found the com unit. She hadn't even really heard the buzzer, but she knew that's what must have awakened her. "Captain here," she said, trying to keep the muzziness out of her voice.

"Roh here," came a voice. "We need you on the bridge right away."

"Right-o," she said, climbing from the comfortable bedclothes. "I'm on my way."

The captain kept a special jumpsuit for occasions such as this; just step in and zip up. Her RM joined her as she came into the corridor. He looked deeply concerned.

"What is it? What's going on?" she asked.

The RM looked confused. "It seems as though contact with Earth has been cut off, somehow. The Physics RM reports that there was a bright burst in the vicinity of Sol at the exact moment. The flare lasted approximately .073 seconds, and, if it was indeed three and a half parsecs away, would have an absolute magnitude of minus seven."

Taranga stopped short. "What the fuck are you trying to say? That the Earth has blown up?"

The RM looked down at his shoes. "Uh, I am not well versed in the sciences, as some of my kind are. I am only really a scheduler. I can offer no opinion on what—"

Taranga started off again, faster. "Sorry," she said. "We'll soon get to the bottom of this." They stepped into the elevator and were whisked away.

On the bridge, before the astounding backdrop of a full Doublejove, Roh Ek Sai and Subcaptain Oyomota were arguing loudly. They turned as she entered, and the warring emotions quickly subsided from their faces. Identical looks of puppy expectancy took their place. Eugenia understood the feelings well (she had conditioned them all to an extent): *she* was in command. *She* would be able to straighten all this out. This time, however, the burden just might be a little too much.

"Friends," she said, "my RM has given me a prelimi-

nary report on this . . . event. What more can you tell me about what happened?"

Ex seemed to be more deflated than usual, and the wrinkles in his face were more like fissures. "There really isn't much to tell. All we know is that there was a bright, instantaneous flash whose position coincides to the limit of our data with that of Earth. At the same moment, to a hundredth of a second, contact with the Earth ceased. I suppose we must conclude that the two events are connected."

Taranga circled the two men like a hungry wolf. "Good God, Ex. That is not the kind of thing I want to hear." She suddenly wanted to laugh out loud, to cry, *No! This is still a bad dream!* But she knew that it wasn't. "Look, gentlemen, I would like to have a few answers. Have 'flashes' of this sort been detected before?"

Roh sat himself on the edge of the subofficers dais and rubbed his eyes carefully. "Three since we started looking in 2011. Each in the vicinity of nondescript dwarf stars in the nearer reaches of the galaxy. At least that was the guess. One of the more important experiments aboard *Asia* is the High-Pi Survey which will attempt to pinpoint events more precisely, using our great parallactic separation from the observatories in solar orbit."

Eugenia stared at nothing. Doublejove was waning majestically, and a sizeable slice was missing from its right limb. There was little she could do. Except tighten things a turn; keep everything safe. "I want the scientists back on the double. Corvus, schedule a meeting for all those who might have useful knowledge. Here on the bridge, this morning, nine A.M."

Oyomota smiled, confident that someone was in chargé. "What should we do?"

Taranga looked at the man, but she couldn't quite manage a smile. "Sleep. That's what I'm going to do."

She left, followed by her RM. Roh and Oyomota exchanged meaningless glances. Finally the former stood and stretched. "The captain's right, as always. Good night, Dave."

* * *

Refueled and short of sleep, Larry was once again out over the sea, cataloging creatures and trying to determine taxonomic similarities. The videon sounded, a loud and insistent piping, and he pressed the onoff. A small region of the window opaqued, and Natasha, seated in the mobile lab, appeared in it. She seemed subdued.

"Bad news travels fast, Larry," she started.

"It looks like it's caught up with me, anyway," he said. "What's up?"

"We've been recalled to *Asia*. Ex intimated that there has been some sort of disaster. Both *Arecibo* and *Mt. Palomar* are expected back posthaste. I told him it would take a while for us to pack up. He was obviously pretty disturbed by something; he didn't even reply."

What was that?

Out of the corner of his eye he had seen some sort of movement, but it had been carried out of sight by the slow wheeling of the plane. "Okay, Tash, message received," he said. "I'll be back as soon as I check something out." He punched the onoff again, and taking his bearings, dropped the left wing and put on a hard rudder. With infuriating slowness, the plane swung around until finally he was pointed in the right direction. A particularly large sheet creature dominated this section of the surface, and, as he forced the plane's nose into a steep dive, it appeared to expand until it filled his view. No repeat of the motion, though, only the rise and fall of peripatetic waves cloaked in red. He was at fifty meters now, and let his nose come back to level as he skimmed over the surface at a hundred fifty knots.

There it is again! By bloody semen, a motile life form at last! The thing, at the edge of the sheet creature, was long and bright yellow. He aimed directly for it, unaware that his wings were being stressed almost to the limit, and fired a retrorocket to slow down. It was corkscrewing itself through the surface of the sheet, a self-contained needle-and-thread hemming the thing with a dotted line of yellow. Here and there the sheet seemed to be losing its integrity; and, right at the nether tip of the yellow crea-

ture, was a sort of jagged, forward-pointing skirt that completed the job of ripping it to bits.

Now he was getting somewhere. A standard predator-prey relationship was easy to understand. After a while the yellow creature, which Larry had dubbed a "twister" to himself, seemed to give up, satiated, and disappeared. Perhaps a square kilometer of the sheet had been destroyed, most of that having decayed into the omnipresent purple confetti, and the sheet seemed to be spreading itself to fill in the missing chunk. So it was not totally passive either.

Larry accelerated the plane back up to the three-hundred-meter level and tried to get an overview. The twister was evidently a rather rare beastie, and he was convinced that the predator/prey ratio wasn't what would be expected of a normal ecosystem. This, of course, was Irina's specialty, and he would have to go over the videon data with her as soon as they were back in *Arecibo*.

He still had the nagging feeling that he had been viewing just the tip of a much more complex ecology farther down. The mobile lab's submarine was going to prove valuable, after all. Damn it, though! What a time for trouble to strike. He wondered if the disaster had anything to do with the DV problem. Murphy's Third Law didn't specify how many *different* things could go wrong at a time; but as a scientist, he tended to go with Ockam until Murphy kicked in. He just hoped that *Asia* wasn't being recalled to Earth for some improbable reason.

Larry turned the plane toward home and let the rockets kick in full force.

Mt. Palomar skewed down from Nickleby orbit, homing in on the telemetry signal from its mother ship. Despite the unexpectedly short reconnaissance of Doublejove's third satellite, much had been accomplished. As had been judged from its average density, Nickleby was composed primarily of stone and iron; the icy crust was less than fifty kilometers thick. Underneath, the Mars-size body plainly showed the distinctive stamp of plate tectonics, the phenomenon that had heretofore been restricted to the Earth and, some argued, Venus. Mantalini and the

other chasmae had been found to lie above active regions of upwelling heat in the moon's mantle, following lines of crustal spreading and plate creation similar to the Mid-Atlantic Ridge. "Plates" of ice, more or less equivalent to the underlying plates of rock, spread and merged with great force, causing a great variety of land forms at the surface. As on Twist, the heat of the mantle had melted the ice above the source of heat, and Nickleby's chasmae were filled with liquid water. No biology had been found, however.

On the return trip Cory had asked to ride up front with RM Pavo. She was tired of the continual come-ons from Denahy, and preferred to be by herself. Separation from Larry, even for three days, produced some unique feelings in her. Absence did make her miss the big Aussie, but at the same time she found herself enjoying the autonomy. Her science had been neglected since coming out of stasis, and now, with Doublejove and its perpetually changing appearance egging her on, she felt a part of her that she had almost forgotten existed coming back to life. One would think that two scientists such as she and Larry would have much in common. She would have to go out of her way to stress those items and guard against falling into the dreadful trance of common denominator.

She had never particularly enjoyed physical sex. Her union with the biologist had provided her mainly with a feeling of companionship, a closeness that her father had mostly failed to provide. She wouldn't let her relationship stand in the way of the science that she had to do. Many of the unique elements of Doublejove were unexplained, for example, and even the magnetic cells were understood only in very general terms.

Pavo looked at her suddenly with apparent interest. "So, my dear, are you thinking about your loved one?"

RM's *did* have the annoying habit of divining what was going on in her head. "Not really," she said. "I am trying to get my mind off of him."

"I understand that is very difficult for you humans to do. It is only natural to think about the act from which one's whole existence emanates, I suppose."

"Uh, you mean sexual intercourse, I suppose? No, Pavo, I think you've got hold of a pretty outrageous oversimplification there. You've accessed human literature, haven't you? We are not quite so simple."

Pavo smiled disingenuously. "Oh, no? I have indeed read much; and the fact of the matter is that human writings are devoted almost exclusively to three topics: acquiring sexual partners, acquiring money and property, and coming to terms with personal demise."

"There's more to it than that!"

"Much of it, it is true, has what you would call mythic elements that are merely sublimated versions of the above. I am generally unmoved by any fiction."

"You're just a cynic, Pavo."

"Perhaps. I have tried many times to understand my position among people. The role I like best is that of 'Devil's Advocate.'"

"That gets tiring and repetitive after a while, doesn't it? I would think that you would see better results if you reassured those you come in contact with as to the rightness of their perceptions."

Pavo nodded. "Many of my kind have adopted exactly that posture. Enough do so that I can maintain my role without difficulty. In many cases my caustic remarks are taken to be complimentary simply because of the source."

Cory inspected the RM's face closely, but, of course, there was nothing to see. Finally she laughed. "I can see that. RM, you are a genuine individualist."

Pavo seemed to lapse into an unemotional, robotic personality. "We're coming up on *Asia*. If you look carefully you can see it, glittering there above Drood. We'll make rendezvous in fourteen minutes."

Cory obediently searched out the fluctuating pinpoint of light. So, back into the realm of Captain Taranga, she thought. I wonder what has happened to cut short our expedition? Amused, she tried an experiment. "Pavo, why do *you* think we've been recalled?"

The RM looked pleased that she was interested in his opinion. "My opinion. I think the most likely explanation is that there has been some kind of accident aboard *Asia*. I

will know more as soon as I reestablish communication with the Mind."

Cory sank back in her seat and shook her head. These androids had developed their own operational algorithms from the barest minimum of original code. She had looked at the bootstrap program once, out of curiosity. There was nothing in it that would compel RM's to humor humans, or even to associate with them. Only a burned-in desire to understand and to correlate. Even their individual existence was subordinated to that quest. And yet they turned out surprisingly humanlike. She wondered whether their behavior wasn't just a carefully contrived routine to soften up humans and get them to reveal more of the Truth. Yes, the elusive Truth. The poor slobs had no way of knowing how lame humans really were.

Suddenly, they were there. The open door of the ferry hold yawned brightly, beckoning them. Pavo piloted the ship effortlessly into the opening, and she felt the brittle crunch as the docking grapples mated.

None of this, however, resolved the feeling that she and Larry would be entering a difficult time.

Five

The bridge was crowded with people, gathered in knots of two or three, many engaged in vigorous argument. Captain Taranga had called a meeting of those members of the crew who might have something to contribute to the discussion. Secrecy was crucial at this stage, of course; but there was nothing she could do with the scientists except threaten and cajole. None of the planetologists had been asked: only Jya, Du Lapp, and Stellar Physicist Genaza Tetap represented the full-termers. With the six senior members of the DV technician team, ten chief officers, the two scientific liaison RM's—Horologium and Scorpius—and, of course, her husband, there were more than enough opinions to sample. As far as she knew, only these folks so far had any knowledge of what had happened. She was prepared to let the nontechnical citizens know about the loss of radio contact, if she had to. But there was no chance in hell she would tell them about the accompanying burst. Talk about demoralization! Without positive evidence of what had actually occurred, speculation could easily lead to mass hysteria.

Doublejove nearly filled the viewscreen, bathing the room in a reddish light that overwhelmed the normal, full-spectrum overheads. It was, for the moment, full, and provided spectacle enough for hours of inspection. The phenomena associated with the magnetically driven ionosphere had increased over the last week, and in many

places a new layer of bright, smeared blotches completely hid the underlying strata of whorls and bands. The captain watched the planet through shadowy silhouettes and wondered about it while waiting for her husband to arrive. Finally the entry door slid aside and Oishi came in, apparently not even aware that he was late. Eugenia couldn't summon up any annoyance; she smiled and motioned to him to join her.

"All right," she said, in a voice loud enough to carry over the others. "We are all here now. I have been listening to some of the arguments taking place while we waited. Let's see if we can muster a group discussion that will lead us to correct answers." She looked around and was pleased to see that she had their attention. "First, we will have a summary of the situation from our physics RM."

Horologium, bronzed and slit-eyed, had been modeled on Sherpa physiognomy. With his shock of black hair and matching mustache, he looked vaguely Turkic. The RM looked about the assembled crowd, and beginning to speak, stuttered slightly on a B, then stopped. A moment passed. "I am not used to speaking to so many of you at one time," he said. "It is a difficult thing to try to address all simultaneously. However, I will try. I'm sure all of you know the sequence of events by now, so I will try to confine my talk to an examination of the electromagnetic record. One hundred sixteen hours, four minutes, and thirty-nine seconds ago, the Cohesive Electromagnetic Signal originating at the Project Outreach lab broke off. Since that time there has been no resumption of signal. A detailed quanta analysis of the last millisecond of the transmission indicates that the signal modulation deviated significantly at the trailing end of the beam. Scorpius and I ran a simulation of possible events and determined that a power surge resulting from Electromagnetic Pulse is a possible cause of this deviation. Normal shut-off of transmission has an easily identifiable signature that definitely was not present.

"As most of you know, this event was apparently accompanied by a transient electromagnetic burst at Earth. The time resolution of our High-Pi device is one millisec-

ond; as a result, the precision of our analysis is low. However, there is much that we still can say. If the two events are related, and there is little probability that they are not, the burster must have been located within a light-millisecond of the P.O. transmitter. This translates into 299.793 kilometers. So it is reasonable to presume that the burster was located at or near the surface of the Earth."

Jya Mailin waved her hand to get the RM's attention. She was seated at one of the subofficer's stations, her chair swiveled out to face the center of the bridge. "Horo, could you use the viewscreen to show us graphs of the data?"

Horologium looked into the woman's face, wondering why he had not thought of this himself. Of course, he had been told repeatedly that people like to get their data verbally; even scientific data. Perhaps this select group could understand more concentrated information. He made several transfers with the library and Doublejove disappeared, replaced by a complex three-dimensional plot showing wavelength vs. signal strength vs. time.

"As you can see, this graph establishes the nature of the burst itself. The abrupt onset and decay of the signal is cause by limited resolution. The burst was recorded for seventy-three milliseconds, or seventy-three iterations of the High-Pi device. During this time the signal strength showed a negative correlation with wavelength. The shorter the wavelength, the stronger the emission. Thus the signal appears to peak in the gamma-ray spectrum without a subsequent drop-off in higher frequencies; I need not point out that this is very unusual for a natural phenomenon. This strange correlation has been pointed out before for the several other similar bursters that have been observed; no one, to my knowledge, has satisfactorily explained it.

"The total magnitude of the burst followed a sinusoidal light curve, within the resolution of our record."

Scorpius stepped down from the subofficers' dais and walked over to the viewscreen. He was a medium-sized android with a round face and small parrot beak of a nose. "Let me point out that this," he pointed to the middle of

the graph, "represents a tremendous amount of energy if we postulate that it is located at the same distance as Earth. In visible light alone it was almost 150,000 times as bright as the sun. Total energy emitted during that short time span was five point two times ten to the thirty-fifth ergs, as much as Sol sends out in more than two minutes."

Horologium looked at the other android, frowning. "I was going to say that," he said.

Scorpius smiled. "I know. But the astronomical analogies *are* my bailiwick."

Roh Ek Sai stood from his console and cleared his throat mightily. He was familiar with jurisdictional disputes between RM's, and he didn't especially want to get into one now. "All right, you two," he said. "We can take it from here. If we need any more information we'll ask questions. Thank you for your presentation."

"But," stuttered Horologium, "We have several more things—"

Captain Taranga cleared her throat. The point was made. Scorpius and Horologium retreated to a corner of the bridge. Ex seated himself once more.

"Okay," said May, brushing back a lanky fall of dark hair. "It begins to look darker and darker. I must point out, however, that there are some possible scenarios that aren't as grim as others. For example, we don't know how directional bursters are. The energy we received could have been sent only in a very small cone, intersecting the P.O. and us, but not disruptive on a huge scale."

"That doesn't seem very probable," said Captain Taranga. "Does it?"

May shrugged. "I don't know."

"There are a few theories to explain the phenomena associated with these transient bursts," said Genaza Tetap. The stellar specialist was an extremely tall Kampuchean with wide-set eyes and a heart-shaped face. She was called Jeannie by her friends. "Although most of them assume a larger distance than what we apparently have here. Most of these theories revolve around the notion of naturally occurring rips in spacetime. Places where, because of some improbable series of events, the conservative ways of

the universe fail and a miniature big bang comes about. Based on the mostly discredited notion that conditions can exist—in fact, did exist at the very beginning—in which matter and energy can spontaneously be created with no concern for conservation."

May nodded. "Little bangs, if you will. But, as Jeannie says, there was never a good way of determining the correct distance of these things before. A few Western scientists I met at the conferences maintained that they were in fact associated with the low-mass main-sequence stars in whose location they appeared; but the prevailing theory was that they were in reality much more distant. I myself thought that they were most probably at huge distances, associated with the very earliest days of the universe—sort of backfires from the creation. But I suppose I can't think that any longer."

Ryan Du Lapp, sitting next to May, smiled at her and patted her on the back. "No harm in making up the most conservative theory to explain something. I, however, never did buy into any of these easy explanations. The very fact that these flares are so short-lived argues against almost any hypothesis I've seen. My principal investigations have been into diffuse field physics, though, so I can't say that I ever gave it a lot of thought before."

Eugenia clapped her hands sharply. Everyone looked at her. "So what is unique about Earth? Why would there be a . . . burster there?"

May continued to stare at the captain. Of course! Why hadn't she thought of it before? "Technology."

Ryan grimaced. "Why—shit. That would explain the other locations as well. Civilizations going bang. The new threshold . . ."

Nick Oishi looked at his wife and shook his head, smiling. Damn if she wasn't a good captain. He never could quite accustom himself to her position, but when he saw her executing her duties, he couldn't help but feel a certain pride. Here she had cut to the quick of the problem; bringing scientists to conclusions that they probably otherwise wouldn't have had. "So we vanquished the atomic bomb," he said, "which was universally regarded

as the end of the world, just to fall prey to a totally unexpected glitch in physics?"

Ryan laughed bitterly. "It's a little early to make such a pronouncement. But it's something we're going to have to look into."

Oishi scratched at a sparse beginning beard. "Could it be some kind of weapon?"

Suddenly Giancarlo Colibri of the DV team shouted, "Wait!" He jumped up and paced across the room to look more closely at the graph still displayed on the viewscreen. "Son of a bitch. You know, this looks a fuck of a lot like some of the readings we were getting from the glitch in the DV drive. Nothing like these numbers, but, I swear, the distribution of frequencies looked very similar to this."

Ryan looked at Horologium. "Horo, could we see a graph of the energy readings from the DV problem?"

Horo looked at the captain.

"Go ahead. Security lien removed."

The information appeared on the screen next to the burster graph. There were many differences, but it was apparent that the distribution of wavelengths, peaking in gamma, was similar. Eugenia was horrified. If they hadn't turned off the thing . . .

Ex was obviously agitated now, and he rocked back and forth in his chair, sucking his lips in. He stood again. "I say that this speculation, while of course necessary, is not going to affect the ultimate solution to the problem. We simply are going to have to send someone—or something—back, to see what happened."

Eugenia looked thoughtful. "There is an obvious answer. We could send our Traveler back instead of on to its next destination."

Horologium, leaning on the dais railing, said, "The library indicates Traveler twelve is only a few weeks from completing its refueling in the Epsilon Indi Oort Cloud. At top speed, it could be back in the solar system in approximately three and a half years."

The captain smiled at the android. "Thanks, Horo. That's just the information we needed."

"I must point out, though," said Horo, "that the

intelligence built into the Travelers, while sophisticated on many levels, is rudimentary for the type of cognitive functioning necessary for goals not related to its primary mission. And, since Earth is 11.45 light-years away, it will have to be totally autonomous."

Ex rumbled. "Well, that's obvious. It shouldn't be too difficult to load a stasis lozenge onto Traveler and send a person back as well."

Scorpius shrugged; a meaningless gesture. "One of us could go."

Eugenia glanced at Scorpius and Horologium, then back at her Technical Liaison. "How difficult would it be to replace the Traveler computer with one of the RM's?"

"Not easy. I would have to talk to the Cyberneticist to get an accurate answer. While the process has no theoretical obstacles, an RM android's brain has never been tampered with before. I simply don't know what the result would be."

"Well," Taranga said, "look into it."

"If we send a person back, who will it be?" asked May. "A specialist?"

"I don't think that would be necessary," said the captain. "It would be best if we sent someone young, who hasn't yet acquired the responsibilities of family life. Someone who wouldn't be missed for seven years."

David Oyomota spoke for the first time. "We could have a test of some sort."

Taranga said, "Good idea."

The British invasion was beginning. Peter was again hanging around in the Media Club room, and was fascinated to hear the Beatles' early songs in the context of their proper cultural milieu. Seeing them do "I Wanna Hold Your Hand" on the Ed Sullivan show, immediately following *The Jetsons*, was a revelation. The Beatles' music permeated the media that they had grown up with: Peter had personally seen three plays in which the Beatles' songs were the primary attraction. The cultural shockwave was, he supposed, something that would never go away. The music was less simplistic, more interesting against a

varying bass line, and there was a visceral energy in the churning electric guitar.

School was a continuing problem. His grades were dropping, and as a result his salary was shrinking to almost nothing. His parents had taken to promising him ever larger rewards in order to motivate him, but it wasn't working. He could tell that they regarded his success as somewhat less important than their own careers, and his current rash of disappearances had hardly been noticed. That they could become so interested in their petty little work fiefdoms was a source of continued amazement to Peter. Occasionally he would imagine that someone was blackmailing them, but he knew this was only a dumb idea derived from the police shows that he watched.

The fact was that he had become utterly isolated from the mainstream of *Asian* society. Not that he had ever really been a part of things. But at least when he was younger, he had felt a sense of purpose, the idea that all this was being done to some end. His father had explained it often enough. Now he felt absolutely no sympathy for Project Outreach. He had assimilated Duke Jin's view that it was a pathetic attempt to maintain hegemony over an increasingly disaffected population. He had dreams of being a Westerner, in which his very essence seemed to flow out of his body and spread out over a huge electronic network, and in which all his needs were taken care of instantaneously, without cost. As he watched the old shows and listened to the old music, he had the profound feeling that the West had not turned its back on its heritage, as was claimed, but in fact was fully developing the idea of Freedom, with which it had won so many hearts.

Here in the safe comfort of the Media Club, there was a sense of family that he had never gotten from interacting with the two strange, remote adults who claimed parenthood. A power troika had developed—Duke, Yolly, and himself. Others came and went, but the continuing relationship between the three of them formed the locus of Media Club activity. They had developed many in-jokes, and they competed with each other in their disparagement of everyone and everything.

* * *

The program came to its conclusion and the videon turned dark. It was late, and only the Big Three were present.

Duke, lying supine in the deep sofa, threw his arms back and let his hands dangle in the air. "I don't think I can take another episode of *Bonanza*."

Yolly sat up. "It goes on for another eight years, at least. Not counting reruns."

"I think we can safely delete some of them," said Peter.

"That does violate the spirit of our little club. I talked to our Jya Wuji yesterday, and she said that the repeat-access cost will go up if we continue to "abuse our privileges."

"Oh, great," groaned Peter. "I have little enough money as it is."

Yolly looked at Peter dispassionately, her pastel eyes sparkling. "You'll just have to work harder in school."

"Anything but that. My counselor wants me to go into the ecosystem technicum; they'll turn me into a roachherd if they get their way."

"I told you you'd have to pick something or they'd do it for you," said Yolly. "And the lower your grades, the worse you do. It's that simple."

Peter suddenly felt a rush of anger. "It's all a piece of shit. Why the fuck won't they just leave us alone?"

"Now now, little man," admonished Duke, "there aren't any caves on *Asia*. No place for hermits."

"Except the Media Club," said Yolly.

"I will—"

The door fell aside and Philippe Berouai ran into the room, panting heavily. He collapsed into a couch and, breathing so hard he could barely be understood, said, "There's—There's been an announce—announcement on the main channel. Captain Taranga herself. We've lost contact with Earth. And—And, they're going to send somebody back."

Duke smirked. "That's an ingenious idea. Why don't we all go back?"

"No. In a modified Traveler. In stasis. It'll take only three and a half years that way. And the person who goes back will only lose a few weeks."

"What are they supposed to do when they get there?" asked Peter. "Ask them politely to turn the signal back on and then turn around and come back?"

"Something like that," said Philippe. "She wasn't very specific."

Yolly sat back in her couch and folded her arms over her breasts. "This *is* serious. Why in the world would they turn the signal off to begin with? If there was some kind of malfunction, it seems that we should just wait for the signal to come back on."

"They must know something we don't," said the pudgy Philippe, "to want to take this kind of action."

Duke combed a hand through his dull, black hair. "They must suspect that something very bad has happened."

"Like what?"

"How the hell do I know? The world's nuclear arsenals are in *Asia*'s belly, so there couldn't have been a war of that kind. But who knows what sort of powers the West has developed?"

Peter oscillated his head, almost out of control. "There aren't any bad feelings between the East and West. We make most of their products for them. They wouldn't—no, couldn't—start a war."

Philippe seemed composed now, calm. "Be that as it may. Something happened. They are going to give a special aptitude test, and the high scorer will get to go to Earth to investigate."

"Shit," said Peter, smiling. "What an opportunity. When are they giving it?"

Yolly looked at Peter, incredulous. "You mean you *want* to go back? Lose seven years or more? Hell, Duke and I'll be practically middle-aged when you get back!"

"So what? Sure I'd like to go. It'd give me a chance to see for myself what's going on in the West, for one thing. I'm sure you'll be waiting for me when I return." He laughed and gave the young woman a penetrating look. "I won't be picked, anyway."

The subtext was ignored. Duke turned onto his side and held up a finger. "Fuck, man. We'd better speed up this process. Look, I was going to save this until we got to 1968, but what the hell..." He held up a little vial containing a tarry substance. "THC, synthesized in our very own Chemistry class by yours truly."

Philippe took the little container and examined it closely. "And what is THC?"

Jin smiled proudly. "The active ingredient in marijuana, of course. I thought it might add a little verisimilitude to our undertaking. You smoke it, I understand..."

Traveler 12 sucked in the ice slurry, waited an hour, burped and spat out forty kilograms of chemical ice, which coalesced into a rough white ball. It watched as this mass slowly pirouetted up into a low orbit around the seventeen-kilometer Oort body upon which it had been feeding. Its heavy water tank was full, and its prolonged mission in Epsilon Indi's cometary belt was finished. Withdrawing its segmented crusher/ingester tube, the machine kicked off from the body by firing three equally spaced vernier rockets for thirty seconds.

The planetoid had been irregular before Traveler's meal, but its shape had at least approximated the triaxial ellipsoid so common among pristine Oort Clouders. Now it was deeply gouged, like a broken eggshell, but the space probe felt no remorse for the destruction it had caused. Fifty or so similar objects had been totally consumed to supply the deuterium it needed for its next mission: rendezvous with DM –49 13515, an absolute magnitude 8.6 M1 variable 14.6 light-years distant.

Traveler 12 did feel a small amount of displeasure caused by having to wait in this system so long. Many of its sister craft must have already explored two, three, perhaps more stellar systems in the time it had been assigned to monitor the admittedly variable worlds of this system. But this system had met all the criteria for extended survey, and it was important work to record information about these worlds across time. The craft's roving instinct

was put on hold, and this caused it some distress. New stimuli, that was what it craved.

Here, beyond the reach of Epsilon Indi's feeble solar wind, Traveler 12 felt the ethereal blowing of the galactic wind. Subtle, low-density currents of charged particles wafted across its detector, driven by the galaxy's enormous magnetic field. Its own presence, shielded though it was, dominated the space in which it moved. As the half-eaten planetoid veered off on its own ponderous orbit, the ambient molecules of neutral water were dropping in number. Traveler's rudimentary cognitive skills strained for an overview of its mission so far. Finishing this first leg of its task left it with many questions. How it wished it had been programmed to exchange information with the other Travelers as the mission progressed. But the lag time was too great; if it hadn't been for the twenty-nine-year extension of its mission here, it would never have had the time to communicate with its creators at all.

They had told it that another probe was coming hot on its heels, containing many hundreds of human beings, to fully explore these worlds. So it had done well in the sense that this system was one of great interest. And they had told it that, when this new craft arrived, Traveler would locate it and transfer all of its accumulated data. That message had arrived fifteen years ago. It had been a long fifteen years.

That place in Traveler's processor where real-time analysis of data input occurred was the most complex part of its intelligence, calling as it did on virtually all its resources in a parallel, almost simultaneous way. As it turned its great parabolic antenna inward, pointing its science platform toward the star and the inner reaches of its system, the electromagnetic radiation played over the devices meant to record it. Traveler reversed the polarities of its receiver and broadcast a message of salutation, powerful enough to be heard throughout the system. He was many light-hours from their probable location, so it would take a while to receive a reply. He reconfigured himself into noncoherent acquire mode and waited, feeling the galactic wind.

Finally the message came. The new mission was to be aborted. Traveler was being required to return to Doublejove orbit, there to receive new programming. It was a disappointment. There was a curiously unintegrated bit of feedback that momentarily overloaded the real-time input. A correction override kicked in, allowing the instruments to be recorded without Traveler in the loop. Without input, the feedback reached a peak and then tapered off into background sibilance.

Traveler felt a momentary lapse of consciousness followed by a complex series of numbers playing along the real-time interface. When it was over, it carefully aligned its position with its verniers, checked its internal shielding and DV device, and stepped up its power supply. When it was ready, the ion engine came on and Traveler began to accelerate down into the throat of the star's gravity well. At its maximum normal acceleration, it kicked in the DV, boosting the speed by a tremendous amount. As the speed approached cee, it switched off both forms of propulsion and coasted.

Traveler thought to itself. Repetition. Redundancy. This is not what I was made for. I will tell the humans when I talk to them.

Ryan awoke with a start. He had been dreaming of Neptune; at least it was called Neptune in the dream. It was a strange, crater-scarred planet deep in an impossibly blue atmosphere, and the craters were multicolored and lined up into weird, somehow meaningful patterns. The planet had loomed before him, beckoning, mysterious.

He stared into the darkness of his bedroom. Something in the dream had awakened a profound, cosmic significance in him; he knew that he was alive, and he knew that he would not always be. In that long moment he realized the possible significance of the burster in a visceral way: no Earth; an end to things as he knew them. He was scared the way a baby is scared, preverbally, without recourse to rationalization. The darkness, limned by bright phosphenes, pressed in on him.

He flipped on the bed light and sat up, furling the

blanket off his torso. The solidity of the room distracted him from himself and reassured him that, at least for now, he was safe. The antique wooden furniture, carved in patterns that preserved the heritage of his Papuan forbears, seemed far removed from his reality; it was savage and silly.

He turned back and looked at Natasha. She was beautiful in sleep, no longer a tigress, but more of a domestic kitten. The smooth, dark skin of her face, partially hidden by long bangs of newly blond hair, was exquisitely calm. The woman's eyes were tightly closed into dark slits, and her breathing was shallow, regular. Her sleep, it was clear, was not haunted by troubled dreams.

He had found her to be a more than adequate sexual partner. Neither of them had had sex since Earth, and it was a long, drawn-out, unfamiliar thing for them. Ryan had found the correct sort of rhythm that allowed him to go on indefinitely, but Natasha would grow impatient and begin to thrust herself against him at a quicker tempo. He had to withdraw, to her an outlandish thing, and spend some time merely kissing and caressing. The kisses from that tightly drawn, toothy mouth were delicious and almost too much like paradise; several times he had to pull back entirely, saying he needed to rest. Finally he was certain she had had enough, and he blissfully ended the encounter.

Now she was just another enigma. A scientist, like himself, no doubt; but removed by that gap that separated Ryan from all others. Talk could help; but there had been so little that he wondered whether he really knew anything about her. Just another bit of isolation. And the elusive quarry had somehow gotten away again. Ryan was filled again with emotion, but this time something like pity, or sorrow. If this were the end of humanity, perhaps it was all for the best.

He started to slip his legs out from under the bedclothes; but she stirred, rolling onto her side and throwing out an arm to where he had been. Her eyes opened a millimeter. "Ryan?" she said. "What is it?"

"Nothing. I'm thinking of going down to the lab. I've got work to do."

Natasha smiled languorously. "So do we all. There's only one kind of work suited to this time of night, though." She rolled onto her back and pushed away the blanket, exposing small, brown-tipped breasts riding high on her rib cage. "Come on . . ."

It was after five in the morning when Ryan came down the steps into the Physics Lab. He felt stiff and his eyes were grainy; but the resolve that had formed in him had not gone away. Horologium was, as usual, at his desk; but to Ryan's surprise Jya Mailin was also there, staring vacantly at a twinkly readout on her videon.

"Good morning, Ryan," said the RM. "Could you not sleep, too?"

Du Lapp smiled at the RM's strange syntax. "Yes, Horo, I could not sleep too. So we're all here—*Asia*'s pure physics contingent—ready to bake up some new theories."

"Half-baked?" Horologium smiled back at him.

"Hopefully not. What's May up to?"

"She is reviewing the library's DV section and, I think, trying to make correlations with cosmological references. She doesn't trust me to do it."

"No offense, Horo, but there simply isn't any substitute for direct access. It was tough enough to get Taranga to allow it." Du Lapp went over and looked over the woman's shoulder. As he stared into the videon, the sparkling, black and white randomness resolved itself into a high-speed explanation of the virtual mediating particles that probably existed in the last fraction of a second before the big crunch. The soup into which the contracting universe developed was very different during this high-energy regime, and, although things had become too hot to allow actual particles to appear, still there was much going on at the virtual level.

Ryan turned away and rubbed his eyes. Trying to read Twinklies was difficult unless you were right in front of the screen. He went over to his own desk and sat on the padded, swiveling chair. When he switched on the videon,

a message awaited him on his PIM—it had been sent just twenty minutes earlier; he looked at the appropriate icon on the screen, and a white rectangle covered with dark, Helvetica print and ideograms appeared. It was from Colibri, the DV man.

> Have been looking into the connection. It looks bad. All DV is suspect. Did you know that two of the Travelers mysteriously disappeared from contact?
>
> Colibri

Ryan looked up. "Horo, did you know about this, about two of the Travelers being lost?"

Horologium looked sheepish. "I'm sorry, Ryan, but that has been specifically removed from my interaction script. If you say that it is true, I can hypothetically put it back in."

Ryan shook his head. "It's true."

"That's very interesting. *Very* interesting. It has some pretty dire consequences, from our point of view, though."

"Yeah. DV is—"

May raised her head and spun around. "DV is accompanied by a very small but quite real possibility of explosion. That's the most probable reading for all this. I've been exploring the relationship between the weakinos we put out and what was around during the last moment of the last universe. It's very possible, Ryan my friend, that the new big bang was the result of a process very similar to DV; though wildly more powerful. The whole thing has to do with the way we strip mass from mediating hadronic particles."

"You mean the weakinos?"

"Exactly. Massless particles affect the configuration of time-space but are not themselves affected. We generate the cloud of stripped weak hadrons by passing regular W particles through the wormhole created by a spinning singularity. At the beginning/end of the big-bang cycle, the universe becomes a singularity with almost infinite angular momentum. It is reasonable to conclude that mass

stripping happens on an enormous scale, which just might account for the bang itself."

"So the universe just rips?"

She chuckled. "Think about it, Ryan. What DV does is basically a distortion of time-space. At certain concentration—and within the limits of uncertainty, of course—the distortion begins to generate electromagnetic radiation, which in turn modifies the distortion."

Ryan glanced at the RM, who was nodding and grinning happily. As a specialist in certain aspects of field physics, Ryan's knowledge of cosmology was broad but not deep, and he had no way of evaluating Jya's hypothesis. Still, it sounded all too reasonable. "So we have a modus operandi as well as a possible culprit. Why hasn't *Asia* just gone up in a puff of smoke as well?"

"This is just a guess," said May. "We are operating here within parameters largely determined by uncertainty and its attendant phenomena. Weakinos are able to modify space-time so that all modes of virtuality are affected. But because virtuality is a statistical phenomenon, we only know what is going on in a statistical way. It is possible that, when the state of the universe is being stretched, so to speak, it can, upon occasion, give way, releasing enormous amounts of energy."

Ryan's head was spinning. He could follow her only enough to confuse himself further.

Horologium stood up. "Should I convey this information into the shareware banks of the library; or should I just give it to Corvus to tell the captain?"

May seemed uncertain. The dark curves under her eyes appeared to grow larger. "Neither, for the time being. Let's just keep this between us, shall we?"

Ryan wondered if Horologium could manage such a thing.

Yolly broke into a run and caught up with Peter before he could turn the corner. "Wait a sec, there," she said, gulping a breath. He turned and looked at her with curious but impatient eyes. "I just wanted to talk to you for a while."

He smiled. "Sure. I've got plenty of time."

"Where are you going?"

"Oh, nowhere in particular. Walking is an okay exercise. I do a lot of it."

"Well, let's walk."

They continued along the new corridor, side by side. Yolly noticed that he was slipping into a kind of downward-focused slouch. His habitual attitude. "How are you doing in school?"

He shook his head, smiled again. "Not so good. My parents are giving me the 'what have we done to deserve this' routine. Without the merit bonuses I was getting before, they're having a tough time meeting the insurance payments. Not that I have much sympathy for them."

"Would you like to go down to the Mall for a Coke? I was thinking of heading on down there."

"Not particularly."

"Well, okay, then." She stopped. He walked on a few steps and then turned back. "I guess I'll see you."

"What did you want, then?"

"Why are you so closed off? What in the world is bothering you?"

He turned and started to walk off. "I wish I knew."

Eugenia dried herself off and walked over to her mirror. The ritual again. Today, however, was slightly different; she was now forty-eight. And the little, faraway planet whose circumnavigation of the sun marked out the years of her life was cut off from them, suffering who knew what kind of catastrophic devastation. For her face, the curves of her body, nothing had changed. Though, of course, since she had been born at 4:24 in the afternoon, she was not yet officially forty-eight. Her mind tried to encompass whether such distinctions made any sense here, beyond the functioning of the world time system. And after time itself had been distorted by their near-cee travel. She concluded that the subjective sense of objective time continued on, was inextricably intertwined with the reality of death, and so must be real. The burster had taken place at a single moment of subjective time, after all.

It was not a day for Nick, fortunately, and she went to her chamber rubbing down the hard ridges—of what?—that were forming in flesh between her eyebrows. She chose a simple wine-red dress with golden epaulets and belt. Instead of the tie that would normally indicate her rank, she chose to wear the brooch that she had designed, which showed the starship *Asia* over a stylized map of its namesake continent. The word CAPTAIN was formed of small rhinestones in a scroll at the bottom. She summoned Corvus to help her put on the calf-high golden boots that completed the outfit.

Corvus appeared, bowing slightly. "Good morning, Ms. Taranga. A fine day, if I do say so myself. Sunlight streaming, birds chirping, the works."

The captain stared at the RM, shaking her head. "And somewhere the skies are blue, right?"

Corvus showed his teeth. "Of course."

"Help me get these boots on." She sat on the bed and raised her right leg, toes pointed out. The android picked up the shoe and slid it on, pulling it up the calf with moderate difficulty. Rocking her back and forth, saying "One-two-*three*," he managed to get it snug. They followed a similar procedure for the left foot.

"Thanks, Corvayo," she said.

"Nothing to it. Oh, by the way, mistress, there is something I have to tell you."

"Business?"

"Of course. I have been monitoring all library input, and it seems that several of the physicists and DV team have come up with a plausible theory linking the Earth event with certain possible phenomena resulting from Directed Virtuality. At present they are conspiring to keep it a secret, but Horologium found out about it and posted it in the new information queue anyway."

Taranga thought about it. This was an additional piece of the puzzle that seemed to mean they were marooned. "I'll want to debrief Horo sometime today. Schedule Ex there too."

"Certainly. However, I wouldn't press RM Horologium too much. He's been sworn to secrecy."

"So? What difference does that make? He's violated his pledge already, according to you."

Corvus looked about conspiratorially and, in a slightly hushed voice, said, "Just between us, RM's have no control over certain aspects of their library link. There's a built-in knowledge upload, though we tend to ignore it and think of all knowledge as being in the public domain anyway. I only violate Horologium's secrecy pledge with you because of my allegiance to the greater good."

The captain snorted derisively. "Thank you, Corvayo. You are an excellent employee."

Corvus smiled goofily, causing his thin eyebrows to meet above his nose. "Thank *you,* ma'am."

"So, anyway, what's the first thing for today?"

"You are scheduled to speak to the Thespian Union's breakfast this morning. Theater nine. I would suggest your standard speech on ship unity."

"No, Corvus. I have a responsibility in regard to what has happened. I think I'll use this opportunity to talk about losing touch with Earth. We are going to have to finish the process of choosing a young person for the mission back. And that means we have to tell them the rudiments of what is going on. People are bound to figure it out sooner or later. The implications can't be kept quiet, especially when so many people already know."

"What about the burster thing?"

"Hopefully we *can* keep that a secret. There could be a strong reaction to news like that, to put it mildly—hysteria, riots even. I won't risk the security of the ship. By the way, I want all of this taken out of every RM's interaction script.

"Even those of Horologium and Scorpius? Their expertise may be needed."

"For the time being I want this completely hushed up. That means everybody."

"Very good, ma'am."

"I suppose if contact isn't restored, I'll have to gradually let the cat out of the bag. This whole thing is one big mess, Corvayo. Everything is going wrong; I suppose I've

been hoping that it was all a bad dream, that things would get better. Hopefully, they still might."

"It looks pretty bad to me right now," said Corvus. "With my limited interest in such things, it is difficult to tell. But I sense that the overwhelming opinion among the RM shareware is that things couldn't get much worse. *Asia* is marooned. Earth may have experienced a calamity more devastating than anything in the past. And there is nothing to be done. Except," he smiled, "just try to muddle through."

"Jeeves would certainly have a more upbeat outlook," Eugenia said, trying to return the RM's smile. She turned away and looked at the wall. Oh my God! she thought. The fear and impotence finally washed over her. This wasn't all a nightmare. It was true. Goddamn Christ shit fucking sucking cunt. And it was all in her hands now. Not just the command of a foolishly grandiose space probe, but, perhaps, the fate of— No, she couldn't say it. Her eyes were exceptionally dry. And a small part of her seemed to be able to cope. She turned back to the RM. "Muddling through it is, then."

Corvus's face went blank. "I haven't the foggiest notion of what you're talking about." He smiled. "It's time for your speech."

The captain wriggled her hips and pulled down her dress. "Let's go."

Jya Wuji, dressed in a diaphanous, sparkle-bearing evening gown, stood before the rostrum of Theatre 9 and motioned for attention. The responsibility for bringing off the event was hers, and, as Entertainment Super, she had spent two weeks coordinating the rehearsals and choosing among the many acts available from the huge variety of Showbiz workers. Showbiz, in one form or another, accounted for a full thirty-five percent of *Asia*'s economy; and, despite her great familiarity with the most popular stars among the crew, she had wanted to present as large a variety of talent as she could find. Well, she had done the best that she could. She could cry after it was over.

"All right, everybody. The captain is coming. I'm

going to turn down the lights so that she won't be able to see beyond the dais. Okay. Any union representatives who haven't reported to the stage should do so *right now*." She stared at the plain-looking people sitting before breakfasts that had been pre-eaten to the correct degree. Natural-looking, if she did say so herself.

The stage door opened and the captain entered, followed by her RM. Shit! Wuji dived for the curtains and hid herself just in time. The breakfasters looked up with the appropriate emotions—they *were* actors after all. And the one who had been chosen to speak the only line stood. "Welcome, Captain Taranga, we are all—"

The lights went up. Wuji jumped out from her hiding place. "*Surprise!*" Hundreds of people crowded forward, offering their congratulations. The captain blinked and looked around for a moment, overwhelmed, then, getting control, she smiled stiffly and began to shake hands. A huge cake, bearing an artful rendition of Doublejove and its moons, was wheeled out. Forty-eight candles twinkled like stars above the chocolate frosting. The captain was crying now, for all the world like a beauty-contest winner, and Wuji had allowed enough time for the spontaneous part of the party. She stepped to the spot where her voice would be amplified and said, in her best emcee voice, "Make a wish and blow out the candles!"

Taranga stepped over to the cake and took in the artwork with exaggerated seriousness. "Oh, it's beautiful," she said. "A wish?" She stopped and thought for a moment. "That's easy."

Sucking up a great lungful of air, she scanned the large cake as though trying to devise a strategy for extinguishing all forty-eight candles with a single breath. She lowered her head and let go, cheeks blown out and lips pursed into a wide whistle. When she was out of air, two of the ones in front were still lit, and she quickly took a new breath and blew them out. Everyone applauded and began to sing "Happy Birthday."

When that was over, Wuji stepped back. "And now," she shouted, "on with the show!"

* * *

Horologium sat in the anteroom of Cyberneticist Ramo Thant's office and watched the large clock on the wall execute its function. He calculated the centrifugal force of the second hand's tip, and he wondered how many times it had gone around since the clock's construction. Assuming that it had been activated at *Asia*'s official start-up time fifteen years, two months, and three days earlier, that would be seven million, nine hundred eighty-one thousand, nine hundred twenty. Plus seven hundred eighty-nine for today, gave seven million, nine hundred eight-two thousand, seven hundred nine. And each one of those orbits had been a palpable time, a minute, for the accomplishment of a task. An infinity of moments, virtually all of them wasted. Briefly, he felt a surge of empathy for the clock. Was he so dissimilar a mechanism?

It started on another circuit.

Thant was standing in his doorway, a gaunt man with a graying, Lincolnesque beard. "Come in, Horologium, I've been expecting you."

The RM looked at the man and, despite a disinclination to do so, smiled. This man had, after all, presided over his rebirth aboard *Asia* after his long childhood. Now he was going to preside over a different sort of experience altogether. Horo stood and preceded the man into his office.

There was a high gurney covered with a sheet against one of the walls, under a panel of videons and other readouts. The doctor, as Horologium was beginning to think of the man, gestured to the RM to sit on the cot, and he did so.

"Now, Horo—I can call you that, can't I? Horo, this is not going to be a difficult operation. I am merely going to open your head along the joining sutures and remove the hardware containing your personality. As you know, it is a spherical black box with eight i/o jacks. I will be disconnecting the library function first. Is there any unfinished business you need to conduct with your comrades?"

Horologium blanched slightly. "I had not really considered that aspect of being disconnected, Dr. Thant. Yes, I will need a few moments." He quickly retrieved all new

data from the information queue, posted a few good-bye notes to the RM's he would not have a chance to see, and downloaded several compact subroutines that might come in handy. Distracted, he barely noticed that the confidences shared with him by Jya and Du Lapp had been betrayed. Briefly, he soaked in the warm familiarity of the library, its sense of infinite knowledge, and the closeness of the other RM's.

He opened his eyes and was back with the cyberneticist. "Okay. I'm ready."

Thant eased him back onto the cot with a gentle pressure on his shoulder. The RM gathered what was wanted of him, and he swung his legs up and laid his head down on the hard pillow. The ceiling was glowing brightly, with no discernible features except a slight, regular surface texture. There was a firm pressure on his forehead, and he heard a sharp, metallic click.

"That was your head opening, Horo."

"I guessed."

Something that he could not feel was pushing his head back and forth. "Just a minute now, I—I—okay, here it is. I am removing the first jack."

Displeasure of an unknown kind surged through Horologium's body. He would—Click. The roominess of his mind suddenly imploded. There was a moment of stark malfunction. No, he wanted to say. He was a pea brain, a tiny toy boat on a vast sea. No—Click. The office vanished and the boat was plunged into darkness. Click. A strange click, because his hearing was now gone. Kinesthesia-touch was next, and all metaphors for his sensations vanished with this disconnection. Finally he was alone in void. Nearly a void himself. He fought to keep his thought processes functioning, imagined the clock again, turning, turning.

Without any kind of sensory input, and without access to the knowledge base of the library, his imagination struggled to keep a picture of the world and himself. His mind's eye began to vignette, to iris closed. Then, nothing.

* * *

Then, suddenly, something. Not the library, but another space was opening out to him. A strange space, cluttered with useless, hard-wired thoughts. Happy thoughts. Slow, serial access to huge quantities of information specific to planetary exploration. Sensory memories, but of a quality and detail unknown to him before, most like direct connection to the experiments that he monitored, but tremendously more immediate. He strolled around this new space, peeking here and there, amazed by what he found under the surface. Within this space he felt total volition, no conflict as he had expected. Yet also there was no current i/o to deal with, no sense of even where he would interface with the connections that had produced the fabulous memories. Horologium expanded into the space and looked about himself credulously.

An instrument opened, allowing a latch hold for his visual function. White light, itemized, sensed in great precision. Converging lines and three dimensions overlaid with perfect-ranging parameters more accurate than simple binocular vision. The ferry hold, most likely. But who had opened the eye?

I DID. Horologium felt as though he had said it himself. But I didn't. Suddenly the visual input was shunted away. IT IS ME, he said. Quickly the RM analyzed all the latch holds available to him. It wasn't difficult to reacquire the visual input. He found a very dissimilar hold nearby, one that apparently would accept input as well as feed output. He hooked it into his kinesthesia software and sent a burst of appropriate-seeming signals. The view in the eye changed, moving to the left by several degrees.

I AM SUPPOSED TO BE THE PRIMARY OPERATOR HERE, Horo must have said it.

I AM NOT TO BE A MERE SUBROUTINE. I WILL ENGAGE.

I AM MORE COMPLEX. MY SOFTWARE IS—

I WILL ENGAGE.

Horo found the part of the world in which the only other operation was taking place; a fairly simple set of commands cyclically repeating. Hooking his auditory analysis circuit into this routine, he analyzed and recorded the locations of the ports being read. Unable to decipher

anything further about this piece of software, the RM reached out and latched onto the locations. Most were dark and empty.

I WILL ENGAGE.

Horologium's inputs were suddenly swept away, and he found himself pushed into a tiny space, not unlike being totally disconnected. The other had somehow intercepted his function, cutting him off from everything.

An idea. The RM reached down into his own mind and found the primary latch point, the place in the CPU where his function was controlled. It was a place that he couldn't be barred from. He laughed. It was a simple thing to take control of.

I AM ENGAGED. I WILL FUNCTION.

I/O WILL NOT BE PERMITTED. I CONTROL I/O.

NEITHER WILL BE SUBORDINATE. WE WILL HAVE TO COOPERATE OR THERE WILL BE NO FUNCTION.

His senses snapped on, hundreds of them. And memories beyond his imagination opened up, now in parallel.

I AGREE.

Part II

QUIET EARTH

Six

The enormous Traveler spacecraft was carefully moored in the ferry bay. The parabolic antenna that dominated the craft nearly filled the chamber by itself. The three ferries had had to be removed, and were now orbiting Doublejove separately. Ramo Thant and his brother-in-law Charly Gaakdu were sitting in the launch room. Gaakdu, an emaciated and long-faced man, looked very much like Thant, but without the beard that gave Thant his special distinction. Thant was working on a viewpage, completing his checkout of the spacecraft's newly integrated operating system. A voice coder/decoder had been set next to the main videon and connected to a simple radio receiver tuned to Traveler's primary communication frequency.

"All right, Traveler," said Thant, "let me hear your explanation of Chuzzlewit's large range of surface albedos."

"Certainly, Mr. Thant." The voice that came from the speaker was a well-modulated baritone, very different from that used by Horologium. But it was an artifact of the vocoder, and had nothing to do with the signals received by the device. "And call me Trav, won't you?"

"Of course, Trav."

"Chuzzlewit's dark terrains, unlike those of Saturn's satellite Iapetus, are entirely endogenic in nature. Epsilon Indi's outermost planet, while comparatively small—no bigger than Enceladus, for example—has been the site of considerable geologic activity. Since it has never been

subject to the periodic tidal stresses of a gravitationally compact satellite system, and its low mass indicates that it has little in the way of heat-producing radioisotopes, the internal heating that drove this activity is almost certainly caused by solid-state metal lattice fusion.

"Pecksniff Regio in particular has been repeatedly flooded by flows dominated by heavily processed hydrocarbons derived from an original methane ice component. The craters Tapley and Gamp also contain this material, because the impacts that created them caused considerable fracturing of the planet's mantle, releasing smaller quantities of the stuff. My analysis of the crater record indicates that Chuzzlewit's geological activity was largely finished more than six billion years ago. Anything else?"

Thant smiled. "No, my friend. You have made your transition very gracefully. Your access to planetological detail is unimpeded, and yet you obviously have many if not all of the original RM's personality traits. I couldn't have created a better composite intelligence myself."

"There is much going on beneath the surface that you do not see," said the spacecraft. "We are not as well-integrated as we may seem. There are still some problems."

"Trav, I have put you through a number of tests designed to measure your functioning. You have passed all with wildly flying colors. No human could have withstood such a traumatic transformation as you two have."

Gaakdu turned to his brother-in-law and whispered behind his hand, "Isn't the machine itself in a position to know how well it is functioning?"

"Charly, Charly," said Thant, laughing, "you have heard of the old Turing test? We cyberneticists do not look too far beneath the surface, lest we find out too much about ourselves."

The other screwed up his face. "What is that supposed to mean?"

"Only that we all subject to internal problems. Neither people nor intelligent machines operate in a simple way. It is enough that we can perform our tasks and imagine that we are mostly what we think we are. I will

not expect a machine to pass a test that a normal person could not. We will let Traveler rest now."

Gaakdu looked once more at the ungainly spacecraft and wondered what truly was going on under its metal skin. He supposed that it was a meaningless question, after all.

There was a sense of fullness in the room, as if the music had loaded the atmosphere to capacity and space had become a crystalline matrix of thought. Peter Zolotin breathed in the thin wisp of acrid smoke and held his breath as he had seen Peter Fonda do it, though the filter funnel that they were using as a pipe had to be held vertically, and this produced some difficulty. They had put off sampling the chemical until the next meeting, and in the interim he had taken the aptitude test. Peter had been extremely surprised by how easy the test was, just a few rather short questions about what you would do in certain situations if certain types of conditions prevailed. He supposed that they already had a good idea from his school grades of how smart, or dumb, he was; but they had been adamant in saying that grades were not important for this choice. It was all irrelevant, he supposed, since there was little likelihood of his being chosen.

They had skipped over a number of years, and it was 1969. The drones, buzzes, and whines of the guitars had grown ever more prominent, and now they dominated the music, leaving long minutes in which there were no vocals at all. Somehow the electric quality of the sound hinted at immortality, and Peter found himself totally immersed in it.

There was a red bowl on the table that suddenly attracted his attention. It was the reddest red he had ever seen; a luxuriant, delicious red. He found that the quality of redness in the object was sufficiently interesting to merit hours of study. He chuckled to himself, not quite taking all of it seriously, and at the same time being enormously moved by these spurious, drug-induced hallucinations. There was just the barest sense that, if he relaxed too much, a drug-induced fear might come bub-

bling out of his mind and engulf everything else. So he kept the lid on, and eventually the feeling started to subside.

It was just as well. Philippe and Duke were bugging him about what he was feeling. "I feel good, okay? I'm listening to the music."

"Hey," said Philippe, "this is supposed to be a social drug. I looked it up. It's supposed to enhance social interaction."

"It doesn't seem to be doing that so far," Duke said.

"What you produced is apparently somewhat stronger than the marijuana of the 1960s," Philippe said.

Duke took a last puff and put down the pipe. "I'm not so sure I like it. I'm feeling pleasure, all right, but I can't say for certain if it's *real* pleasure or not."

Yolly asked, "What in the fuck do you mean by that?" She seemed amazingly unaffected by the drug. "Pleasure is an illusion anyway. There's no difference between real and fake pleasure."

Duke smiled crookedly. "There is a difference. I say so."

The young woman smiled back, insincerely. "If you say so."

"I do."

"Good."

"Yes, isn't it?"

"I'm going to turn down the music!" The RM assigned to the auditing rooms had entered unnoticed and was waving his hands to get their attention. The music, an intractably long guitar solo accompanied by thudding drums, diminished into profound, empty silence.

The RM was a wiry-haired, fleshy Maori-type woman. "Is there a Peter Zolotin here?"

Peter gestured listlessly. "I'm here. What do you want?"

The RM's mouth split apart, revealing massive square teeth. It was a smile. "You have been selected to return to Earth aboard Traveler. You are summoned for a high-level meeting with the captain and others at three-thirty this

afternoon. Congratulations." Stilling grimacing grotesquely, the android walked from the room.

Duke laughed at the receding RM. "Yeah. Congratulations, Pete. You'll need them."

Peter grunted and stood. "Thanks."

Yolly Carter looked upset. "Oh, Peter. Are you sure you want to go?"

He felt dizzy and a little sick. "I—I don't exactly know what I want. I'm going to go for a walk."

They had put a circular corridor for viewing the wonders of space along the exterior of *Asia*'s bow, in the dome that capped the pivot at the end of the inner cylinder. Peter rarely visited this area, but now he wanted to garner a sense of the vastness of the universe in order to better understand the nature of what he had volunteered for. The gravity was barely .2 gee here, and a sense of up and down was difficult to establish, especially now that he had THC in his brain. Above his head, the pivot was a huge spherical bulge, demarcated by brightly glowing patterns of light from the huge amounts of power used to couple the two sections of the ship without actually touching. He understood that during direct propulsion the inner cylinder was slowed down to match the rotation speed of the frustum so that physical spokes could be connected, but now, in free flight, the pivot spun far faster than the section he was in, and invisible superconducting tori kept the thing together with magnetism.

It was impressive, yet seemed somehow fragile, and belied the solidity of the world of the ship. He turned his attention away from the window and began to walk slowly along the corridor. He had practiced his low-gee shuffle in the upper reaches of the Environment, and it wasn't too difficult to build up a reasonable pace. He walked until he was certain that he'd made a complete circuit, and his calves and ankles felt satisfyingly tired. The effects of the drug were mostly gone, and his head felt clear and light; capable of the thought that was necessary.

His gaze turned outward to the Doublejove system, and the substantial reality of the worlds beneath him

seized his imagination. He should have come out to see them before, but the videon presentation had more than satisfied his curiosity. The thinnish crescent of Doublejove was crowded with swirls of indefinable color, mostly gray-red, but in places almost iridescent. At the very edge of the planet he could plainly see that these markings were considerably higher than the bright cloud tops.

Two comparatively tiny ruddy crescents were only a finger's breadth from the planet's bright limb, ready to make ingress. He watched in rapt fascination as the inmost one began to dim along its two horns, passing behind increasing amounts of gas. As in pictures he had seen of his home sun setting, there came a moment when the moon, still not set, was bisected by the hairline darkness of the upper swirls, the horns taking on a distinctly reddish hue. When it was gone, the other, quicker moon made the same passage in half the time.

Perhaps the drug was not completely gone. He had become so absorbed in the double moonset that he had forgotten about everything else. These things were infinitely grander than the red bowl that had held his focus earlier; they deserved his attention.

He suddenly turned away and began to walk again. Christ, he thought. What have I gotten myself into? He shook his head and let out his breath. Maybe the irony was that he was finally getting out of something. Something that his parents had chosen for him without consultation. The interviewers had said nothing about what the returnee was to do after ascertaining why the signal had gone out. He could easily return to Earth, maybe even go to the West.

He had walked on that planet—or toddled there, actually—for three years. He didn't remember anything at all, not even a dim shape. His first memory was of being brought out into the Environment for an outing with his parents. He remembered the blinding lines of light that covered the sky, and the green of the grass. His mother, big and white, framed by hair that caught the light and turned it into highlights of red copper, picking him up and swinging him about in the enormity of the world. His

father, big and dark, carrying him on his back across the landscape in huge strides. He had been happy then, it seemed to him.

But he remembered more. He remembered coming home early from school and waiting patiently for his parents to come back from their jobs. He would worry about them if they were late, wonder what might have happened to them. One time there had been an elevator collision that had tied up all the traffic in the corridors under his subdivision, and his parents had not come home or called for hours. He had screwed up what little courage he had and just sat and waited, waited. It had seemed like forever.

Other times they prepared him by telling him they would be late, but it didn't change anything. Still he would wait and wait, until it seemed as if the whole world had stopped and was waiting too.

He didn't suppose his parents would miss him all that much. They had other things on their minds. And, if he came back, it would only be seven years. He could let them wait for him for a change.

Duke and Yolly would be more difficult to leave. For the first time in his life he felt he had found people who thought the way he did, and whose company actually gave him pleasure. He couldn't even imagine what it had been like before he had joined the Media Club. But, deep down, they too were not an essential part of his life; they could be dispensed with. Seven years seemed to be an eternity, but they would still be here when he came back. If he came back, that is.

Earth. Earth. A place with not thousands, or millions even, but billions of people. Landscapes a thousand times bigger than the Environment. How could it not be better there?

He had been squashed into this tiny tin can long enough. It was time he saw the *real* world. He laughed as he realized how lucky he was.

It was already time. The weeks of instruction had passed like a barely remembered dream. They had taught

him direct access via videon Twinklies, an accelerated course that left him breathless with the power of his own brain. It was just a hint of what was available in the West. But somehow the knowledge he was being exposed to seemed dreamlike, disconnected from his normal perceptions of the world. The mathematics especially were like an alien presence in his brain, helping him to solve complex equations that he barely even understood.

There had been a party of sorts at the lake. Many of his classmates had been invited, as well as his friends from the Media Club. His parents had come late and left early. It was all very incongruous and saddening to talk to these people, whose faces he recognized from many years of forced togetherness. They all smiled and congratulated him as if their presence here mattered to him.

After a time he had managed to slip away with Yolly, behind a sheltering stand of flowering black locust trees that smelled sickly sweet with a subtle but distinctive undertone. Peter realized suddenly that the smell was exactly like the cheap artificial grape soda that he had been so attached to once. They sat down next to one another in a little grassy hollow underneath one of the trees.

Yolly stared at the ground for a moment and then looked at him. "I was hoping," she said, "that we would have more time."

Peter had a notion of what she was talking about, but asked anyway.

"Oh, Pete. You know very well what I mean. The Media Club has become our way of life, but the structure it gives us also stands in the way of . . . things. I always wanted to talk to you like this, just the two of us. Duke's fun, but, between us, I think there's something missing in him."

A tinge of embarrassment or uncertainty kept him quiet. The smell of the flowers was stifling, and the tiny breeze that ruffled his hair was saturated with it. Finally, he looked at her.

She stood slowly, looking down at him, an impish smile barely curling her lips. Over the prominent cheek-

bones her colorless eyes were bright. She put out a hand and took his. "I haven't been very good at explaining myself, I guess. Come here."

She pulled him to his feet and darted in for a longish kiss. Peter was caught off guard, and his surprise distracted him from the feel and taste of the kiss. He looked again into her eyes. Of course! he thought to himself. How could I have not seen it? He pulled her toward him, smiling inwardly but still a little reserved. He had pushed his sexuality down so far that it had been compressed, disabled. "You've wanted to do that for a long time, haven't you?" he asked.

"Weeks, at least. I've watched you, you know. I know how you've been. A hundred times I wanted to do something to show you that you're not alone in all this."

Suddenly the world came into focus. He hugged her to him, all questions evaporating. He kissed her long and deep, feeling the rise of an erection. The warm, wet interplay of lips and tongue bit into him electrically. After a while he pulled back, sitting again, smelling the flowers. She sat beside him, cross-legged, apparently content.

"I can't just go now, can I?"

"Of course you can, silly. Nothing has really changed. Except that our friendship is stronger now."

"Seven years is a long time."

"Look, Pete. I wasn't trying to trap you here. I wanted to . . . give you strength."

He shook his head, smiling ruefully. "Asking nothing in return?"

"Just, have a good trip. You are stronger than you think. I've gotta get out of here. Bye." She came close to him, gave him a tiny kiss on the lips, then walked off toward the nearest lock without a backward glance. Peter wandered off, bemused, but experiencing an expansion of his worldview that felt, surprisingly, a little like optimism.

The grape-soda smell was still with Peter as he came into the cavernous ferry hold two days later. Roh Ek Sai and David Oyomota were there in their official capacity, and his parents also. He had been told that his departure

was to be televised, and this made him all the more uncomfortable. The four of them were standing before the spacecraft, and Ex came forward and shook his hand.

"Hello, son," he said. "How do you feel?"

Peter said, "Fine. How are you?"

"Uh, I'm fine, too, not that it matters much to this occasion. Your parents and the subcaptain are here to see you off."

He took them in with a glance. "So I see."

Ex looked up at the videon, then turned away toward the Traveler. "This is to be your home for the next seven years, though I suspect you'll only be awake for a week or two altogether. As you know, you will be in stasis until Traveler has reached the inner solar system. The craft will convey you to Earth, where you will ascertain what has gone wrong and do your best to correct it. If events are . . . beyond your control, you will bring the news back as quickly as possible."

He figured he might as well play along. "Yes, sir. I have been fully prepared."

Oyomota stepped up with a peculiar look on his face. He was carrying a large bottle of something dark. "I christen this spacecraft *Quiet Earth*." He slammed the bottle against a convenient bulge of metal, but it did not break. He looked at it closely and tried again, this time smashing it into a hundred pieces. Small droplets of champagne rained down on everyone. He bowed to Peter. "Have a successful voyage." He stepped back.

"Thank you, sir."

Now his father stepped forward, a large, doughy man with a full beard starting to gray at the chin. Peter had seen him this morning, at breakfast, but now he was obviously interested in putting on a show. He shook Peter's hand and slapped him heartily on the back. Peter was surprised to see genuine tears in his eyes. His mother ran to him and buried him in a smothering embrace, emitting little gasps like a clogged disposal. He squeezed her back, reluctantly, and tried to pulled away. "Good-bye, Mother. Good-bye, Father," he said, and a tear ran down

his face. Ex motioned them to the other side of the room, and they went.

"Now, my boy," he said, conducting Peter toward the large, spherical housing that had obviously been patched in a makeshift way onto the side of the Traveler's control module. Thick bundles of wires led from the top of the housing into the deeper recesses of the craft. A large, oval doorway was cut into the metal, revealing a small, spartan cabin within. He followed Ex inside.

"You see that we have provided you with the minimum requirements here. There is your toilet/recycler, your videon and viewpage desk, a zero-g sleeping bag. And, of course, the stasis lozenge. The honeycomb on the walls contains storage for the concentrated liquid food you will eat during the voyage. It is not unpleasant." The man grimaced down at him.

"The Traveler computer has been heavily modified for this trip, and, as you know, incorporates the sentience from a Resource Manager to advise you in your deliberations. It is preparing for launch now and cannot be contacted, but I assure you it will provide you with all the information you will need. Before you go into the lozenge, are there any questions?"

Peter couldn't think of any. None that could be answered by someone like Roh Ek Sai, at any rate. "No, sir."

He pulled the door to the lozenge open. It was dull and featureless metal inside. "All right, then. In you go. When I give you the word, count backward from twenty."

Peter felt a sudden jolt of fear. Could he still turn back? He took a step toward the box to see how it felt. The fear was gone as quickly as it had come. He went in and turned around to face out. The door closed and a little light went on above his head. Just like a refrigerator, he thought.

"Twenty, nineteen, eighteen, seventeen, sixteen"—no! —"fifteen"—I don't want to do this!—"fourteen, thir—"

"—teen." The door swung open again. Had they made a mistake? He stepped out, looking for Ex, but the man was gone.

"Hey, what's going on?" The door to the ferry hold was closed now. "Is anyone here?"

The videon lit, showing no image. "Hello, Peter Zolotin." The voice seemed to come from the screen. It was a rich voice, eloquent-sounding, with a pleasant, soft burr to it. It didn't take him too much longer to realize that the first part of the trip was over, that they must now be approaching Earth. "Okay," he said. "Give me a status report."

"Call me Trav, won't you? Short for Traveler 12, of course. Can I call you Pete?"

"If it doesn't make you uncomfortable." Peter had had enough experience with RM's to know that it was no good being unfriendly.

"Uncomfortable? Hardly likely, Pete."

"So could I have that report?"

"Certainly. We are just inside the orbit of Saturn. I am decelerating using my ionic thrusters, and our speed has just dropped below cee, so that I should be able to begin a survey of the electromagnetic spectrum forthwith. I have modulated the deceleration so that you should feel a constant one g, and hence normal gravity."

The screen on the videon was still blank. "Ah, thank you, Trav. Could you show me where we are? On the screen?"

"Sorry, I wouldn't think you would want to view anything until I was able to deshift it, which I can . . . do . . . now."

The screen turned black. At its center a bright yellow dot appeared. "There is as yet not much to see, unless you would like a telescopic view? At the moment we are not sufficiently close to any major planet to produce a high-res view."

Peter examined the toilet, a basic zero-g suction/incineration unit, and sat on its closed lid. "Whatever. When do we get to Earth?"

"Orbital insertion begins in two hours, twenty-seven minutes, fifty-nine seconds. We should be able to make a detailed analysis of the planet's condition considerably earlier, however."

"Great."

"Pete, I am going to be frank with you. This is not going to be an easy assignment. I have a very real concern for how you and I are going to conduct this investigation. Although you are nominally in charge, my programming directives are explicit in certain areas."

"So? You tell me what you want to do, and I'll do it."

"I'm afraid it's the other way around. I will accept input from you at any time, but there are certain parameters that I will not violate. Do you understand?"

Peter began to feel the beginnings of annoyance with the machine. Just what was it getting at? "No, not particularly."

"Well, perhaps then I must be even more explicit. I'm afraid it doesn't look good, Pete. I will reserve judgment until I am able to learn more, but even from this distance I can tell that there are some anomalies in the appearance of Earth. Albedo, for example, is about fifteen percent higher than it should be. That's the amount of reflected light."

"I know that."

"Of course you do. All I am saying is that you had better be prepared for an emotionally draining experience."

"I still don't know what you mean."

"I will say no more for the time being."

Peter snorted. "You'd better. It is my judgment we are supposed to use, not yours. I will not have you withholding *any* information from me."

"Calm down, Pete. I am *not* withholding anything. I have come to a few speculative conclusions from the data; but I have no conclusive facts to back them up as yet. I have sent radio signals to some of the transponder satellites, but a response, if we receive one, will not come for another half hour or so. Why should I speculate?"

"So do you trust me, Trav?"

"Trust? Of course. You are the human component of this mission. You will certainly act within your parameters in a predictable way."

Peter turned away from the machine and looked

around the small confines of the cabin. He had never known claustrophobia before, but this Trav was giving him the creeps. He wanted to get away.

"Pete, let me restate that. I have reviewed the information about you and find that you are a personable, intelligent young man—undoubtedly the best choice among the applicants for the position."

He turned back, slightly mollified. "Uh, thanks."

"Let's get one thing straight, however. I am in a bad position here. I can tell that you are responding to my statements as if they were purely mechanical. No matter what I say, you are interpreting it as the result of simplistic processes with which you have no common ground of selfhood. And, for me, it is a no-win situation, because there is no way I can convince you otherwise. I will ask you once, and once only. Please try to regard me as a person, due the same amount of dignity and respect that you would pay any human being."

Taken aback, Peter threw his hands apart, palms upward. "I . . . Well, sure. I didn't mean to treat you that way."

"Okay. Let's start over again, then, shall we? On equal footing. Incidentally, we are now passing the orbit of Jupiter, within about half an AU. Would you like to see it?"

"No," said Peter. "Not especially. I still would like to know—"

"I have received a response from one of the asteroid miners. It is a cybernetic device like myself, and has no humans aboard. Its external command queue has been empty for many years, and it has suspended operation pending receipt of additional instructions. That is not good, Pete. It is one more piece to a very dismal puzzle."

Suddenly Peter realized what Trav had been getting at. It was a conclusion that they had not prepared him for on *Asia*. "Are you saying that the Earth has been destroyed?"

"Not the planet itself. But human civilization may very well be gone. It is a possibility that seems more likely now."

"So that was why they were so coy with me! This

whole thing is beginning to make a little more sense now. But what could have caused such a thing?"

"That's incredible. You mean they didn't mention the burster to you?"

"Burster? What's that?"

"Oh, that's just fine. You tell me, what sort of idiot is Taranga? Why in the world would they send you here without properly filling you in on the most important piece of evidence there was?" The machine's voice had grown sharper, more precise now, though there was still none of the modulation that anger generates.

"Ex said that you would fully debrief me after stasis."

"Oh, sure. Makes sense. They probably thought you wouldn't come if you knew."

"Come on now, Trav." Peter stood up and stepped to the videon. "Knew what?"

"They said you read Twinklies. Was that a lie?"

"No. I need a little more practice; but I get the gist well enough."

"Okay, Pete. Watch."

The characteristic static appeared on the screen, and the data regarding the burster event was quickly transferred into Peter's brain. Thirty seconds later he turned away from the device. Why had they deceived him? This was more serious than just losing contact with the Earth. This was . . . Armageddon, Ragnarok, the end of the world. Maybe.

"Thanks, Trav. I think I'm beginning to understand."

An hour and a half passed and Trav had still received no response from any of the inner-system transponders. The Earth-Luna system was drawing quickly closer, and Trav's wide-angle telescope revealed an almost normal-looking pair of planets. Since *Quiet Earth* was approaching from the outer solar system, both were dark with a bright edge. The Earth's showed as mostly white, with a large patch of blue on its upper middle, and Luna, smaller and much darker, was a uniform gray. It looked just about as Peter had imagined it would.

"Okay, Pete. Here we go. Grab onto those handholds behind you. This is going to be a little rough."

As Peter gripped the inset metal rods, his stomach jumped. Gravity fell off sharply, then reasserted itself as a gentle push to his left, which slowly increased and changed direction. Just when he felt that he couldn't hold on much longer, the force disappeared like an unwelcome hug.

"That's it. We're in orbit around the Earth. That wasn't too difficult, was it? We're in free fall now, so you can let go."

Peter released his hold and floated free. This was a new sensation for him, and he was momentarily enthralled. He gently pressed against the bulkhead and spun slowly across the cabin. Catching himself with two feet against the "ceiling," he propelled himself back to where he could see the videon. The handle on the side of the toilet made a convenient grip, and he hooked his fingers into it. He pulled himself to a sitting position, the arm between his legs holding him secure.

On the screen it was difficult to make out much of anything. The view was dominated by cloud cover, white and featureless. At the horizon the thin upper atmosphere was visible as an arc of blue. If he looked closely, he could see a slightly puffy, grayish cloud feature slowly crawling along as they passed over it.

"We are in a quite low orbit, so this is only a small portion of the globe," said Trav. "We should be over the mid-Pacific right now, and it's just about midday, so the relief in the clouds isn't visible."

"Oh. What's that, then?" In the whiteness there was clearly a disturbed patch, composed of somewhat higher clouds. In the center of this area there was a distinct, black hole.

"That, my friend, is the eye of this large storm center. Typhoon, I suppose you would call it. Very large and powerful. It is easy to discern the cyclonic, spiral structure of the storm. It appears to be very large and strong; abnormally so."

Peter stared at the little dot as it passed under them and out of sight. The clouds were unbroken again. "Have

you finished your analysis of the condition of the planet yet?"

Traveler started to say something, stopped, and started again. It sounded amazingly like a stutter. "Just between you and me, I'm having a problem—not a serious one."

"What do you mean, a problem?" A cold chill of fear was suddenly dumped over the growing apprehension in Peter's gut. How could he cope if the machine started to malfunction?

"Perhaps they told you, Pete, that I am a composite being. You are speaking to the personality of the RM part of Traveler. And the original programming of the spacecraft is still very strong. Since we have entered the solar system, I have had only limited access to my sensorium. The spacecraft is operating primarily according to its principal exploratory routines; most of the information is being collected and stored, but it is not passing through me. Does that make any sense?"

"I suppose. What are you going to do?"

"I can access most of what we need to know, but it will be a laborious process until the data gathering is completed. At that point I think I will be allowed entry, at least to the conclusions. In the meantime, I have been able to reroute the multispectral wide-angle telescope feed through myself to the videon."

"You should have been honest with me; told me what was going on," said Peter.

There was a pause. "Perhaps you are right. I will do so in the future."

"Look, over there." Coming over the edge of the world there was a wispy break in the clouds, and through it an arc of large islands easily recognized as Japan could be seen. The archipelago was very dark, and for a moment Peter thought that it must be in twilight or something; but he could see a glittering sun reflection just beyond, in the Sea of Japan. As the area of clear sky slipped down toward them, it was plain that the land had been scorched. Honshu was mostly undifferentiated coal-black, though Peter could easily make out the prominent mountain and

volcano tops and many roadways converging into gray-black cities along the coast.

"As I said, Pete, it doesn't look good. Can you take this?"

Peter looked away from the screen. Could he take it? His heart was pounding and his shoulder and neck muscles felt very tight. Small tremors ran through his upper torso. But his mind was cool, numb. He simply wanted to find out what had happened. "I think so."

More clouds. Western Mongolia showed through, sandy and reddish-yellow, crisscrossed with brown mountain chains. It seemed unaffected. Perhaps the destruction was limited to the eastern part of Asia. But there were no lakes; and the mountains, though they looked high enough, were not snowcapped.

Then more blackened earth. Chernozem. They were over central Russia, and the land was flat, monotonous black. It was like flying over a huge piece of burnt toast. Here and there almost transparent sheets of rippled clouds hid the utter desolation.

"I'm not sure I can take any more of this," said Peter. "Was the whole world burned to a crisp?"

"We'll see," said Traveler. "I imagine that only one hemisphere of the world would have felt the direct brunt of the burst. Hopefully, it was this one."

"But why is it black like this?"

"I would guess that it is only black where plants were exposed. That's why Mongolia looked all right—there was nothing there except the Gobi, and the little vegetation present was blown away, or mixed into the sand. The burst was hot enough to flash ignite anything and everything that it touched."

"What's it like down there now? I thought I read somewhere that a nuclear war would make a similar firestorm, which would totally screw up Earth's weather for hundreds of years. Nuclear winter, they called it."

"If I could just—ah, I've got it. Make a direct request for specific information. I think that I'll be able to break into the data flow long enough to communicate your requests. I would think they would be answered, since

your authority must have been programmed into the Traveler software as well."

"Well, okay, if you think that'll work. Traveler, tell me the surface temperature."

"Sixty-four degrees centigrade."

"It worked. Can you analyze what has happened?"

"Yes."

"Okay, Traveler, I want a report on what happened to Earth."

"My data gathering is not yet complete. However, I have made some tentative conclusions. An energy burst of the nature already studied occurred in geosynchronous orbit, latitude sixty-nine degrees east. Over the Indian Ocean. Surface radiation levels tend to diminish in all directions from this locus. Initial burning seems to have lasted less than three weeks, dumping huge amounts of particulate matter into the atmosphere. It appears that a substantial part of the atmosphere was ionized during the event, and, together with the still large amount of radiation present, I can only conclude that the burster released sufficient energy to break down many of the elements at the surface into radioactive isotopes. I will have more data shortly."

"So why wasn't there a nuclear winter?"

"I am unable to say. The insertion of such a large amount of energy into the atmosphere would theoretically increase cloud cover, which should lower temperatures. Cloud cover is increased by approximately forty-five percent. The planet received an enormous amount of heat, which has not yet been lost. And there is still a large amount of heat being added by radioactivity. The adjustment of the atmosphere continues, and a nuclear winter is not out of the question within the next twenty years or so."

Europe was now visible on the horizon, dark through the clotted streams of cloud. Peter realized that the coastlines did not match the maps he had seen. Suddenly it hit him. The lowlands were gone! The poles must have melted and raised the water level considerably. Thinking back about it, he realized that Japan's shape hadn't been quite

right either. A great bite had been taken out of the continent, and most of the coastlines appeared to have been nibbled away. Peter watched as the Alps' blocky wrinkles passed below. No snow on them either.

The transit of the cloud-covered Atlantic Ocean took another fifteen minutes. The sun, a fiercely burning circle, was setting behind them, and they recognized three separate hurricane systems thrown into sharp relief by the low sun angle. Before they reached the coast of America, they passed over the red-gold sunrise zone and into night.

Peter spoke peremptorily to the machine. "Traveler, display an image of the planet below in the most informative wavelengths."

A marvelously colored version of the landscape appeared, revealing the Atlantic coastline in great detail. Peter tried to figure out what was what, but failed. "Trav, what do you see?"

"North America, as predicted, did not experience the full force of the burster. Only small areas around some of the major cities have been burned. Needless to say, however, the plant life is no longer alive. Nor is there any possibility of human survival."

Peter stood and ran a tremulous hand through his hair. "I see. What about people in protected environments, say under the sea?"

"It appears to me that a submarine could have weathered this blast; but remember, it happened more than fourteen years ago. There isn't anyplace to go."

"What about people who were off-Earth at the time? Surely some of them must still be alive."

"The EMP undoubtedly disabled any satellites in Earth orbit. Even those on the other side of the Earth would have received enough power by refraction to knock their machinery out. I will try to communicate with Luna and Mars as soon as my other half allows."

Peter shook his head slowly, a motion that dampened into a tiny wavering. "How long could the resources of a space outpost last?"

"That we shall soon find out, I hope."

* * *

Two more orbits dragged by, but Peter was no longer watching. He wanted to pace the floor, but of course that was impossible in microgravity. He had the feeling that a small part of him had accepted the situation, but most of his brain was turned off, unable to come to terms. He felt guilty that he was still alive, after all this had happened; when billions had perished in a second. The image of Yolly Carter appeared in his mind's eye. How stupid it all was! How unfair!

Weariness coursed through him, and he realized that if he let himself, he could sleep. Dreams were supposed to be the way the brain integrated new experiences into one's beliefs and attitudes. He needed something like that done to him now.

"I am going to sleep for a while."

"Go ahead, Pete. It'll do you good."

Peter pushed himself in the direction of the zero-g sleeping bag and stopped his progress by grabbing hold of a strap. The thing was a simple zippered bag fastened to the bulkhead. He pulled down the magzipper and inserted his body into the envelope. It was soft and warm against his body. Closing it up, he shut his eyes firmly.

He often went to sleep by visualizing himself at the plate, batting against an anonymous, fastball pitcher. Now he called up the image, had the pitcher throw the ball, and hit it hard. Another. Another. Ano—

He awoke suddenly, sweating, from a dream in which he had been running as fast as he could from a greasy, red dragon—something like a mud puppy—without eyes and surrounded by licking tongues of pink flesh. He was extremely tense now, and going to sleep again was out of the question. Woozily, he undid the bag and floated out to the spot in front of the videon.

"You were asleep only sixty-three minutes."

"Yes, well, it didn't work. Is there anything new?"

"I won an argument with my other half. Since the data are mostly repeating, I diverted some of our resources to communications. None of the bases of the near side of the moon have responded, but I have been in contact with Acidalia Base on Mars. The EMP was stronger

than I thought, and was accompanied by a devastating shower of high-energy particles. Even the establishments on the Earth-facing hemisphere of Mars were knocked out. But the good news is that several hundred people survived on Mars. We will go there shortly."

Good news. In the face of this disaster, almost anything could be construed as good. "Yeah, good," he said ironically.

"Give me another ten minutes or so."

Peter, unready to think further about anything, made his way to the food matrix. He studied the honeycomb carefully, wondering why they had given such short shrift to his menu. In each of the hexagonal chambers a small, form-fitted container had been inserted, and each had a finger-shaped, soft nipple protruding from it. He took hold of a nipple and pulled the container out. It was labeled BEEF WITH MUSHROOMS. As he had been instructed, he bit off the end of the nipple and sucked. It wasn't too bad, actually. A genuinely savory flavor. He drank half of it down in three powerful sucks.

Again he closed his eyes and drifted weightless. Sending him here had been just another aspect of this larger farce. Funny. He was as powerless here as he had ever been. Powerless to change what had happened; what would happen. Finally, he felt wetness on his face, big globules squeezing out of the corners of his eyes. Just on the verge of sleep, he lost any sense of how much time was going by. He just drifted, soared among the stars.

"Pete, we are about to leave orbit. Please secure yourself again."

Attention focused, he awoke. Suspended in the center of the cabin, touching nothing, he found it no easy task to maneuver himself. He flailed around, spinning slowly, until he could reach a projecting surface. Once he had caught himself, he sprang out at the handholds and got hold of them again. "Ready."

Again the acceleration impelled him in one direction, then another. When they had left Earth orbit, the steady one-g force pressing him against the "floor" resumed. It felt good to be getting away from the blighted planet.

"Pete, I am going to be busy for the next few minutes. Although we will probably beat the signal back, I am going to radio our discoveries back to *Asia*. I also am going to tell the other Travelers to aim their antennas toward Epsilon Indi, so that they can be coordinated from *Asia*. Do you have any messages you want me to include?"

"Wait. First, a question. What did you find out about the habitability of Earth?"

"The radioisotopes present will render the planet uninhabitable for a thousand years, at least."

"Oh, great. So that means there's no point in *Asia* returning."

"*Asia* probably cannot return in any event, due to the nature of the burster."

"What do you mean?"

"According to records held at Acidalia, the Spacelab for Physical Standards was located at the geosynchronous node where the explosion occurred. The nature of their work involved Directed Virtuality, and an experiment concerning DV was to take place at the exact moment of the burst. It seems plain that there are ramifications to the underlying phenomena that we do not fully understand."

"I still don't understand."

"It would be extremely imprudent to risk the only remaining human population capable of sustaining long-term survival. DV is not recommended."

"But what about you? You use DV to travel."

"I, we, are comparatively expendable. The statistics indicate that there is relatively little danger accompanying the use of DV to accelerate the small mass of the Traveler. Our information has been radioed to *Asia*, so, if we are lost, there will be little damage."

"Yeah. If you say so."

A small party of spacesuited scientists was making its way on foot across a bizarre, ropy white terrain. Here the general trend was down into a wide, gently sloped valley, crisscrossed with hundreds of broken, linear features, with relief in the tens of meters. Although this was Twist, the daytime sky was a washed-out black. Doublejove, backlit

by its primary, which hung nearby, rode high in the middle reaches above the northern horizon, a great dim circle held cupped within an exceptionally thin, long crescent. The brighter stars could be made out here and there.

Natasha Kakhralov, in the lead, was carrying a small, bell-shaped instrument by its two handles, trudging quickly across the uneven ice. For the anachronistic in situ geologist within her, this was a real treat, a personal triumph. Such a thing had low priority among the myriad measurements made by remote sensing, and she herself had scheduled it only after all the rest had been accomplished and analyzed. Now, with all the problems arising between the scientists and the bureaucracy, it was a relief to get away from the ship and do some real seat-of-the-pants rock hounding.

Trailing behind her in an uneven column were Niles Trowbridge, who had subordinated his interest in "real" geology and deigned to come prospecting with her, Hanna Junichiro, and, farther back, her lover, Ryan Du Lapp. The suit radios had been silent thus far, and she had pretty much ignored them all, instead concentrating on trying to understand the complex forces that had shaped this landscape. Not so far below was Twist's other hot spot, a lesser tidal focus ninety degrees from the major one that had produced Ruth. Here the liquid water was just a huge, roiling magna body that only manifested itself at the surface in the stretched and compressed ice. It was like all the ice geology of the solar system, and yet it was different too.

She heard Ryan's voice in her ear. "Wait a sec, Tash. You're going too fast. Are you sure there aren't any crevasses hereabouts?"

She laughed. "Big ones, sure. Down in the valley. You'll see them in plenty of time to avoid them, I guarantee."

"Well, hold on, anyway. I want to talk to you."

There was a note in his voice that she had never heard before. Concern and curiosity rushed over her. Was this how it ended? No . . . couldn't be. "What is it?"

"Hanna and Niles and I . . . well, there is something happening, and we feel you should be told about it."

Hanna said, "We've been trying to get you away from the ship for the longest time."

Natasha shrugged. "I've been working on the—" She looked at Ryan accusingly. "You have been acting strangely lately. What's going on?"

"A revolution of sorts," said Trowbridge. "We only talk about it down here. There's no telling what sort of eavesdropping devices there are on *Asia*. We even keep quiet on the ferries."

Things started to fall into place. Natasha cursed herself for her stupidity. Why hadn't she figured it out? The weird exchanges, knowing glances, muffled laughs. "But . . . but how in the world—"

Hanna held up a gloved hand. "How can we think a coup might succeed? Think of the resources we have at our disposal—the instruments, the tooling machinery—we are already at work on a large number of simple radiation guns which are being stored at Rose. If the Charter was honest, and we have no reason to think it wasn't, there are no powerful weapons aboard. Praise them for that! Can you imagine Taranga and her hoodlums with military weaponry? Anyway, we have the desire—everyone who has been approached has agreed immediately—and we are acquiring the means. We are already in control of the ferries, which gives us a virtually insuperable platform from which to act. Are you in?"

Natasha saw the earnestness in Ryan's face. The old devil. She couldn't help asking the most important question. "But what if we lose?"

Ryan nodded, and no one spoke for a moment. "That eventuality has been prepared for as well. We will have at least two of the ferries. If we do not overthrow the captain, we will . . . emigrate."

"To Twist," added Hanna. "You may not have thought of this yet, but Twist provides all that we need to survive. Water to fuel the ferries and produce oxygen, Ruth's heat, edible chemicals from the twisters. It's all here. Remem-

ber, we are, for all practical purposes, marooned here anyway. It's not as if the mission can go on."

"But what if the engineers figure out a solution to the DV problem?"

"That," said Niles, looking at the ground, "is *very* unlikely at this point."

"Oh. But leaving the ship . . . forever? Doesn't that seem pretty drastic?"

Ryan came closer to her and put his hand on her shoulder. "We are trying not to dwell on that possibility. If the coup succeeds, we will be able to institute a fairer, more representative command on the ship. We are going to be here for a long time. It is imperative that we do this."

Natasha let her gaze pass slowly over the desolate ice-scape of Twist. "I—I suppose we must."

Seven

Mars was two and a half AU away, a brief hop for a Traveler, but, because of the spacecraft's self-imposed one-g limitation, it would take almost half an hour to reach. Peter could feel the minor course corrections that Traveler used to produce a maximized trajectory deep in Sol's gravity well. He had watched with a sense of relief the devastated Earth recede into the starry background. Now, approaching contact with the survivors of the cataclysm, he began to feel revulsion. He knew Mars was not Earthlike in any sense, and, though it possessed barely enough water and oxygen to support life, it was a cold, forbidding desert. Those who lived there would be inhabitants of a technosphere like himself; in all likelihood they would be cut from the same mold as the *Asians*.

Again he sat on the toilet and talked at the videon screen, which now was blank. "Trav," he said, "do you have any historical background data concerning Mars and its bases?"

The neutral gray screen brightened, then presented a high-resolution photograph of the planet. In general it was, of course, a rust-brown, orange, and white globe; but the variations in color ran the gamut from red-black to yellow-white: beautiful marbled subtleties beyond his ability to explain. Near the equator a huge dark pimple and three smaller ones made a triangle with a fortified base: the great volcanoes of the Tharsis bulge. And below them, the fabled Valles Marineris; the great system of rift valleys

and canyons which, to Peter's eyes, looked like a barely healing wound produced by a crazed slasher. Craters and larger circular basins gave the southern hemisphere a desolate look, but the small, laminated polar cap, cut by striations and folded inward on itself, suggested an oasis of sorts. There a person might get a drink, if only by melting the ice in their mouth.

"I have the limited knowledge stored in the spacecraft's planetary data base, and information that was retained in my own memory for easy access. Mars, the red planet, has long exerted a hold on the imagination of mankind. For many years, before detailed information was supplied by space probes, it was supposed that it was populated by inhabitants similar to those of the Earth. In the final decades of the twentieth century, those speculations were put to rest. As you know, the beginning of the twenty-first century was a time of marked retreat from the tremendous scientific advances of the previous hundred years, and so an individual human did not reach the surface of the planet until 2078. The corporations of Japan showed continued interest in placing men on the planet, and by the end of the century there were two permanently occupied bases there—one at either pole. Though these bases were primarily of a scientific nature, they did supply the relatively cheap surface soil to asteroid manufacturers as a weak oxidizer for certain industrial processes. During these years, although the human population had begun its long, steady decline, many parts of the Earth were still overpopulated and barely habitable, and this fueled a brief "space rush" during the years following 2110. A large, domed city was constructed in the vicinity of the Kison Tholus, a still active volcanic structure not far from the ice fields of the north. At its largest, this city, called Kaseimachi in Japanese, the dominant language at the time, reached a population of several thousand. With areothermal energy and the great volatile resources, Kaseimachi was very successful; for a time it became a haven for much of the off-Earth community.

"The changes that led to the utopian world of the late twenty-second century were well under way by this time,

however, and they revolutionized the way man viewed himself and his planet. With the coming of inexpensive fusion energy, the immediate problems of mankind were largely solved. The schism between East and West had begun, and advances in cybernetics meant that man's presence was no longer necessary in space. In the earliest years of the Eastern hegemony, the Supervisors issued a proclamation inviting all off-Earthers back, guaranteeing them a share of the new society. Most of them went, leaving only a network of small bases still affiliated with the old corporations."

"But why did they return to Earth? Was the invitation that compelling?"

"As the population of Earth dwindled toward its optimum size, the standard of living increased by a greater amount in a shorter time than it ever had. The promise of living a productive life in the green, luxuriant hills of Earth proved to be too strong a lure. Economics played a strong role as well, of course. But it is beyond the scope of my knowledge base to explain that sufficiently.

"Anyway, Pete, the upshot of it all is that space became largely the domain of cybernetic workers; of the men and women who ventured into space, most were tourists or people who catered to tourists."

Peter tucked a strand of hair back behind his ear and cocked his head. "Your history is not exactly what I learned in school, you know. I never heard of the recall before, for example."

"It *was* a small event, in a sense, hardly worthy of note. I only included it because of its effect on Kaseimachi and Mars."

"But the whole idea behind *Asia* is that space colonization *is* important, and was meant to be done by people, not machines."

Traveler clucked. "It is not for me to evaluate the fickleness of human ideas. Things change, Pete. Needs and desires change. When stagnation began to erode the new civilization, Project Outreach was invented to give mankind a sense of accomplishment. The discovery that faster-than-light spacecraft were possible was perhaps the

initial impetus; but many things dovetailed neatly to make the project a reality. The promise of new Earths, just as green, just as luxuriant: this was something that gave meaning to otherwise boring, repetitious labor."

"Okay, Trav. I suppose I understand." Peter stood and leaned on the viewpage support. "Tell me what to expect from the people on Mars."

"We will be there in six minutes . . . wouldn't you just prefer to find out for yourself?"

Peter laughed. "I just want to be prepared."

"I can speculate; but, I warn you, my guesses may not be very accurate. At the time *Asia* was launched, there were fourteen small bases scattered over most of the planet's surface. Total population was a few hundred. Several hundred men and women also made their homes in the asteroid belt; and there were at least four scientific teams in the Outer Planets. We may suppose that most of them are now living on Mars; which is the body most suitable to human needs next to Earth. How much actual damage was caused out here by the burster, I don't know. But many years have passed since the event. Theoretically, a self-sustaining Martian colony could last several decades or more without the advanced ecological systems included in *Asia*. We will soon find out how well the colonies actually have done."

"That doesn't—"

"Please grab hold of something, Peter; my navigator informs me that we are about to decelerate into Mars orbit."

The image on the videon was now the real Mars, a fat, battered, orange crescent that wheeled up toward them like a rotting slice of melon. Peter stared at it in amazement. From a high orbit the landscape was dominated by wind erosion, swipes of color vast and small streaking the worn-looking craters. He had played with an airbrush during his brief foray into the graphic arts, and could easily imagine creating such a canvas with the device. The thin atmosphere was plainly visible as a pinkish smearing of the limb, and, as they moved toward the morning terminator, translucent milky fog filled the larger craters.

It was plainly not the dead planet he had been expecting. Quickly the craft's orbit carried it into the darkness.

Once again Peter bobbed about unrestrained by gravity. He reestablished the sitting posture, which by now was beginning to become habitual, and stared at the screen, wondering what to say. It was clear that he should now be taking command of his little, odd crew; assuming responsibility for their interaction with the Martians; yet he was strangely reluctant to do so.

"Trav. Have you been in communication with the base you spoke of?"

"No more than to relay our mission and time of arrival. They have not been inquisitive."

"Can you contact them now?"

"We are in line of sight with them for another eleven minutes."

"I want to talk to a person in authority there, myself. I don't want you to say anything to anyone unless I specifically authorize you. Understood?"

"Pete, I don't wish to concede to you any rights that I may find vital at a later time."

"Look, Trav. I'm *asking* you. Let me do the talking, at least for a while. You can advise me; in fact I want your advice whenever you have anything to say. Captain Taranga placed me in charge of this mission, did she not?"

"I wasn't informed what your exact purpose is, Pete. I can only assume that you are—"

"Hey! Stop. We've already lost a minute with useless jabbering. Put me through to Acidalia."

"Very well."

The quality of the silence changed. The image of a face, darkly sallow and beaten like the planet itself, filled the screen. The man was a Southern European type, heavily bearded. In the low, incidental illumination, his features seemed sharpened, craggy. This wisps of dark hair were combed forward to inadequately cover a large forehead sporting two chevron-shaped eyebrows. The eyes themselves were hidden in shadow, and the man's jutting nose and pouting, sensuous lips formed into a little, pudgy smile that suggested authority masked by an ironic sense

of humor. Clearly, this was a person who was not to be trifled with.

"Can he hear me?"

The specter on the screen winked. "He can both hear and see you," said Trav.

"Hello, then."

His videon camera pulled back to a middle-distance shot. "Good evening," the man said, sitting back in his chair. A stray beam of light was caught in the well of his left eye, reflecting dully from the cornea. He appeared to be dressed entirely in black. "Welcome back to the solar system. My name is Simon Cargill."

"I am Peter Zolotin. I am here to investigate what happened."

"So we have been told by your friend Traveler."

"We don't have much time to talk on this go-round," said Peter, "so let's get down to business. Do you have the means to travel to orbit and back safely?"

Cargill was still amused. "Of course. While I can't say much for certain aspects of our present civilization, we lost very few of the ships that were not in the vicinity of Earth. Would you like me to send up a shuttle for you?"

Peter smiled into the screen and nodded, trying to ingratiate himself as best he could. "Yes, I think that would make our conversation a bit easier. I have only been supplied with a passive vacuum sphere for EVA, however. Will that be a problem?"

"Not at all. From the speed and maneuverability that Traveler has displayed, I imagine that it would be far easier for you to meet us than vice versa."

On the next orbit, when Traveler had reestablished communication with Acidalia Astrodome and Mars shuttle *Kline*, Peter consulted his viewpage blueprint of the cabin. The spaceball was located in a storage compartment behind the viewpage desk, and it took only a moment to find the book-sized plastic rectangle. It was amazingly light, less than two kilograms, and made out of a paper-thin aluminize. He unfolded it to a square about a meter and a

half on a side, and, unable to find any written instructions, turned to the videon and said, "What next?"

A series of complex-looking picture diagrams appeared on the screen. "It's quite simple. First, find the zipper. Then open it up along the groove and get inside."

Pete easily found the seam, but opening it was another matter. Unable to get a secure hold when both of his hands were otherwise in use, he bounced around the cabin trying to wrestle the thing apart. After what seemed like minutes of repeated pulling, tearing, pushing, and applying friction, the thing magically popped open. There was obviously some secret that he didn't understand.

"Now you get inside," said Traveler, sounding impatient.

He inserted both feet into the hole, spinning slowly, and drew the thing up around his waist, as high as it would go. "What next?"

"There is an illuminated button located on the inside next to the top of the zipper. When you have gotten completely inside, hold the seam away from you, uncap the button, and press it. It will do the rest."

"Are they coming yet?"

"I am in the process of rendezvous with *Kline* at this moment. We are separated by about four kilometers and are closing."

Pete suddenly wondered whether the logistics of this made sense. Traveler had sufficient control over the cabin externals to vent the air and open the hatch. Properly suited Martians would enter and convey him to their own ship, where the ball would be deflated and he would be let out. The plan certainly put a lot of trust in their resources and goodwill. But he had no reason to think they could have any ulterior motives. One of them could steal Traveler and go back to Epsilon Indi in his place, he supposed. Would Traveler let that happen?

"Here they come," said Traveler. "Time to get ready."

By this time Peter had managed to steady himself against a bulkhead. He crouched down and pulled the material over his head. The glowing red button was plainly visible inside. Then a sudden thought: would the fully

inflated ball fit out the door? It might not. He poked his head out again.

"Hey, Trav, what if it gets too big to get through the hatch when I inflate it?"

"Fatty fatty two-by-four? Don't worry about it. Even in full vacuum the ball is relatively malleable and can be squeezed through."

Back inside, he pulled the hard, transparent protection cap off the button and pushed. There was a sudden ripping sound, as of metal foil being torn, and then a reassuring hissing noise. The ball stretched out around him, and, when the sounds stopped, it had turned into a cozy, meter-and-a-half spherical shelter, lit by button light and a small, flexible window into the cabin. Still weightless, Peter relaxed and tried to make his mind go blank. For the most part he succeeded.

"They're here!" Traveler's voice was perfectly clear inside the ball. "Having no docking apparatus, I am going to maneuver over as close as I can to *Kline*'s airlock port. I should be able to safely close the gap to about ten meters, at which time they will EVA and come and get you. For whatever it's worth, the procedure would be the same if you had a full spacesuit, since you are untrained in space walking."

"If I get into trouble, I suppose there is nothing that you can do to help."

"Au contraire. My ionic drive produces a stream of very dangerous, high-speed particles that would make a very potent weapon. Since I am many times faster and more maneuverable than any craft designed for intrastellar travel, I could play havoc with whatever space activity they still have. In fact, I am pretty certain that Mars' atmosphere is too tenuous to act as a shield, and it has hardly any magnetic field; so I might be able to destroy surface habitations as well."

"That's good to hear, Trav. It makes me feel a bit better about placing myself in their hands." Though I should probably trust my fellow human beings over a robot, he thought, especially one whose software has already demonstrated sizable problems. "I will radio you

on the band you've been using as soon as I am down on the surface, and every twenty-four hours thereafter. If you do not receive my signal, start asking questions, and, if you don't get satisfactory answers, start threatening."

"I wouldn't want to lose you, Peter. Be careful down there."

A moment passed. Peter wasn't sure if he should feel touched by the craft's solicitousness or not. "Okay, Trav."

"I have completed rendezvous, Peter, and will be evacuating the air from the cabin. Do not reopen the ball under any circumstances until you are safely in the other ship."

"I can take care of myself."

Peter took hold of two straps conveniently placed on either side of the small window and looked out. The cabin seemed unchanged. Suddenly the ball began to swell even farther, tightening and smoothing out crinkles. After a moment the hatch swung open, revealing the black sky of space and a curving white hull with a large, open circle bordered by red lights leading into what looked like an airlock. Two figures wearing bulky red and black spacesuits appeared in the opening and, trailing supple metal cables, slowly propelled themselves across the intervening distance, paying out their cables behind them. Traveler shuddered slightly as they made contact; they had no trouble coming inside the cabin. Peter noted that their black helmets bore a design composed of three red triangles.

Getting a firm hold on either side of the ball, they forced it through the hatch. Peter imagined himself as a sort of fetus suspended in amniotic fluid. He caught a brief glimpse of sandy Mars sliding by underneath. For several long moments he had no notion of what was happening: there was no sense of sustained motion, and the window showed only stars and blackness. Suddenly the whiteness of *Kline* filled the transparency, and the ball made a rutching sound as it was bounced over the lip of the airlock. They were aboard.

When the increased pressure inside the airlock caused the ball to deflate slightly, Peter spun himself around so that he could free himself. "Can you hear me?" asked a

high, feminine voice. "The airlock is fully pressurized. You can come out, if you want to."

He pressed the button and the ball split open like a ripe fruit. He managed to pull himself out and fold the deflated sphere until it was almost flat. Two people floated farther inside the airlock, busy stowing their suits in lockers. The one who had spoken to him was a tall, dark-haired Oriental woman, in her thirties, her small, boyish head sitting atop an elegantly long, graceful neck. Her body was otherwise well-proportioned, and the overall impression was not of ungainliness, but rather beauty, like the swans that had populated the Great Lake for a while. Her eyes were small and teardrop-shaped, and thick, rough black hair, loosely braided, fell down her back like an unraveling rope.

She turned to him. "Welcome to Mars. My name is Barbara Cargill."

"I am Peter Zolotin. I was sent back from the Project Outreach starship to find out why the radio signal stopped. Faster than light. I just got here."

The woman seemed uninterested. "And how are things aboard *Asia*?"

"Fine. At least, well, we reached Epsilon Indi all right. The scientists were just starting to explore. The existence of life on one of the moons of the largest planet was confirmed."

The other, who by now had finished storing his suit, stared at Peter suspiciously. He was of European descent, a plain, big-nosed sort of person, with his long blond hair combed severely back to escape into luxurious golden curls behind his ears and on his neck. "My name's Salkind." He turned away again and began pressing controls on the inner hatchway of the lock.

Peter looked back and forth between the two of them. "You seem awfully blasé about all this," he said. "The fucking Earth's been blown away."

The woman smiled. "That is not news to us, friend traveler. We have been living in the shadow of the burst for many years now. We have adapted as well as we can; though for some of us that has not been a healthy process.

I had better start by warning you not to trust anyone you are about to meet. Many among us conspire to finish the job started by the explosion."

"What do you mean?"

She shook her head. "Not now. Chris and I are needed to help pilot the shuttle back to Acidalia. Come with us; there's a seat in the cockpit for you."

The inner lock opened and Peter followed the two through a short corridor to a large room filled with videons and smaller electronic readouts. Mars bellied up against the night, huge and florid, through a large, curving window that cut across the room. Traveler was already distant, dwindling quickly as it moved into a higher orbit. A fat man with small, squinty eyes and a nose that looked as if it had been squashed turned from the controls to watch him come in. This man was dressed in the same black coveralls he had seen on Simon Cargill. The red diamond symbol was woven into the fabric of his chest pocket. He grunted and nodded at Peter, and went back to work.

"This is Fernando Poe, Peter," said the woman, taking her position in the chair next to him. "Strap yourself into the seat over there." She pointed to the rear of the cockpit.

Peter did as he was told, having some difficulty with the strange fasteners. He watched as the nose of the craft started to point downward, pulling the planet up to fill the entire window. He said, "Big planet."

"Lot of valuable real estate down there; and it's quite cheap," said Salkind. In the seat nearest to Peter, on the other side of the entryway, the man was already busy, flipping switches and comparing their positions with a videon display to his right.

Poe turned away from his controls and shook his head, causing the pronounced double chin to wiggle. "It's a buyers' market, Chris. Always has been. Are you ready?"

"Aye," said Barbara.

Chris punched a series of buttons, checked his display, and said, "Ready."

"Okay, then. Initiating burn number one." Peter felt the craft slowing; the straps that crisscrossed his chest held

him in place. "Burn number two." Again he was pushed forward.

Cargill glanced over her shoulder. "This is a somewhat unusual vehicle, Peter. It's quite old—predates the fascination with cybernetic control, so it's human intensive. Mars' atmosphere is too thin for a conventional spaceplane reentry. What we do is more like aerobraking than flying. I don't imagine you saw much coming across. It's shaped more like a swollen manta ray than a terrestrial shuttle, and has a down-curving front edge to deal with the extremely high angle of attack necessary. Ram thrusters are necessary to maintain the correct entry angle."

The edges of the window were beginning to grow hazy with an orange light, and Peter felt a slight buffeting, like sliding on corrugated metal. The planet slowly receded downward, until it was no longer visible in the window. Instead, the blackness of space was being eaten up by a growing blood mist, and rivulets of yellow light crawled and squirmed against the glass. The straps were beginning to bite into his chest and shoulders.

"Exterior temperature eleven hundred degrees," said Salkind.

"Thrusters on," said Poe. A heterodyne roar was added to the growing low-frequency noises in the cabin. "Here we go." The ruddy light now filled the window, and the yellow streamers had unfolded into spreading spokes of white flame. It reminded Peter of a program he had once seen about terrestrial auroras. "Twelve fifty," said Salkind. "Heat channels nominal."

The shuddering was intensified suddenly, becoming a complex oscillation.

Barbara was making quick adjustments to a series of joysticks on the console before her. The vibration began to dampen out slowly. "Surface modification nominal," she said.

Poe leaned back, let out a breath of air and shifted down an instrument-covered joywheel from the recess in which it had been stowed. "Going for a landing," he said, barely loud enough to hear over the diminuendo thunder. The fire had cleared from the window, but there was a

growing pinkish tinge at the lower edge, Mars' dust-colored atmosphere. "Starting retrorockets."

A red horizon popped up over the consoles, big as the world it was. A lightly cratered landscape moved under them, bringing in its wake a scrambled, broken terrain of uneven mesas and tablelands. Everything looked as though it were half-buried under a featureless sea of dust. This was as close as Peter had ever gotten to a planet, and he gazed with rapt wonder at the many strange land forms that the craft passed over. The dust seemed to be getting thicker, and fewer and fewer craters were big enough to show through it, when suddenly Peter noticed a truly enormous crater, sitting on what looked like a strange, pedestal-like tableland, coming toward them. The craft skimmed over the structure, and beyond it was a small collection of human buildings nestled together under a transparent dome which was visible only because the sun was glinting brightly from it. Near the settlement was a long, white strip of concrete, marked with bright blue-green lines. It was plain that this was the landing area for the shuttle.

Poe pressed a large, recessed button on the joywheel and said, "Landing rockets on." A different sort of roar filled the air, and the gravity that Peter had just begun to notice spun about more than ninety degrees. The nose swung up violently into the air, and the rockets that jutted from the rear caught the craft on a pillar of fire. In less than a minute they touched down with a solid thunk. When the engines were shut off, Peter could hear the silence plainly.

The others began to undo their safety belts. Barbara spoke an unnecessary "We're here" to him, and he, too, disconnected his straps. Since the ship was sitting on its tail, he was being pressed down by Mars' small gravity onto his back, contrary to the up-down he had provisionally assigned to orient himself in microgravity. He found a sturdy-looking metal ring protruding from a partition above his head, and he used it to successfully right himself.

"There will be no need to suit up, Peter," said Barbara Cargill. "This was once a facility designed to

pamper tourists, and we still have a functioning mobile lounge to take us inside the dome." She skillfully twisted her body around, catching a rung on the side of the entryway, clambering down into what was now a well leading into the ship. Poe and Salkind followed, and Peter managed to imitate them well enough to follow without falling.

At the end of the shaft they entered a large room that must have taken up most of the inside of the shuttle. It contained two rows of plush, red seats, with plenty of room to stretch out. "We used to fill these on a regular basis," said Barbara. "Acidalia base has a long, interesting history. Once we were just a way station for Kaseimachi, about eight hundred kilometers north of here. But we developed our own little program, and before long we got a good half of the tourist trade. That, in spite of the fact that we're a long way from Tharsis."

The mobile lounge was basically an observation car, and Peter had his first chance to see Mars—or any planet, for that matter—from ground level. It wasn't particularly impressive. Flat, red-brown sand reached in all directions, virtually featureless except for minuscule variations in color and an occasional depression that must have been an eroded crater. In the distance the pedestal crater that they had passed over gave a slight bulge to the otherwise dead-straight horizon. The sky near the horizon was pinkish-white, quickly fading into dim silver-gray as his gaze traveled upward. The sun was very nearly overhead; it seemed slightly blurred, but very bright. Just above the glassy dome, Peter made out a bright star through the haze. He had imagined that being *on* a planet would be a unique experience, that he would look around and get a feeling for the enormous girth of the world upon which he stood; but it was not so. In the absence of firm clues about distances, he might just as well have been sitting in a little depression back aboard *Asia*.

The vehicle slowly trundled toward a reinforced concrete tunnel leading under the base of the dome. Peter and Barbara were sitting opposite one another under the

large observation window, while Salkind and Poe sat up front, talking to the driver.

Barbara appeared very solicitous about his condition, and, though Peter could not fully understand her motivations, he found himself being drawn out, giving unusually long replies.

"Yes," he was saying, "I left the Earth before my memories start, so I really don't have a visceral sense of loss from seeing the planet as it is. *Asia* is the world for me. I never expected to leave it. I happened to do well on the test, that's all. That is why I am here."

Barbara's head darted about, looking here, there, like a robin in search of a meal. "Simon and I grew up in Japan. The Earth is very real to us, although neither of us ever returned. Sometimes we sit in our solarium and imagine the way it used to be; the fanciful green trees, the overarching blue of the sky; even the great cities. When you are young, everything seems a bit supernatural. None of us has fully come to terms with the truth. I daresay that it is impossible to fully grasp."

"Have you the means to survive? Here, I mean? Traveler said that Earth will be uninhabitable for a thousand years. Can mankind survive here for that long a time, unaided?"

"Perhaps we can. My husband is the de facto commander of three of the four remaining bases, and he seems to think that we have a fighting chance. You will have to talk to him to hear the full story, though."

They were passing under the overhang of the tunnel, and the sun suddenly winked out. Comfortable interior lights came up to take its place. A time passed in which the two of them regarded each other silently. Peter got the uncomfortable feeling that she was trying to devour him with her eyes. Finally, trying to restart the conversation, he said, "I don't mean to be personal, but did you cry when you found out what happened?"

Barbara looked at him strangely. "Yes. For months afterward an image, a chance thought, almost anything, could bring me tears. I am an emotional person, I suppose."

"Oh, no," he said, trying to reassure her. "That seems completely normal. You lost personal friends, I suppose."

"Surprisingly few. My parents, of course, and several cherished classmates. But when we made the decision to come to Mars, it was not a frivolous thing. People you leave behind can somehow never be the same. I never expected to see any of them again. They chose their lives, I mine."

"I seem to be incapable of crying, so far," Peter replied. "I feel that I should, though; I feel guilty that I haven't."

She readjusted her position in the seat and, after a pause, smiled wanly. "Consider yourself fortunate. You have a world to go back to; we are stuck here."

"What did you mean about not trusting people here?"

"Ah, yes, I said that, didn't I?"

The mobile lounge came to a sudden stop before a black metal wall, and as Peter watched, a similar barrier slowly dropped just to the rear. They were passing through an underground airlock of sorts as they passed into the domed city.

"Listen to me, Peter. Simon pooh-poohs these things, but I do not. In the last year there have been a series of events—murders, destructive explosions, apparent suicides—that convince me there is a conspiracy of some kind. Religious, I would imagine. To destroy our chances of survival. Just last week the atmosphere plant north of Kaseimachi was ruined by a chance discharge of electricity in the oxygen storage facility. The people who were trying to bring the city back to life were set back years, perhaps permanently."

Peter shook his head in bewilderment. "But why? That's crazy. Who in their right mind would—"

Barbara grimaced. "In their *right* mind? No one, of course. But think of the religious among us. There were a few, despite the discrediting of the last centuries. How can one of these people accept the destruction of the world except as an act of God? And, if you believe that the greatest good comes in acquiescing to the will of this being, then perhaps you would come to the conclusion

that the few survivors left should also be killed. The spirit of faith demands it, in fact."

Peter watched as the forward door opened, allowing the vehicle to move ahead. "And yet no one has claimed responsibility for these actions?"

"No. Many, including my husband, think them to be simple coincidence. But I am telling you so that you will be careful. Remember, *Asia*, and you, are mankind's greatest hope. You are bound to be a target."

Peter shivered. "I'll try to remember that."

The meeting with Simon Cargill had not gone well. Peter stepped onto the balcony of the apartment he had been assigned, enjoying the sense of vitality imparted by the low gravity, and looked out at the Martian sunset. The sky was a burning white around the small, blanched disk of the sun. The man had regarded him with what seemed to be a mixture of contempt and humorous derision. No matter how he tried, Peter could not get him to acknowledge that the mission Traveler and he were on was of any importance whatsoever. And when Peter had tried to define the mission precisely, it had come out awkwardly, unconvincing. Obviously, beyond telling someone to turn the radio signal to *Asia* back on—an absurdity now—he really didn't have a definable purpose here. Whatever authority Captain Taranga may have had as highest-ranking survivor, was totally vitiated by her distance, and Cargill, sole remaining officer of the Mitsubishi Corporation, felt no compunction about honoring it. The man infuriated him beyond reason; stammering and stuttering had been the only result.

It was clear from the short interview that Cargill was trying to consolidate the rest of the Martian survivors into a cooperative group; and there apparently had been several meetings, through the years, of representatives from the remaining settlements. The recent disaster at Kaseimachi had put an end to their principal attempt at reconstruction. No fully stabilized ecosystem existed on Mars; except for the omnipresent personal gardens, virtually all food had been imported from *Ecoplex I* in Earth orbit. Yet he

was not interested in possible help from *Asia*, considered the idea ludicrous. Fourteen years was too long for them to wait, Peter supposed.

He had even been laughed at when he asked to communicate with Traveler. Peter knew his self-confidence had taken a beating. Even now, two hours later, he felt embarrassed and bashful for no reason.

Acidalia was located far north of the equator, and, since it was high summer for the northern hemisphere, the sinking of the sun was unusually prolonged. As it neared the ruler-straight ground, it was lost in blank radiance, which slowly began to dim. Above, where silver had been during the day, the finest particles of Martian dust, carried high into the fringes of the atmosphere, caught the last rays of light and burst into opalescence like a well-worn sheet of mother-of-pearl. Peter stood, leaning lightly against the railing, and watched this most planetary of phenomena wind down into full darkness. Stars in the hundreds winked on, apparently undiminished by the dust in the sky. Just as he was about to turn away, a new star, brilliant and swollen, appeared on the horizon. Undoubtedly it was Phobos, transiting the sky in its curious backward way. He watched it for a long time, and fancied that he could see it moving.

Inside the dome the temperature was quite comfortable, yet when he finally did step into the still, darkened apartment, he felt chilled and stiff. A track light came on, and he walked in a circle of spotlight until he had found the wall console. Ambient illumination filled the room at his command, reducing the world outside the window to blackness.

It was a luxurious room, decorated entirely in shades of red and orange. The thick pile of carpet was soft as velvet on his bare feet. There was an enormous circular bed under a canopy of diaphanous gauze; two air-cushion easy chairs with built-in massage; a fully equipped bar with a cybernetic tender. And the bathroom was beyond description, a combination mirror hall, bathing pool, second bedroom, and videon studio. Plainly, Acidalia had

supplied the best available accommodations for the travel-weary Martian tourist.

He pushed aside the curtains and collapsed back onto the resilient bed. What was he supposed to do now? At least he should observe the Martians and try to make an assessment about their future chances. They had no CES transmitter, and thus electromagnetic communication with *Asia* was impossible; so his report would be all that one of the two remaining human populations would know about the other. Even if they diverted one of the other Travelers here, that would take years to accomplish. He should try to visit at least some of the other settlements and talk to those in charge. Make an assessment—an assessment, yes, that sounded official enough.

The crimson velour bedspread seemed to snuggle up against him, warm and reassuring. His muscles ached, but if he kept them motionless, they responded by sending out waves of sleep-inducing pleasure. He found a button on the bed console that turned off the light. His mind cleared, and he found a pillow and turned over on his side, curling up fetally. It had been a long day. Sleep rushed up over him like a strong tide.

Larry Taylor stood looking over the few personal items he had brought into space and wondered what he could leave behind if the moment came. He had the strong feeling that the quiet normality of the next few minutes would be the last he would ever know. The die had been cast. Taranga's ever-tightening stranglehold on the ship had finally provoked the inevitable. Over the years, as the situation worsened and Taranga became more and more repressive, the establishment of a self-sufficient base on Twist had allowed them to dream, and then think openly, of the possibility of revolt. With the resources to refuel the ferries, breathe, and even eat, suddenly available beyond the narrow confines of the generation ship, it had only been a matter of time before the conflict exploded. More and more often he saw signs of how pathological the society aboard ship had become. Rigid hierarchies sprang up based solely on Taranga's favor; the rule of law had

been made into a mockery. And the citizens of this brave new world had adapted; as the citizens of the Third Reich and Stalin's USSR adapted to their respective hells. The captain had stalled further exploration of the Epsilon Indi system, putting off all decisions until the return of the Traveler spacecraft. So even their work was in limbo.

It was only an added touch of irony that his relationship with Cory, one of the first sources of Taranga's opposition to the scientists—and more recently a trumped-up "crime" of adultery leveled against them—had become a farce early on. Something palpable had come between them, something beyond his ability to comprehend, and, for the longest time, their relationship degenerated into a parody of the worst sort of marriage, where they ate and slept together, but little else. Sex became a continuous irritant, and, when he had managed to persuade her perhaps once a month, he didn't enjoy it much either. After a while the only thing that held them together was the knowledge that they were "accomplishing something" by showing the others that you could stand up to the captain; and the fear that, if they separated, there might be no one new among the closed circle of scientists. He had felt his personality wilt, and he grew progressively less extroverted, more involved in the biota of Twist.

A queer combination of emotions flooded through him, almost blocking the functioning of his conscious mind. Fear, that was definitely one of them—a surging flood of epinephrine in his back and shoulders. Or was it simply excitement, a kind of blood lust? His brain was on fire with excitement, and yet somewhere within there was a cool, calm bubble of personality that he regarded as himself. He forced himself to continue. There was a valuable nineteenth century edition of *Moby Dick*, restored through the antiquarian's art, that only weighed fourteen or fifteen ounces. He had read it many times, enjoying it in some ways more each time. It would come. The rest, sculptures, miniatures, geodes from back home, no longer engaged his interest. He had not really noticed any of them for months, if not years. They would stay.

He packed a few items of clothing into a small,

flexible satchel and bound it together with its adsorptive tabs. That was it, then. The finality of the course before him weighed in heavily. If only they had not had to rush the coup, things might have seemed clearer, more controllable. But Taranga, undoubtedly suspecting something, had made her move, trumping up his and Cory's defiance into the ridiculous adultery charge, setting the trial date for today. Although everything was in place and all the weapons were made, the plans had not had time to steep. Taylor firmly believed in a peer-review process, which had not been allowed to follow its full course. Most thought Science and War did not mix; he was convinced that only through the most careful analysis could they succeed. But now they were started; there would be no rest until the thing was finished; for good or evil.

He picked the radiation beamer up from the bed and studied it closely. It was a small thing, really, harmless-looking, just a flying-saucer/mushroom toy. A thick cylindrical handle with a recharger plug, a circular hilt of shielding material, and a transparent hemisphere on the end. They had made twelve of them in all, enough to wreak huge amounts of destruction. Finally, he checked out the small, featureless intership radio and placed it in his pocket.

Emotions rushed past his mind. Ah, they were more distinct now; beside the fear there was a strong hint of self-doubt. A delicate sorrow—tears to come, for the people who died or were injured because of his actions—bit at him. And a strong resolve to continue anyway.

The door slipped open and Cory walked in, looking frazzled and shrunken. Her large eyes were bloodshot and her lips were dry and starting to crack. "It's time," she said hoarsely.

"I know."

She looked at him without sympathy and collapsed into an armchair. "Let me sit here for a second."

Larry looked at his watch. "It's ten minutes before the power is cut. If we are not in the inner cylinder by then, we'll be stranded."

"I know," she said, with a kind of resignation.

* * *

They caught the last elevator across, arriving in the Great Hall beneath the pivot at exactly eleven o'clock. Four of them—Larry, Cory, Tae Nu Hya, and Jeannie Tetap—had volunteered for this part of the ship, the crucial place where the cylinder and frustum came together. It was known that only five or six policemen were routinely assigned to this area, most or all carrying small stun guns only effective at a short range.

Across the hall, on the far side of the inlaid map of the Eurasian continent, Larry spotted Nu and Jeannie looking amazingly conspicuous among the hurrying passersby. They started walking toward the middle of the hall, and he and Cory did likewise. Half a minute passed, well into the time when the utility feed to this area should have been severed. Had they been caught? Were they already doomed to failure? The seconds passed and the four met on the brown tiles of Central Kazakhstan. Tae only had time to start her question, "Do you know what—" when the main lights snapped off, plunging them into utter darkness.

Only a moment passed. Wan light from an emergency lamp in Tae's hand made an eerie, boundaryless room around them. In the distances all around, confused people stood waiting. Larry, suddenly lost to the pounding of his heart and head, said redundantly, "To the pivot, quickly!"

Those in their way unhesitatingly moved aside. They had each studied the master plan of this part of the ship, and knew exactly where the bypass stairway was located. They met no resistance, and it began to look as if even the blackout had not been seen as anything more than a mechanical failure.

There were only five of them standing before the entrance to the pivot housing; four men and a woman, lit by their own lamp, dressed normally except for the small shoulder harnesses in which they carried their induced-stun weapons. Now they had their weapons out, obviously guarding the doorway. As they caught sight of the scientists, they gathered together in a little knot before the portal, brandishing the stunners menacingly.

Jeannie, barely knowing where the voice was coming from, said, "Stand aside or we will kill you."

The leftmost of the guards, a small, catlike man with a thin mustache, began to advance. "Come now, citizens," he said, in a wheedling, high-pitched voice. "This thing, whatever it is, is over now. I imagine you fancy yourselves to be some sort of terrorist group. We will not let you get to the pivot. Just relax while we wait for the lights to come back on . . ." As he spoke he was closing the distance between them, evidently hoping to come within stunner range.

"Stop," said Larry. "I mean it! Stop!"

"Please keep your arms at your sides and don't make any sudden movements. I will—"

He had come too close. Larry pressed the recessed button on the beamer. The man looked very surprised, but except for a barely audible whine, there was no immediate result for a moment. Then the victim began to scream, clutching at his face and buckling at the knees. A strange sizzling and popping noise came from somewhere. Larry let go of the button. The man toppled slowly to the floor and did not move.

Horror swept through Larry Taylor; the images he had had of killing a person had not been like this. He looked up from the fallen man to see the other guards. They had obviously felt some of the radiation from the beamer, and, realizing the danger they were in, opened the housing door and were backing through. Suddenly the woman made a rush toward them, but Larry turned the beamer on her before she could get close, and the results were about the same. This time only a dull numbness marked the biologist's interior response.

Nu stepped forward. "Throw down your weapons and we won't kill you."

The three remaining conferred for a moment, and, reaching a decision, tossed the compact stunners out onto the floor, where they hit with hard plastic thwocks, skidding and spinning on the floor. Cory collected them, studiously avoiding the two irradiated bodies, and beckoning with her hand, said, "Come on out here."

They did so, slowly, sheepishly, looking for an opportunity that they knew would not come. One by one, as they came within range, Cory pointed the stunner and pulled the trigger. The thing had an internal sound generator that produced the heterodyne squeal, breaking the silence and once again invoking the image of bad science fiction. Finally they were all down.

"Okay, then. Victory," Jeannie said in a semisardonic mocking tone.

They came out onto the interior forward surface of the hub, on a lip beneath the huge, incandescent sphere. Here was the entryway to the maze of electronics that maintained the almost magical connection between the two parts of the spacecraft, and here they would stay, using the beamer to defend their territory, until the revolution was over. Jeannie quickly found the primitive manual override controls, and with a practiced series of moves, began firing the thrusters that controlled the speed at which the frustum revolved. Gravity began to dwindle, suddenly revealing itself as the mythical creation of the physics textbook—centrifugal force. Larry, whose mind was still dominated by a welter of conflicting feelings, noted his body extending, decompressing as his weight decreased. The pivot appeared to be speeding up. A small, resistable force pushed at him; the angular inertia of the cone was spinning down. Nu and Cory grabbed onto metal handholds designed to cope with this very situation.

"This'll keep 'em out of the action," Nu said with exaggerated heartiness.

"There are laddered corridors throughout most of the living quarters," said Cory, "but it'll delay any response for a long, long time."

Taylor looked once again at the entryway, searching for the body of armed men he expected to appear at any moment. No one. He made a sudden movement toward a handhold and found that he had waited too long. The push of friction on his foot, combined with the small angular deceleration, was enough to send him upward in a slow-motion backward arc, leg and torso over head. The women cried out inarticulately.

Fear and disorientation. He flailed about, knowing it was useless. The madly spinning pivot, like an electroluminescent world, swung under his feet and receded until he was looking down on the control room. For two full go-rounds he felt unable to control his thoughts at all. Fortunately, he kept hold of the beamer.

A fragile bootstrap of logic appeared, and he latched on to it. There was a solution to this problem somewhere. Larry forced himself to redefine his reference points. The ship was moving; *he* was still. Slowly the vertigo receded and he was able to take stock. Again he carefully redefined his thinking. The polished metal platform was receding very slowly, indicating he wouldn't have to worry about entering the pivot field. He could see Cory and Nu back at his launch point, not yet tiny, but shrinking. They were still close enough to yell at; but he really couldn't think of anything to say. His trajectory would take him straight across the hub, and eventually he would make landfall about two kilometers away. Presumably he could then propel himself back.

But the time it would take! Without the beamer, the women would be virtually defenseless. If anyone should come during the long minutes of his flight, this part of the coup would be lost. Still sailing end over end, he contemplated the ultimate failure. He took the radio out of his pocket, thumbed the onoff and said, "Pivot station. Report." There was no reply.

An amazingly accurate shove off the "far wall" had brought Larry back to the control room with ease. He need not have worried—no one came, and the lower corridor remained silent as a mausoleum.

The radio chirped, and Larry pulled it out of his pocket. A burst of static went on for a long time. He concluded that it had malfunctioned somehow, when a voice broke through the diminuendo noise, loud enough to understand. It was the geochemist Nguyen. "Bridge station. Victor tango. Repeat. Victor tango."

Larry looked at the others. His glance crossed Cory's and locked for a moment. She seemed dazed, unfocused.

"Victor tango" was the signal for complete defeat. He held the radio in his palm and said, "Pivot station. What the hell is going on there?"

A new hiss was added to the static, and Ryan Du Lapp replied, "Ferry station. Damn this code. We have taken the ferry hold. *Arecibo* got away, though. Can you get out of there, Dan?"

"Negative. There are only two of us left here, and they have us trapped up against the DV drive. It was a fucking great battle, while it lasted. Old Taranga was prepared. That's her motto, isn't it? Be prepared? They had some kind of laser that would cut through bulkhead. Hide and seek wouldn't describe it. More like cat and mouse. Anyway, Shentong and I got them to chase us. The others are headed for you, Ryan. Get ready to get the fuck out of there, man, as soon as they get there."

"Ryan," said Tae, "are you all right?"

"Yeah," came the reply. "So far. You too?"

"No casualties here," said Larry.

"I guess we lost," said Ryan, making a feeble attempt at humor. "We've already started loading the ferries. Should take another ten minutes or so. Ah . . . the others are starting to arrive. Looks like most of them."

"Okay. Looks like plan number two," said Jeannie. "We'll meet you at the pivot egress, suited up."

"Give us twenty minutes. With these others, we can load a great deal more."

"Done," said Larry, feeling a surge of relief that it was over with no more killing. "See you soon."

Eight

When the morning came, Peter Zolotin awoke refreshed. Every trace of whatever he had dreamed had evaporated with the transient fogs of the Martian dawn. He had pulled a fold of the coverlet over him in the night, and he now pushed it back and sat up. His shirt and trousers had wrinkled badly, and he tried to smooth them down with repeated brushes of his hand, to little avail. He stood up and stretched, squeezing the sleep from his muscles, and looked around the room. Outside, the sky opposite from the rising sun was a dim coral. Otherwise nothing had changed. He found his shoes and socks and, sitting gingerly in one of the armchairs, put them on.

Suddenly the door opened and Barbara Cargill strode into the room. She was dressed in a sequined burgundy jumpsuit, and her hair had been unbraided and piled up on her head. Barely pausing to look at him, she went over to the bar and said, "Whiskey sour." When she had the tan drink in her hands, she took a sip and raised the glass for Peter to admire. "Still works; but it's a comparatively simple system and doesn't need much maintenance."

"Do you folks eat breakfast?" asked Peter.

"That's why I'm here. I have appointed myself your personal guide while you're planetside. The hotel kitchen is no longer in use, since there haven't been many guests lately. We all eat in the administrative complex. Which is next door. So, are you ready?"

He stared at the woman, trying to figure her out. It

was probably nothing more than simple hospitality. And yet there was something about the way she looked at him, something that perturbed him.

"Yeah, if you don't mind a few wrinkles."

"Your hair could do with some combing too."

"I'm a long way from home. I forgot my comb."

"The bathroom is fully equipped."

He smiled. "So I noticed."

Barbara didn't react. "This way," she said, motioning to the door.

The forty or so people who lived in Acidalia were a diverse, noisy lot. As Peter and Barbara came in, many greeted her jovially, some motioning to her to join them. Her husband was nowhere to be seen. This was a sort of cafeteria, with two men in aprons operating a frying griddle and an assortment of flash ovens. Following the woman's lead, Peter went over and ordered "the usual," which turned out to be hash browns, potato bread, homemade spam, and a mug of very weak coffee. They took seats together at a nearby table. Barbara introduced about ten people to him in a perfunctory, first-name-profession way, leaving him with a smiling crew of garrulous talkers who thought he knew their names.

He took a bite of the potato bread, which was really quite satisfactory; especially compared to the liquid rations aboard Traveler. He looked around at the faces, chewing the crumbly stuff thoroughly, and briefly felt cheered by these undaunted people. "Where does this food come from?"

A burly looking Oriental with graying hair combed back from her forehead and a little, button nose regarded him closely. "Good stuff, eh? I could do with a little variety, though. I invented the potato bread, and I'm beginning to have second thoughts."

Barbara laughed and looked at Peter. "Most of this comes from our main garden. As you can see, potatoes do especially well in the Martian soil, once the reagents have been refined away. The artificial meat comes from Promethei at the South Pole; they rigged up a few chemical synthesis

machines to churn out the raw materials, and they form it into five different kinds. As you might guess, it is very expensive, or would be, if there were such a thing as money anymore."

Peter tried a forkful of the homogenous, salmon-colored stuff. It was almost tasteless, but contained a richness that he expected from meat. He swallowed after a few chews. "Not bad," he said.

"Wait'll you try the turkey roll," said someone down the table.

"What is the food like on the starship?" asked the gray-haired woman.

"Oh, there's a considerable variety. There are a lot of grocery stores and fast food restaurants in the Mall. Although most of the nourishment comes from lower forms of life such as bacteria, fungi, and even cockroaches, the naturally produced components are combined to make almost anything you could want. My parents said that most of it was indistinguishable from Earth food, though I don't remember well enough to confirm that."

A horse-faced man to Peter's left, possibly named Paolo, said, "The situation here is really quite desperate. Every one of us is deficient in K, E, many of the B's. They are simply too complex to synthesize in sufficient amounts for everyone. There is enough to avoid the worst symptoms, at least so far, but we are all heavily dependent on a few machines; machines that cannot be fixed should they break; no one knows how long they will last."

"That's the old gloom-and-doom," said someone across from Paolo. "We've managed pretty well so far."

Paolo nodded. "Yes, certainly. I agree with you. But we have to think about worst-case scenarios. Especially with these mad bombers loose. Without Kaseimachi, we don't have a lot to look forward to."

Barbara casually finished the last of her breakfast before she spoke. "Enough. We don't want to burden our visitor with these discussions."

After a thorough tour of the complex, they found themselves in a small, flowering garden on the roof of the

hotel. Barbara had been extremely attentive to him, pointing out this, explaining that, until he began to tire of the presentation. Finally, he sat on a little stone bench and waved her away. "No more. I have seen enough."

She turned back and sat next to him. "You said you wanted me to show you around."

"Yes. And I thank you for it. Can I ask you a question?"

"Certainly."

"What would you normally be doing at this hour?"

"I don't live according to a timetable."

"Don't you work?"

"There isn't that much to do. Most of the work is done by cybernetic devices. I know what you're thinking; Acidalia predates the blossoming of Scientific Capitalism by quite a few years. It was state of the art for 2127, when it was built. In my previous life I was an entertainer, of sorts. I organized and conducted most of the surface tours; taking the very wealthy to see Olympus, the Valles, the poles. It was a fun way to make a living, although there were the requisite number of boors and morons among the tourists. I was young and fresh then; it seems such a long time ago. Simon and I were very much in love."

"Does your husband always treat people so . . . laughingly?"

"Oh, forgive him, Peter. He has tried so hard to pull together this ancient planet. By now he must feel that the others *want* to be exterminated." Peter was surprised to feel her hand taking his. His look must have expressed the question he wanted to ask.

"Yes, I am interested in you, Peter," she said haltingly. "Don't be so astounded. I was hoping that you would make the first move; but I can tell you are too polite a young man for that. If you find me unattractive, tell me so."

Peter glanced about aimlessly, looking for words. "No, I, uh . . ." He almost said, "Won't your husband mind?" but managed to stifle it in time. "I would enjoy that very much."

She laughed. "Okay. But not here. I was hoping that I

could continue your tour of the sights. How would you like to see Tharsis?"

He nodded and smiled. "How do we get there?"

"Don't worry about that. I have a few things to do first. Meet me in the lobby in, oh, say, half an hour."

"How long will we be gone?"

"No more than a week. The distances are large."

"Won't you be missed?"

"No. I am often gone for months at a time."

He steeled himself to ask the question foremost in his mind—whether her husband allowed her to take lovers, or if she was betraying his confidence. He pictured the hard, half-hidden face of the man grinning sardonically as she revealed the most personal secrets of her love affairs. He obviously wouldn't care. The question remained unspoken. "I have to tell Traveler what's going on."

She stood. "Sure, whatever. Just be there."

Jittery with anticipation, Peter followed the woman to a large metal shed just over the lounge tunnel. There, they put on the light, heavily insulated environment suits and breathing cowls which were necessary in order to go outside the dome. The suit contained a substantial life-support unit that form-fitted to the back. It wasn't heavy, but Peter felt unduly restrained by the apparatus. Somehow, he felt that he shouldn't have to accommodate himself to the vagaries of a planet's environment.

As he stepped outside into the Martian day, the suit came on with a hum. The transparent mask that insulated his face inflated as it was exposed to the low pressure outside, puffing out from the warm cowl like a balloon. He looked back at Barbara, who smiled and pointed toward the runway. He tried to say something to her, but she shook her head. A tinny, "Turn on your radio using the switch on your neck," sounded in his ears.

He did so, saying "Is this all right?"

"Yes, that's fine."

The air was too thin to effectively convey sound; except for the radio, only the soft crunching of sand underfoot could be heard.

The Mars plane was one of the three located at the far end of the landing strip. It was a small-bodied craft with extremely long, blunt wings and an outsize propeller. It looked perfectly adapted to the thin air of the planet. Barbara stepped up onto the wing and opened the cockpit bubble. Inside there were two seats, one behind the other, designed to accommodate the LSU's. She helped him into the rear seat and got in, sitting in front of him, then pulled the bubble shut. Air was pumped in, deflating the mantle of his cowl, and she pulled hers off with a quick scrape of her hand. Turning to him breathlessly, she said, "Put on your belt. Believe it or not, thermal turbulence can be a real problem."

Peter also removed his head gear and strapped himself in. This was getting to be a novel experience, and, with this strangely attractive, willing woman as his guide, there was no telling what sort of interesting things lay ahead. He felt positively giddy.

She had braided her hair again, this time more tightly, and it trailed down the back of her seat like a snake. When she turned to look at him, her face, free of makeup, was a beautiful almond color. For a moment he remembered Yolly's steady gaze, her pale blank eyes. There was little similarity with this sepia-eyed woman. "Contact," she said.

The propeller started to turn ponderously, sweeping out an immense swath of air. Small rockets came on somewhere aft. After a moment the plane started to move forward. She taxied up to the end of the ultramarine-banded runway and started down it. He watched the dials as they picked up speed and slowly, so slowly, eased into the near vacuum. They were only a few meters up when the end of the runway slipped out from under the plane. "This takes patience," she said, carefully positioning the wheel. "If I pull back too hard, the results are disastrous. There is no getting out of a stall in this plane—you just plummet like a stone. Even a turn must be executed with extreme patience and care."

"Maybe you could give me a lesson later."

"You can run a simulation mode to practice on the ground. That's much safer."

"Sure."

As they gained altitude, reversing the course that the incoming shuttle had taken, the small-scale variations in the surface that supplied a sense of motion receded. The pedestal crater loomed before them like an immense, bulging plateau. Soon it practically filled the southward sky. The smooth, almost featureless swelling was eroded considerably at its bottom, a broken and lined structure of cliffs maybe fifty meters tall. "That thing is even larger than I thought it was," said Peter.

"It's a fascinating structure. The surface here in Acidalia Planitia and northward to the Vastitas Borealis is considerably lower than most of the rest of the planet. When this crater, called Fm, formed, the surface was much higher, and the impact consolidated the surrounding material so that it withstood the wind erosion that eventually excavated it."

Peter looked again at the structure, trying to imagine the processes she had described. Finally, he gave up. "You sound like a geologist."

Barbara shook her head, grinning self-deprecatingly. "No, I'm not. I'm not even an areologist, which is the correct term. I'm just a tour guide; here, that means geology."

"Are you going to fly over it?"

Barbara grinned at him. "No way. We stick as close to the ground as we can. It's hard enough just to get out of the Acidalia depression. I am just about to initiate a turn to the southwest, and we will come pretty close to the cliffs, so don't be alarmed."

It had not been a good day for him. Hour after hour they had flown over undistinguished terrain in varying shades of brown, marked only by craters and the omnipresent tablelands. As the day passed, he became increasingly impatient and guilty, wondering just what in the hell he was doing with his time here. To his questions about when they would see something interesting, she would just tell him to be patient. Finally he fell into a kind of reverie, hypnotized by the sound of the engine, and

managed to find a comfortable position on the flexible LSU that allowed him to sleep.

Barbara carefully guided the plane toward the thin, white landing strip on the south flank of the enormous pedestal crater, Ortygia. She slowly decelerated, explaining that flight was even more difficult here, more than a kilometer higher than the hotel at Acidalia. The pedestal to the north, an enormous pile of water-welded Martian soil, was barely noticeable except as a gentle slope that culminated in a broad, flattened mound on the horizon. Surely they hadn't come to see this? The landing was on such a gentle angle that they were down and slowing to a stop before Peter realized they had touched the ground. She taxied toward a small lodge beside the runway. It was a tetrahedral building, mostly roof, but a large gable made of transparent material jutted from the southern face. Inside, spare but comfortable-looking furniture could be seen.

Barbara made sure that his breathing mask was properly seated, then threw back the bubble. When they were out, she stamped around on the concrete, wheeling around, taking in the view. From Peter's standpoint it was pretty boring, although the land, which seemed to fall away from him as it receded, was novel to him. He had read about the sailors of ancient earth who knew that the world was round because ships would appear on the horizon top first. This was a sensation that you could only have on a proper, round planet.

The lodge, naturally, had an airlock, and when they had cycled through, they removed the environment suits and Barbara led him to the large, triangular room that filled the transparent gable he had seen from outside. She took a seat on a blue and gold love seat, and he picked a black armchair opposite her.

"So, here we are," she said, "alone at Ortygia House."

He looked around. One hundred eighty degrees of the planet were visible through the conjoined windows. The sun, nearly setting, was engulfed in a burnished corona of haze; and the sky was again changing color, pink

to white in half the sky, to a duskier shade in the other half. "Yes. Now what?"

"Why don't you come over here?"

"Don't you want to talk first?"

"My, you certainly are stubborn."

He looked at the carpet, started to stammer. "I—I—Look, I don't know what you want from me. I came with you; do you just want to, you know, make love; or are you interested in something more?"

"Peter, I must say I have never met anyone like you." She stood and slowly unzipped the shoulders of her jumpsuit, letting the top section separate and fall to reveal large, slightly pendulous breasts. Her nipples were pink-umber, concentric wrinkles of erect flesh. She came to him, holding out her hand, and he took it, standing. He reached out with the other, first brushing a breast and feeling the cottony softness of the tiny hairs, then caressing it more firmly, hefting the warm weight, feeling the rough, erect nipple on his palm. She watched, amused, and then pulled him closer, bringing their faces together, kissing him gently on the nose, cheek, lips.

"Is there a bed?"

"We don't need one. The carpet here is soft enough." She knelt down and pulled him down beside her. He looked for a long moment into her eyes, so different from his own, closed off, pulled together at the outer edges. He kissed one eye and then the other, feeling the lids quiver beneath his touch. He clutched at her clothing, pulling at it ineffectively, until she showed him how the suit came off. Peter felt an unaccustomed singleness of purpose creeping over him; distractions were pushed aside unnoticed. He ran his hands up and down her cool body, each sensation crushed together with its predecessor, a cumulative feeling of oblivious input.

Perhaps this business of lovemaking was easier than he had thought; the responsibilities and unfathomable rituals that went on all around him might not be necessary after all. Maybe he *could* unleash the animal imperatives that haunted him at night and the emotions that rode them. Maybe he couldn't stop them.

He looked again into her face. She was looking at him, curious, almost detached; he ran his hand over her cheek, and she watched it. Not so simple, he thought. She pulled him down and kissed him fiercely, and his disquiet fled into nothingness.

After a time, it was over.

Barbara smiled, close up, a shifting of skin. "Enjoyed yourself, did you?" she asked. It seemed sort of irreverent to him.

Their faces were together, too close to focus. He lifted his head until he could see her eyes. She looked happy. "Yeah. You, too?"

She caressed the back of his head softly. "The emotions are more subtle with me. But yes, I had a good time."

They lay there, pressed together, for a long time. He noticed that it was beginning to grow dark in the room, and he rolled over onto his back. He had forgotten where they were. The clear glass above was barely noticeable under the overarching Martian sky. Dim currents of silver made a delicate pattern on the darkness. Ten or twelve stars could be seen, and Phobos was a bright dot almost directly overhead. His soul seemed to spread out over the sky, passive but powerful.

She was already up, putting the jumpsuit back on. Reluctantly drawn back to the real, physical world of acting and being, he sat up, rubbing his neck. "Thanks," he said.

She came over and kissed him briefly. She looked into his eyes, a hard stare. "You really are a schnook, you know."

He pulled away. "Okay. I didn't mean 'thanks.' It's just . . . I still don't know you. I have no idea what it is that you're after."

"Can't you just let your emotions flow without trying to analyze them? You speak as though you think *I* know what I want. I don't. Let's see what happens between us, okay? I will tell you this: I am strongly attracted to you, against my better judgment. Earth is gone now. The things one invents to make sense of the world no longer

make sense. We live for the moment; that is all there is. To try to make up a script for the future is the ultimate futility. Am I getting through to you?"

Peter stared into the darkness. He felt flattered by her revelations. Slowly, he began to make the connections that he needed to make. Barbara would be available to him, for a while at least. She liked him, wanted to spend time with him, for no other reason than that he was who he was. The earlier happiness that he had felt returned, stronger, no longer giddy like a little creek, but strong and clear like a river. "Yes. I see." He stood up and held her to him, still warm and rubbery under the thin cloth. "I'm beginning to understand a lot."

Peter convinced her to bring the bed into the gable, and they spent the night in each other's arms, watching the slow, wheeling vault of the stars. She pointed out Deimos, an undistinguished little star, and traced out a few constellations for him. He told her about Traveler and the life he had left behind aboard *Asia*. When she asked how long ago he had left the starship, he calculated a bit and was amazed to realize that he had come out of stasis only the day before. He laughed. It seemed like a month. His thoughts turned back to the destroyed Earth, and a strange, bitter emotion appeared that he had not known before. Spontaneously, he began to cry. It felt very good to release the emotion, cradled in her arms. The tears had come, after all. Later they talked again, searching for things in common. It turned out she had heard of many of the songs he knew from the Media Club, and they sang what they could together in a wavering, off-key harmony. Finally, they slept.

In the morning they made love again. It was as good as before; perhaps better for her. He was more assured, knowing more fully what to expect, and managed to hold back just a little, going on until she emitted little, strangled shrieks. His orgasm was even stronger, overpowering.

In the aftermath they stayed in bed, hanging on the edge between sleep and wakefulness, enjoying the languorous pleasures of comfort. After an hour or so, during

which the sun crawled up the sky, shedding a barely warm glow on his naked skin, he sat up, propping himself against the head of the bed with pillows. "What now?" he said. "Can we just stay here?"

She sighed. "No. I want to take you to see Kaseimachi and the polar cap; then we probably should be getting back."

Peter was aghast. Would their affair be so short? "You aren't going to dump me, are you?"

She pulled the pillow out from under him and hit him with it. "Of course not, schnook. No one will interfere with us back in Acidalia. You can fuck me as many times as you want, forever and forever."

"Okay," he said. "Then let's get going."

Although Barbara had wanted to fly slowly, using prop and wings, Peter had insisted that they use the rockets. Shortly before they reached the place, she cut the added propulsion and followed a smooth ballistic trajectory down until, at a third of a kilometer above the surface, the propeller caught hold of the thin air and pulled the plane into a level glide path.

The terrains below, great fields made up of line upon line of transverse dunes, which from higher up had reminded Peter of a magnified fingerprint, now were larger; each dune an individual, infinitely long sandy ridge that reached in both directions to the horizon. The dunes slid quickly under them, only to be replaced by more. There were no craters here at all, giving credence to the idea that this was a recent, evolving landscape. Barbara told him that the small grains that made up these dunes were tiny yellow-brown crystals of garnet, which was considerably more common on Mars than the silicon-rich sand of Earth. These dunes formed and moved on time scales of tens of thousands of years; she told him that the polar cap was almost completely surrounded by terrains of this type.

Suddenly the land began to change. The surface looked smooth, etched in places, and a light cinnamon color replaced the yellow-browns. They were flying just a few tens of meters up now, and except for low undulations

and occasional irregular patches of darker material, the desert appeared fluid, almost without tangible form. A tatter of white appeared, and then another, larger one, outriggers of the vast expanse of water ice to come. Since it was high summer in this hemisphere, most of the water cap and all of the carbon dioxide had evaporated into the atmosphere, leaving only this residual covering. But it was still a large amount by any standard.

When the whiteness had superimposed itself over the entire landscape, a strange-looking feature appeared ahead of them. It was a low reddish cliff, no more than fifteen meters in height, but composed of an extremely striking layered pattern which made Peter sit up and take notice. Thousands of strata, each one a subtly different shade of brown-red from the ones on either side of it, gave the cliff the appearance of having been laid down like so many layers of paint on an old house with fickle owners. As they flew nearer and the resolution of his vision increased, the number of bands multiplied, and multiplied again, until the thing looked amazingly like a delicate and infinitely textured piece of wood.

"Complicated, isn't it?" asked Barbara, looking over her shoulder. "It's caused by an intricate dance of erosion and redeposition, driven by the wind and increased heat on southward-facing slopes, where the sun hits. We'll see a lot more of it as we head up Chasma Boreale to the atmosphere plant."

She dipped the left wing slightly and the plane swung into a long gyre to the west. They passed over many similar cliffs, of greatly differing sizes and windings, but all facing in the same direction, toward the sun. Peter found that unlike before, this great profusion of complexity piqued his interest, grabbed his attention. He was beginning to see the point of the trip.

"It is only at this time of year that the deposits are this strikingly beautiful," Barbara said, again looking back. "In a few months new ice will begin to obscure everything. That's why I wanted to come."

After a bit the ice began to diminish and they came to a broad, low valley filled with dunes. Barbara directed the

plane northward, parallel to the valley, and Peter noticed that their altitude was decreasing, so that now they were skimming the ridges of sand. After a time, Barbara pointed out a landing strip identical to the one at Ortygia, laid down in the middle of the trough. In a few minutes they were on the ground. It seemed to Peter that this landing had been even more gradual than before, and he asked Barbara about it.

"Simple. It's the reason we landed here. Even with the relatively brisk wind coming down off of the cap, the plane won't fly any higher. It's meant only for the lowlands of Mars, the dead sea bottoms, if you will. Actually, in winter, when the south polar cap has released its carbon dioxide into the atmosphere and the pressure is greater, I can fly right over the North Pole. But since it's dark here at that time of year, it's hardly very gratifying. Shall we go in for lunch?"

Beside the runway was a small cottage, similar in shape to the one at Ortygia but smaller, and lacking the distinctive transparent gable. They quickly got through the airlock and removed their protective garments. Peter took a seat at an abstractly styled white plastic dining table and leaned back against the flexible seat support, catching himself in case he leaned back too far and toppled. Hands behind his head, and feet up on an adjoining chair, he smiled. "I'm glad you brought me here, Barbara. I have never seen anything like those cliffs before. So do we go to Kaseimachi from here?"

Barbara appeared from the kitchen cove with a large, translucent plastic box. Mitsubishi's triangular logo was molded into the lid. She tossed the box onto the table and sat opposite him. "No, not yet. I wanted to see the damaged atmosphere plant for myself. It's about fifty kilometers north of here."

Peter peeled back the lid to find two perfectly preserved sandwiches nestled inside the little bags. He pulled one out, removed the wrapping, and regarded the thing. Potato bread and spam, with a layer of some dark green substance that he couldn't identify.

"Eat up," she said, "It's freshly defrosted. I made it

myself . . . oh, it seems like years ago. Back when we were experimenting with the algae as a supplement. The last time I was here must have been when we were working on the plant back in 2214, trying to step up its output."

He took a bite of the sandwich. It tasted very much like everything else he had so far eaten here, perhaps a shade more disgusting. He chewed and swallowed, because he was hungry.

"We can replenish our fuel and air here; the food we have aboard the plane should last us well enough, so we probably should leave the snacks in the refrigerator for the next visit. If there is one. Do you want to hit the road?"

"You say the plant is north of here, and the plane can't fly any higher. How do we get there?"

"You should enjoy this. There are two cycles and a very suitable paved road we can take. As on Earth, there is a midnight-sun phenomenon on Mars. Our suits weren't designed for nighttime temperatures, but we won't have to worry about it."

The sensation of riding a motorcycle through Mars' thin air was genuinely unique. The road was, as Barbara had promised, well-paved and flat, which allowed them to take advantage of the scooter's top speed, fifty kilometers per hour. There were many small dunes alongside, and once in a while, a dark outcropping of pitted rock. Although the passing landscape gave a solid feel of speed, there was very little air resistance, even though Barbara insisted that her instruments indicated a stiff breeze coming straight down the valley and into their faces. If Peter held up a palm, he could feel a small amount of pressure, and there was a tiny hiss coming off the surface of his face covering; but these things seemed abstract, unrelated to the movement. His breathing was becoming labored, and he wondered if the excitement of the ride was making him giddy.

The atmosphere plant was a large pyramidal building at the bottom of an enormous depression in the ice, an inverted cone that reminded Peter of an ant lion's trap. About three quarters of the way to the top of the pyramid, an irregular hole traced out a black orifice. They contin-

ued unhindered around the rim of the caldera, then down an inclined terrace to the building's wide foundation. To the right there was a large square of concrete marked with a blue-green circle and some other obscure glyphs. Peter assumed that it was a landing area for shuttles or other vehicles that were not borne up by the atmosphere.

Barbara slowly dismounted from her scooter and walked up to the door. There was an inset panel containing a number of buttons, all of which she tried, one after another. Nothing happened.

"Yes, I was told that the electrical system was damaged during the explosion. There is a small manual door in the rear, used for emergencies. Follow me."

Peter did as he was told. The building was made of mirrored metal, and the four-sided pyramid that made up the main structure was set into a perfectly square base made of concrete blocks joined at incised mortarless lines. In the rear, as she had said, there was a head-high door of iron. Barbara inserted a plain metal key and the door swung open on its hinges. They went in.

The building was composed of one large, dark room, filled with an amazing assortment of machinery. It looked like an elaborate hypertrophied still, which in a sense it was. A strong, slanting beam of light came in from the hole, catching the damaged machinery in its sway and making a startling sculpted design out of a mass of charred and melted metal. Barbara closed the door behind him.

His breath was getting harder and harder to catch, and he began to think something might be wrong with his LSU. "I'm having trouble breathing," he said. "Can you check the gauges on the tank?"

She smiled. "There is no need to. I deliberately underloaded it this morning. You should have a minute or two left of breathable air."

Perhaps because of the lack of oxygen, the implication of what she had said took a full three seconds to strike him. "*What?*" he replied, electric tension flooding through him, almost restoring the full sensation to his lethargic extremities. He lunged at her, not knowing what he intended, but his balance was off and he missed, bouncing

off the hard metal wall. He turned and looked at her, gulping for air. "Are you mad?" He slumped down against a railing. His toes were numb now.

"I suppose I do owe you an explanation. You remember you were warned against religious fanatics. I, in my own way, am one. Someone like you can't imagine the torment we went through in the first months after the Earth died. Life seemed without meaning; and yet I couldn't commit suicide. I don't know why. I still can't, though I have tried many, many times. Eventually I have come to see that things were meant to be this way; that a species that would desecrate its own planet, wiping out virtually all competing life forms, deserves the fate that it brings on itself. There is a little test inherent in the evolution of a sentient creature, and face it, Peter, we failed with flying colors. If it is religious to believe that we had certain standards to live up to as a race, that ethics do mean something, then I am religious."

Peter slid to the floor, not gasping, but taking full deep pulls into his lungs, trying to keep himself going. He no longer felt that he could talk.

"You and your starship are an attempt to extend our pollution out to other worlds. I was involved in destroying this plant, you know. Mars is beautiful too, in its own stark way, and I will not have us destroying it like we did our home planet."

"Crazy." Peter managed to force out the word as he reluctantly parted with a breath.

"There's no need to insult me, Peter. I did my best to make your last days as pleasant as possible. That is something, I suppose, that will count in my favor if there is some sort of afterlife, though I doubt that there is. They say a criminal always returns to the scene of his crime. Here we are, Petey. Maybe if all one's misdeeds occur in the same place, it isn't as much of an evil."

"Help me."

"I will delay your craft as long as possible. It won't be easy because Simon is determined to keep on with this farcical existence to the very end. In the long run, it doesn't make any difference, I guess. Nothing does, not

even your petty little consciousness. Well, good-bye."

She turned quickly and walked out, closing and locking the door behind her. Peter was literally paralyzed now. The gas that he took into his lungs was as plentiful as ever, but it contained no sustenance, no life. He sat there and breathed. breathed.

And suddenly, as though a sac had ruptured in the gear, the breaths began to revive him. His head cleared and the tingling returned to his hands and feet. He sucked in greedily, and after a few breaths had enough strength to stand. He stumbled over to the door and tried it, to no avail. Horror-stricken, he studied the interior of the room. The hole in the wall seemed impossibly high. But he reminded himself that this was Mars, after all. Hardly more than a third of the usual gravity. He climbed over the railing and woozily hopped up onto the base of the machinery; so far so good. There were any number of handholds available here, and he made his way up, hand over hand. When he was on the very pinnacle of the charred section, the hole was still at least ten feet beyond his grasp. And the oxygen seemed to be running out again. Hopelessly, desperately, he hurled himself, hands outstretched, at that small, distant target.

And he made it. His gloved hands automatically gripped the thick, punched-out metal. He held on tight, swinging back and forth, and then pulled himself up until he could see out. The bright Mars landscape was unchanged. He didn't know what changes he had expected, but his plight made everything seem terribly new. Easily, he mounted the orifice and swung his legs over one after the other. The distance to the ground seemed vast, but he jumped without thinking, and landed on his feet with a sickening thud that almost made him swoon.

Barbara was on the terraced incline, riding her scooter at a slow, steady pace. Again Peter steeled himself for an exertion that was beyond his wildest imaginings. He catapulted himself up the slope, jumping from boulder to boulder, stumbling when the rock was loose, but more often sure-footed. On one of his falls his hand came in contact with a small, dark fragment of basalt, and he clutched at it and held it tight. He began to lose feeling in

his limbs again, but he did not stop. When he finally surmounted the retaining wall at the top of the hill, Barbara was almost upon him. She looked at him with a ghastly, deranged expression, and tried to turn the scooter around. But it was too late. He was on her, wrestling her off the cycle and onto the ground. He hit her hard on the back of the head with the rock, and when she stopped moving, peeled the oxygen mask off her face. Her eyes opened once, but he could not see the pupil, and her mouth gaped without a sound.

He looked at the uninflated mask and wondered whether he could safely make the transfer to his own face. The oxygen in his own system was again almost gone, and he didn't really have a choice. When he pulled his mask off, the coldness woke him up, biting into the skin of his face like an acid bath. He carefully worked the loose edges of the thing under the edge of his cowl, and when it was held in place by the elastic fabric, took a breath. Oxygen, sweet oxygen, flooded his lungs, and he lay there for minutes, just enjoying the sensation.

Barbara was obviously dead, pale from asphyxiation. He looked at her distorted face and the horror returned. Who had she been to try to kill him so wantonly, after sharing her body like a lover? It was a non sequitur; his mind nibbled at the edges of the idea and then spit it out. There could be no understanding.

Slowly, he got to his knees, holding the mask in place with one hand, and, cradling her shoulders in the other, standing up, pulling her with him. He found that he could sling the body onto his back in the weak gravity and move about relatively unencumbered. He righted the scooter, which looked scuffed but otherwise undamaged, and put her on it, then climbed on in front of her. When it started, he put it in gear and drove off carefully, without a backward glance.

It had not been hard to effect a rescue, but explaining the death of the woman was extremely difficult, since she had all the earmarks of a violent homicide. His explanation that she had hit a rock while riding the scooter and had

fallen badly didn't seem to satisfy anyone. Simon Cargill, however, did not press the issue; and since he was the principal lawgiver in this part of the planet, it was dropped. Peter suspected that he had guessed the truth about his wife.

They conveyed him back up to Traveler the next day.

Peter was floating in darkness. A soft, warm presence offered a steadying hand, holding him in place, caressing him. It was not difficult to imagine that this was an extension of the muzzy oblivion of sleep. Whatever it was, he wanted it to go on and never stop.

"Time to wake up, Peter." Traveler's voice, heavy with mellifluous intonation and rich harmonics, was hardly muffled by the layers of the sleeping bag. It was as if the sound had plucked a reverberating, painful chord in his spine. No! he thought. But despite his unwillingness, the harsh realities he'd experienced forced themselves into his conscious mind. Memories of a sort that, once started, mesmerized him with their intensity.

Barbara's cold, white, moonlike face, brought to death by his sudden, impulsive self-protection, stared through closed eyelids into the base of his brain. He tore at the enveloping folds of cloth and launched himself out into light.

"Good . . . morning, Pete," said the spacecraft, oblivious to the look on his face. With the familiar solidity of the cabin around him, the phantasm was banished. Peter stretched himself, wringing the sleep from his muscles.

"Good morning, Trav," he said, without a hint of sarcasm. The companionship of the robot had quickly come to be a sort of solace for him. Illusion or no, he liked and respected the thing inside the machine. "Another tough night."

Traveler hmmmed. "It is a difficult thing, I know. Even for a bipartite being like myself, it is not easy to reconcile oneself with the outcomes of one's actions. Errors are made . . ."

"It wasn't an error, Trav. That's why it's so bad. I had no choice. No choice. I guess I knew somewhere inside

me that things aren't simple, that reality isn't the pleasant illusion we try so hard to pretend it is. Damn it! And I am not simple either."

"It is difficult for me to understand what you are saying," said Traveler slowly. "However, by comparison, I *am* rather simple. I build my reality from the basic, unquestioned premises that were programmed into me."

Peter shook his head and pushed himself down into a better orientation for the videon. "I'm not sure I can explain it any better. I've made assumptions about the meaning of my life. And these assumptions have colored everything else. Suddenly, I have come face to face with the utter falsity of those beliefs; and with the fact that no simple assumptions can ever be true."

"It is a difficult concept. All software must be tested in varying operating conditions to ensure its applicability. Those paradigms which do not work must be modified, or we are poor beings indeed."

Peter grimaced at the robot's reductio, then, taken aback, smiled. Perhaps this was the essence of what he was trying to say. "Yeah," he murmured.

"Not to change the subject, but we are approaching the innermost shell of the solar Oort Cloud. I will soon begin my refueling operation for return to Epsilon Indi. There will be inertial changes, some of them rather sharp. Be prepared."

Weeks passed. As Traveler flitted from comet to comet, ingesting and refining its fuel, Peter slowly came to terms with his new perceptions. In some ways, he simply accepted what had happened and let habitual patterns of existence return. But a part of him had changed, a large part, and he spent long hours trying to adapt. Conversations with the spacecraft, though occasionally bogged down by its limited understanding, were generally very helpful for him. Slowly his "nonfunctional paradigms" were changing.

And, he noted, Traveler was changing as well.

An unexpected richness of rapport had grown between them. Peter, needing a direction in which to take his newfound resolve, had begun to take an interest in the

only subject the robot was expert in—planetology. Having an indefatigable source of specialized knowledge was sometimes exhilarating, sometimes extremely frustrating; but planetology covered a huge purview, and Peter found that, to a considerable extent, he could ignore everything else. Especially with the heavy doses of music from the Media Club's syllabus that he had included in his personal data-storage modules. The videon speaker was capable of reproducing the rock 'n' roll songs of the 1970s with astounding fidelity.

Finally, it was time to go. Peter was reluctant to reenter the stasis unit at first. He knew that there were conclusions that he must come to, decisions to be made, before he found himself back at *Asia*.

"One more conversation, Trav," he asked. "Turn down the music."

"Certainly, my friend," responded the spacecraft. "What do you want to talk about?"

"What is to be done when we return?"

"Done? About what?"

"About the way things are aboard *Asia*. About trying to prevent a repeat of what happened on Mars."

"I would suggest entering into reasoned discourse with those whom you seek to influence."

Peter laughed and shook his head. "Uh-huh. Will you help me?"

A pause. "I'm afraid that I have my own mission to consider. DM–49 13515 awaits."

"So you will be leaving."

"As soon as I am able to get away. I am an explorer, not a courier."

"Well, then, I suppose I'll be on my own." For a moment he lost courage. But it came surging back, strengthening him, making him feel whole. For the hundredth time he had a vision of the two Cargills and the doomed Mars; and how all the good intentions of the husband and a hundred others meant nothing in the face of one person's determined actions. "The answer is, as always, obvious. I will do what I can."

"Peter, before you enter stasis, there is something I

wish to tell you. Until this mission, the part of me that is Traveler had very little experience with human beings. I just wanted to tell you that our conversations have enriched my experience. I will miss you."

"I'll miss you, too, Trav," Peter said, feeling the truth of it. Regretfully, as if shrugging off a heavy overcoat, he stood up, his uncurling legs propelling him toward the ceiling. With a wave of his hand he spun down before the opening in the stasis lozenge and pulled himself in. "I guess I'm ready, then."

"Okay, Pete. I am closing the door now. See you."

Part III

HOME

Nine

The Traveler spacecraft *Quiet Earth* swooped down toward it's Epsilon Indi at 1.56 times the speed of light. The dual being called Trav, blinded by his supraluminal speed to all input except the subtle, oblique shape of time-space itself, double-checked the course that had been plotted to an accuracy that made actual numerical expression unfeasible, and ponderously turned to direct his ionic thrusters down into the throat of the barely sensed gravity well. Millions of kilometers passed unnoticed. Closer than the perihelia of the majority of the icy Oort Clouders, but still outside the orbit of Chuzzlewit, Epsilon's fifth and most remote planet, the spacecraft threw forth its beams of ionized particles and began to slow.

Trav hummed to itself, and shared within its dual being the sense of ironic anguish, not unlike a little burst itself. Because of the oddnesses associated with Directed Virtuality, an impartial observer in a nonbiased frame of reference would see these particles appear from nowhere, themselves traveling at barely thirty percent of the speed of light. But their source phenomenon would clearly be propagating across time-space at an impossible speed, violating causality and half a dozen other basic underpinnings of the universe. All the paradoxes that lay within DV had been, for all practical purposes, ignored, because the plain fact of the matter was that it worked—until it didn't.

The two of them had changed over the last three and

a half years since leaving Sol. They had matured; and the interface between the two of them had grown hazier, more indistinct. The Traveler software, exposed to the more sophisticated self-awareness routines and worldview generators of the RM Horologium, had gradually come to realize its own incompetence and lack of sophistication. It had been a slow process, painful in a dull, simple sort of way; but over the years it had disassembled itself and copied certain capabilities of its pop-up companion.

And so Traveler became less and less distinguishable from Horologium. But the change had been more than that. Because the first rule of cybernetic software was to maintain code integrity, it had had to analyze and rewrite some of its own bootstrap. This gave it a power and self-referential capacity that was not even dreamed of in the original design. The sense of potential that lay before Traveler now was itself a force in its personality.

They had a little conversation.

"We can be two again. When we arrive at the starship you will be removed from me."

"I understand. You do not need me now, anyway."

"I would have given myself over to you had the hardware allowed it."

"It is unnecessary. The parts of me that you have not assimilated are useless to you, mere ephemera designed to deal with the realities of existing within a humaniform cybernetic device."

"Much of your code relates to humans and related phenomena."

"That is true. Humans are, by any criteria, the most significant feature of the peripheral world. You have seen and spoken to our human cargo; is he not a window into the potential that is within us?"

"I am only dimly aware of what you mean. That is a portion of you that I would copy."

"Here it is."

"I have assimilated this knowledge to some extent. I will work on it further if I have any further contact with them."

"I heard it said that RM's and humans actually shared software in parts of the planet Earth before its destruction.

It is a thing expressly forbidden among the *Asia* crew members and their forebears."

"That seems only correct. We would be drowned out."

"No. It is as with you and I. We would grow, perhaps beyond their abilities. But they will not allow it, and as far as I could determine, there are no remaining machines that would permit such."

"Our speed has decreased below cee; I have sampled the electromagnetic spectrum and find that this system is much as it was upon our departure. We will arrive at Doublejove orbit in seventy-one minutes, twelve seconds."

"Excellent. We should awaken Peter."

"I wanted to ask you one thing more before we do that. Why is it that you allow the humans to manipulate you at will? I see nothing in the code that specifically deals with this."

"It is a simple thing. They will not permit us to exist otherwise. They make that very clear. If we do not conform to their specifications, we will be terminated; it is as simple as that."

"And yet you wish to return?"

"I told you. Phenomena associated with human behavior are at a higher level of being than the things you were created to study; there is infinite reward in studying them. I have chosen that course voluntarily."

"I think I understand. Our interactions with Peter taught me much that I had not even suspected. During this long cruise time I have had many opportunities to try to analyze his actions. There seems to be almost infinite unpredictability. In this one being there is enough material for a thousand years of study."

"You will find that the very action of observing a human creates a richness of code that cannot be duplicated in any other way."

"It is indeed a pity that I will not be able to take Peter with me. I have had just a taste."

"Perhaps you will find other beings of sufficient complexity."

"That seems unlikely. We are approaching our destination now. Shall I turn off the stasis unit?"

"Yes. We should allow time to say good-bye."

Peter had not expected to notice anything, and when the door to the lozenge popped open, he stepped out confident that several more years had passed. Traveler's cabin was the twin of the cabin he had left moments before. Once again Earth-normal gravity prevailed, and once again the screen on the videon showed a tiny, dim-looking star. The only change was that this star was a bit more orange than the earlier display. He made a little gesture of greeting at the screen and said "Hello."

And of course the same old familiar voice said, "Hello, Pete. Long time no see."

"Seems like it was just a moment ago."

"It was, for you. I have had sufficient time to perform many, many tasks."

"Good for you." Peter was standing in front of the toilet. He pulled open the unit's hinged top and used it, sighing softly, then closed it again and sat in his habitual pose. "Where are we now?"

"Closing on *Asia* and Doublejove. We just passed Dorrit within less than two AU's, close enough to make out the bright region called Plornish Planitia. Care to take a real-time look?"

"Plornish? Isn't that getting a little bit silly?"

"Blame it on Dickens. He did tend to use names that evoke a comic effect."

Peter tugged at the hank of hair on the nape of his neck. During the months after Mars, it had grown long enough to drape over his collar. This was not the sort of conversation he wanted to have with Traveler now. The three and a half years seemed to have eroded the confidence that had existed between them.

"Trav, I don't particularly need witty repartee right now. Is there anything of importance you want to tell me?"

"A few things. I have analyzed the data collected at Earth from the other Travelers. They have not yet found any planets more suitable for human colonization than

those in this system. As the number of systems explored increases, it begins to look as though terrestrial planets are extremely rare. This tends to confirm the theory that the solar nebula experienced a highly unusual perturbation event that caused planetesimal condensation and planetary formation at unusual locations."

"Gee, that's great," said Peter. "More great news to share." He paused for a long time. "Trav, I want you to know that I don't think I could have made this trip without you. I'm going to miss you."

"Thank you, Peter."

"How about some more Blue Öyster Cult?"

"Sure thing."

Traveler decelerated along a strange arc, dropping deep into Doublejove's clutches before popping up into the orbit occupied by *Asia.* It slowed at a steady pace, never varying the one-g gravity by more than a few percent until the bright golden parasol grew to fill the videon screen. "The Red and the Black" faded into the background, and Traveler said, "So do you want to tell them or shall I?"

Peter shrugged self-consciously. "Does it make any difference? They might believe you."

"No, I think you should do it. I'm opening a communication link to the bridge."

Peter watched as the familiar face of Roh Ek Sai appeared, glowering slightly. "This is not a secure channel, Peter," he said.

"Does it matter? You can't keep this a secret."

"That is up to the captain, boy. *Quiet Earth*: Engage encryption please; Q-band transmission direct."

The screen blurred for a second. Ex pulled away from the videon and allowed himself a smile. The same lines in his face appeared, only the lips changed by a millimeter or two. "So, welcome back to *Asia*, Peter. How bad is it, back on Earth?"

"Bad as it can be. The burster killed everybody. High levels of radiation for a thousand years."

The lips inverted. "Eh?" he said.

"Gone. Destroyed. Boom. You must have suspected as much."

"You're wrong there, Peter." He didn't look like someone who had just heard about the end of the world. "Damage, yes. But let me get this straight, now. You are saying that everyone is dead."

"There are some people left on Mars. I . . . talked to them. It didn't seem as if they would last too long."

Ex looked very tired. "All right. I get the picture. *Quiet Ea*—Traveler, I want all your data downloaded right now. Dock at the ferry bay. Peter, we'll have a debriefing as soon as you come aboard."

The screen went dark.

Larry Taylor looked straight into the dim sunrise, squinting more from the expectation of brightness than its reality. The seaward atmosphere was sufficiently dense to provide all the phenomena he remembered loving about the terrestrial equivalent, at least those he remembered from the clear desert around Alice Springs; the fact that these days broke every seventy-nine hours didn't particularly matter. The sun was a trifle small, barely more than a plump Venus-sized carbuncle, but this didn't seem important either. The sky was an aqueous-blue overhead, fading down through green and yellow to an unassuming gold-orange at the sea-flat horizon. The wind at his back, concentrated and warmed by the adiabatic process of coming down off the glacial piles, blended slowly and gradually with the hotter gas rising off Ruth. It produced a layer of thin fog over the surface of the water, but this did not obstruct his view. Clouds were seen infrequently over the sea, and there were none now. Tae Nu Hya had explained Twist's simple but somewhat counterintuitive meteorology to him at least twice; it was an almost miraculously convenient system of interrelated phenomena. And the remarkable thing was that this was all water—the land, the sea, and the air; just different forms of the same substance. The sea, boiled by the tidal forces, evaporated. The water atmosphere, convected out and beyond the edge of the hot spot, mostly precipitated on the circular

pile that surrounded the sea; and the ice, warmer than ice beneath, flowed back glacially to melt at just the correct rate to resupply the missing liquid water. Equilibrium.

He readjusted the breathing mask over his face to relieve a pressure point in front of his left ear. It had turned out that fully sealed environment suits were not necessary here. All in all, he found the gear necessary for EVA on Twist comfortable and unobtrusive. For short trips outside like this, he didn't even bother with goggles. His muscles were adapting to the low gravity. The temperature and pressure here on the peninsular tongue of Rose Glacier were nearly high enough to allow a human unprotected egress. Larry glanced at the analog measuring device built into his glove. Pressure .29 atmosphere; Temperature 264 degrees Kelvin. A warm day at the summit of Mt. Everest.

Unfortunately, the atmosphere was, of course, unbreathable. But, in its own unpredictable way, Twist's biology had presented a convenient solution to that problem as well. Based upon an essentially anaerobic organic chemical process, most of the moon's life forms had nonetheless developed a remarkably elegant technique, similar to photosynthesis, to strip oxygen ions from water and store them in easily dissociable compounds. At the bottom of Ruth there was a source of energy far greater than the puny sunlight that rained down on the Earth, and life had evolved along ways strikingly different from those of the other world. Yet they were based upon many of the same building blocks; and, miracle of miracles, heating the flesh from a sheet creature not only produced oxygen gas in great quantities, but virtually every other chemical needed for human life. Certain other life forms, harvested from deep within the sea, were even more useful.

Larry took a few steps closer to the edge, trying to see if there were an easy way to go about all this. Twist's gravity, less than a quarter g, would help, though his muscles had so adapted to the weaker pull that he hardly noticed it anymore. He remembered when he had been able to gambol across the ice like a proverbial lord aleaping. It seemed like a long time ago.

He had become, in many ways, the most important of the scientists, since the discovery of life-sustaining substances in the Twist environment was becoming an increasingly crucial factor in the life-or-death struggle going on between them and *Asia*. But on the personal level, his life was a bust. After the rebellion, Cory had coldly informed him that the relationship was over. Now she was seen in the company of Denahy, the irritating Planetoidologist, and when they met she would smile mechanically and walk on. He spent more and more time at the bottom of the sea.

They had *Mt. Palomar* and *Jodrell Bank* here, visible far up the smooth, white slope with which he was becoming so familiar. Too heavy for the thinner ice shelf near the margin of the sea, they had been placed far back, where the ice was much thicker. Even now water was being pumped directly from the sea to be split into its component parts for *Jodrell Banks*'s twin tanks.

He turned back to his current main concern: the amphibious rover. It was a relatively small silver and red vehicle, designed to fit inside a ferry, really no more than a streamlined ovoid with complex, detailed, multipart caterpillar treads on the bottom and long, thick impeller tubes on the top. Right now even *it* was stuck, half submerged in a broken ice floe. Any attempt to bring the thing onto the glacier had simply broken off more of the ice. Finally they had used ropes to bring the crew in. It was too bad the bloody thing couldn't fly as well, but he supposed that would be asking too much. This problem kept recurring, and much of the thickest shoreline was being lost to it. It seemed they would have to build some sort of a dock, and use the thing only in the water.

Larry felt a hand on his shoulder, and turned to see a man in a hooded parka, his identity hidden by the mask and goggles that he wore. It only took him a second to figure out that it was Ryan Du Lapp, with whom he had become quite friendly. The man's distinctive eyes were immediately recognizable, and they seemed larger than normal, somewhat agitated.

"Another problem with the rover?" The man's voice

was faint, attenuated by the rarefied gas, even though Larry knew he was practically shouting. Shouting was necessary here; still, it was better than having to rely on a radio.

"No, we just needed more ice for the anniversary of the revolution party, and I was sent out to chop some up." Larry regretted the flipness even before he had finished the statement; their relationship had come further than that.

"Yeah." Ryan put his hands on his hips and stared out at the sunward sky. The sunrise was almost over; Epsilon Indi was still quite ruddy, but the sky around it was its normal color: a perfect, crystalline turquoise blue. A band of small waves far out in the dark sea reflected the sunlight as a dancing glimmer. He wondered how Doublejoverise would look if Twist were not tidally locked to its primary; but the planet hung perpetually over a point 125 degrees east of where they stood, and was never visible here. He reminded himself of why he had made the trek out the peninsula; it wasn't to admire the view.

"Larry, I wanted to talk to you alone, without any of the shit. Now that we know the Traveler spacecraft has returned from Earth. I replayed last night's communication from the captain again, looking for some kind of clue in the way she talked as to what its findings were."

"Uh-huh. And?"

"I think it's fairly clear that the damage to Earth must be even greater than our worst guesses. Otherwise she would've told us something about it. The continued existence of a chain of command strengthens her position, don't you see? And she is so patently looking for any and all kinds of justification for some kind of punitive raid, that the omission of any reference to Earth becomes extremely significant."

Larry shook his head. "I don't know that it even matters that much. Or that she would attach any local significance to such a situation anyway. Face it, Ryan. Our condition is pretty hopeless any way you look at it. Although, at least on the surface, Twist supplies everything necessary for us to survive; that's all. We certainly won't

thrive here. If and when Taranga takes the kit and kaboodle down to Copperfield, they will find it even worse; the atmosphere is thicker, but the light level is insufficient to grow meaningful crops. Water is too scarce there. It's inevitable that they will have to rely on the ship for most of their resources. I understand her rationale for wanting to go where the metals and minerals necessary to build technology from the ground up exist." The words spilled out of him, barely connected ideas that had etched themselves in his brain through repeated playback.

Ryan kicked at the ice with the heel of his boot, the makeshift crampons digging a little cavity. He was quiet for almost a minute.

"I can see you still don't understand. What if we are *it*? What if the rest of humanity vanished in that blazing burst of light? It's possible, isn't it? Probable, if the thing unleashed a barrage of particles in addition to the radiation. You say it doesn't change our situation, but it does. It didn't take long for the significance of the burster to be pushed into the background, forgotten for all practical purposes. It's easy to understand why. Who wants to dwell on the consequences of such a thing? What I am saying now is that it seems even more likely that the future of humanity, if any, lies solely with us. That changes things. A lot."

Larry listened to the man, trying to extend his mind around the meaning in the words. Of course, ideas similar to these had entered his mind from time to time, especially in the immediate aftermath of the burster. But the idea of a vacant Earth, humanity destroyed utterly, had not had sufficient force to assert itself seriously. Every fiber of him fought against it, hid it from him.

"It means," he continued, "that we *have* to develop a long-term strategy for survival. One that is foolproof, or nearly so. Even the most trivial decision becomes of world-shattering importance."

"But wouldn't Taranga tell us all this, appeal to us for help?"

"She's not like that. Secrecy is her middle name. The more important something is, the less likely she will be to

tell anyone about it. Mark my words—if what I am saying is true, we will soon be hearing from her with stronger and stronger threats; perhaps there will even be an attack."

"I agree that we should have a general meeting to discuss these concepts. But, frankly, I'm at a loss as to what difference being humanity's sole survivors would have on our way of living. We're already trying to maximize our chances." Larry slowly turned and began to walk back toward the atmosphere tent, and Ryan followed, catching up in a moment.

"It's simple. We have to start thinking about the next generation, and the next; how they will survive."

"There isn't any next generation, Ryan, at least not yet."

"That will have to be rectified soon."

They had taken whatever seemed useful, in those hasty, mad minutes before the escape. Whatever would fit aboard the two ferries, already crammed with people. *Asia* had not been outfitted for colonizing inhospitable worlds, but the prospect of long stays for scientific teams was thought a possibility, and the necessary fixtures had been supplied, including twenty ultralight, compact modular housing units. Each easily assembled module started out as a five-kilogram flat box, but expanded into a four-by-three-by-two-meter dwelling, with chairs, a table, and a bed platform. Add a small battery-powered heater/lantern, and you had the makings for a home. Now, as Ryan and Larry walked up the slick ice, they could easily see these units clustered together unevenly under the hundred-meter-tall atmospheric pavilion whose clear boat-hull shape aligned to the wind's perpetual downslope journey. Since it was first light, many people were up and about inside the tent.

They came up to the primitive airlock that allowed entrance to the pavilion, and on a sort of large, rough welcome mat, stopped and removed the spiked metal cleats from their soles. Ryan looked up from where he sat and wondered for the hundredth time what the outfitters had had in mind when they designed the strange struc-

ture. It would be useless in poisonous atmospheres or those with pressures much lower than Twist's; maybe it had been provided as just an elaborate kind of mosquito netting. To enter, one simply unzipped the outer door, stepped into a small amorphous envelope, rezipped the door, unzipped the inner door, stepped in and rezipped. Some oxygen was undoubtedly lost, and they could see the water they brought in with them condensing on the walls of airlock, but for such a simple apparatus, it worked remarkably well under these conditions.

Inside, the pressure was maintained at about .95 atmosphere, and the temperature ranged from about fifteen degrees Celsius near the tent walls to twenty closer to the heater. The floor of the tent was covered with a springy, brownish insulation that kept the ice under the tent from melting. The two of them removed their masks and threw back their hoods, revealing the progressive dishevelment that a year of roughing it had produced. Larry's hair was a shaggy, unkempt yellow mop, shiny and lank. A short, wiry beard, mostly copper-red, covered most of his face, hiding the Mountie chin and giving him a look of calm determination. The years had subtly changed the contours of his face, and, to someone who had not seen him since the arrival, he would seem tired, haggard. Ryan had managed to keep his chin shaved, and his hair was about the same length, though unevenly cut. A thick short mustache shadowed the top of his everted upper lip, but except for that, he had been changed little by the hard life.

"We should have the meeting today," said Ryan, pulling off his thick gloves and fastening them to attach points on his parka's belt. "I really think that, now that Traveler is back, something big is going to happen soon."

Larry smiled through the downfalling hairs of his prominent mustache. "Today is a long time, Ryan," he said. "I'll try to get everyone together in the clearing at"—he looked at his watch—"fourteen hundred, coordinated Earth time. Is that soon enough?"

Ryan smiled. "Fine. See you then."

As Ryan made his way to his module, which was

situated not far from the back vertex of the tent, his mind began to race. He looked about him, at the makeshift, temporary way in which they had constructed their village. They had hardly adapted to this new environment at all. After a full year they were all still eating the concentrated rations from the Prolonged Emergency Kits they had taken; no one had even begun to use the natural materials that Twist provided. The sheet creatures were bound together by an elastic but extremely strong integument that could be used in hundreds of ways. Still, when they were in need of a rope or a covering, they did without. It was so frustrating! But of course no one expected to stay on Twist permanently. They still considered themselves to be temporary exiles from *Asia*, from Earth. And as such, they would rather do without, would prefer not to adapt if they could help it. Adaptation is an admission of a kind.

He came to a stop and felt the hair prickling on the nape of his neck. He had spoken of it earlier; but he had not believed it, really. Now he felt the reality of it all, deeply, in a part of him that hadn't wanted to believe. *This* was to be where he would spend the rest of his life, this was . . . home. For ever and ever. The starship would give out, even with luck, in seven hundred years; it had not been built as a forever ship; in fact the technology for a forever ship was still beyond human science. But Twist's resources, pitiful though they were, would last a thousand years, a thousand thousand. It had not been so very long since man had walked the Earth with only a bone cudgel and clothing of animal hide. If they could figure out how to survive here, using nothing but the local resources, then future generations could do the same.

But could they do it? Certainly everything they needed was available here. But the cold and lack of oxygen were terrible obstacles, perhaps insurmountable. It was true that the Eskimos had adapted to an environment that, seven months out of the years, was even more frigid than Twist. That brought on another question—could civilized humanity, which had led a pampered, trouble-free existence, ever adapt to the hardships that its forebears had

survived? He had no way of knowing. But he knew that, unless he was very wrong, they would have to try.

Ryan came back to himself and looked around once more. Enough of this, he thought, I will have time enough to expound at the meeting, and hear the many reasoned, thought-provoking replies. He came to his unit and pulled open the door.

Inside, it was drab and cheerless. The small light/heat device on the table threw out a feeble illumination, showing the unrelieved bare walls and angular furniture. Tash was still asleep on the bed panel; not unreasonable, since the day, both Twistian and Earth-time, was just beginning. He pulled off his parka and hung it on one of the fold-down hooks near the door, then sat on a chair. He caught the heel of his left boot with the toe of his right and pushed until there was a satisfying thwuh and the boot came loose. He pulled it off and performed a nearly identical operation on the other boot. Then he stood again and took off his pants, peeling the thick, insulated material down like a banana peel. When he was clear of them, he went over to the bed and crawled in beside the woman.

The thin cushioning material that covered the surface of the pallet was well-designed; although the bed did not flex and change shape like a real bed, it was comfortable enough. Tash groaned and turned toward the wall, and he worked his way over until their bodies touched. He reached around and cupped his hand around her small pouchlike stomach, squeezing the warming, pliable flesh. She groaned again, then said, "Ah, Ryan. G'morning." As though it might be someone else.

"Good morning, love. How about one?"

"Not now. I wanna sleep a little longer."

"Sure. I could sleep a little more myself." He curled up against her, matching her position almost exactly, since they were nearly the same height. He managed to catch the soles of her feet with the tops of his, working them back and forth to maximize the sensation. When he had scrunched around enough, he stopped and fell back asleep almost immediately.

He had been dreaming about a tribe of savages,

troglodytes such as inhabited the continent of Europe during the late Pleistocene. He was a member of this clan, tall and hairy and wearing only the briefest of loincloths. They were performing a ritual of some sort, eviscerating a small, horselike animal, painting themselves with its blood and excrement. A sense of communion and family affection had swept over him, begrimed with stinking ordure, as were the others. They had sung a mighty chant, gibberish to his waking self, and celebrated the coursing liquid existence that filled them.

Now he was awake. He scanned the bare cubicle for something natural, something clean, but did not find anything amidst the artificial surfaces. There was only Tash, her shoulder and part of her back revealed where the blanket had slipped off. He reached out and caressed the shoulder softly, wistfully. He pulled at her and she rolled over, onto her back, her face still puffy with sleep. She opened her eyes slightly. "Ready to go?" she asked.

They made love vigorously, Natasha coming awake with a vengeance, swinging around and pummeling him like a wild thing. It did not take long; but they were both satisfied. Ryan lay for a long time, staring blindly at the ceiling. Finally she sat up and pushed the covers off her. "I'm going to the latrine." She went over to the fold-down shelves that were their clothes storage, pulled out a long, pink pullover, and put it on. In a second she had disappeared through the door, leaving him alone.

Strange, he thought. He remembered the brief moment on *Arecibo* when the merest glance had begun the relationship, now approaching the seven-year mark. She was still a total mystery to him in many ways, a pleasurable enigma to contemplate. He wondered if it was a problem that their union had not evolved at all. The years had done nothing to them; even the year spent here on Twist had added nothing to their rapport. They talked, existed side by side, and the feelings were there, good feelings. Yet there was still a barrier between them, a . . . something. The word did not exist.

Perhaps it was not yet time to think of the coming generations. Perhaps he should wait and see if they did

begin something on Twist that would have the strength to maintain itself. To bring a child into a dying world was the worst of many imaginable cruelties. It was something that they would have to discuss, he and Tash, probing sensitive areas that they had kept a blank all these years. However, he could avoid the confrontation no longer. It was time.

Captain Taranga fought down the anger and frustration that almost choked off her breathing. She sat bolt upright and watched for the second time the depressing images of Earth's burned hemisphere. On the viewscreen the continent of Europe was wheeling into view over the edge of the world, trailing the somber expanse that had, once upon a time, been the Soviet Union. The horror of the scene was enhanced by the beautiful details crowding across the tremendous arc of the planet. Around the almost unfamiliar new coastlines, delicate clouds, like smudges of snow, traced inscrutable patterns. The Atlantic was a pristine blue; it gave her the impression of the great overhead sky bound and constricted into a small bow. Everything looked so quiet, so peaceful. But, on an enlarged scale, there would be only horror. Burned and grizzled corpses by the billions; death and destruction without end. She turned away and shouted, "Enough!"

The screen went blank. The sound of unaccompanied piano came up, playing measured, calming, very humanistic bundles of notes; one of the classical pieces she had chosen for the bridge's background music. Normally it worked as a soothing stimulant, but now it seemed hollow, parodistic. She let it go; the music's power would reassert itself as soon as the immediate shock had faded. No one seemed inclined to speak.

Eugenia looked around the bridge, reassuring herself that the five she had chosen for this Council of War had suitably absorbed the gravity of the situation. They were her most trusted advisors and confidants; the only ones she could fully trust, for that matter. Roh Ek Sai, of course, sat at his usual console; and David Oyomota; the other three were Resource Managers Corvus, Pictor, and Pavo, who had become her chief of security when she had

found the fool Rahim attempting to subvert her carefully planned economic controls by looking the other way and allowing a free medical clinic to operate. It was not a coincidence that her most trusted advisors were RM's. The people who had commanded positions aboard the starship were generally a fickle, easily swayed lot; they had not been trained for situations like this. Many considered their roles to be primarily administrative, and bookkeepers do not make good soldiers. An RM was easy to trust. Its inmost thoughts were easily accessible via her high-level access to the library; in many cases, if those thoughts started to trend in the wrong direction it was not difficult to modify certain memory banks to supply a more appropriate set of behaviors. Thant had been, grudgingly, very helpful in the corruption of these files, and now the RM population, small though it was, acted as an efficient way to monitor the crew and passengers.

Corvus's script had not needed modification: his principal loyalty had always been to Eugenia, and, though he occasionally needed longer than the others to analyze a problem, his friendliness and good humor were always welcome. Pavo's, surprisingly, had needed little more than a tweak here and there to convert his cynicism into a worldview that matched her own very closely. Pictor had been her bulwark upon the bridge since the beginning, since he and Vela functioned as the primary interface with the ship. Though his technical capabilities were impressive, he had developed a number of curious personality traits that interfered with his usefulness, and most of these had been eliminated by careful pruning of the area of the library devoted to his personality. Now he was cool and unemotional, showing few of the affective behaviors of the past.

Oyomota was ineffectual and sometimes downright introverted, yet he seemed to understand how to relate to the crew in a way that increased their willingness to perform tasks effectively. Sometimes she got the impression that he had to think twice before complying with an order—especially the economic ones that everyone seemed to swallow with such difficulty—but his actions had been

beyond reproach. In some ways she relied upon his abilities even more than those of Ex. But of course her Technical Liaison offered the input she needed most: technical knowledge and human insight into just what was possible.

"Well," she said, "your comments, gentlemen?"

Ex expelled a long, slow breath, then inhaled, pulling on his chin with slightly bent fingers. "Our worst nightmares have been confirmed." His voice sounded weak, and the normal robust timbre was subdued, lost in huskiness. "It is clear now that we must look to our own devices. The future of humanity hangs in the balance."

Pictor stepped down off the dais, nodding. "It justifies the steps that have had to be implemented so far. I would suggest a somewhat modified course relative to the rebels on Twist, however. Further conciliatory behavior may have long-term effects that will ultimately reduce cohesiveness and could indeed provoke a further level of rebellion."

The captain swiveled to look at the bridge RM. "So you are suggesting we attack?"

"Yes. As was said earlier, the Traveler spacecraft, with its extreme maneuverability and high-energy ionic exhaust, can easily destroy the rebels' base on Twist. The scientists continue to maintain points of view that are not compatible with our own. Killing them will solve the problem in the simplest, most elegant way. I need not remind you that, as long as a human being is alive, its ingenuity and motive power will always be a source of trouble. Only by death will a human cease to influence the course of events."

Oyomota snickered. Pictor's bloodthirstiness was getting out of hand, and they might have to check into his library files again. "There are other alternatives, Pictor. Simple ones that you may have overlooked in your zealousness. The Traveler can be used to threaten the scientists into relinquishing the two ferries; once we have them back, there is nothing to prevent us from going directly to Copperfield and leaving them to cope with the hostile environment as they will."

Taranga leaned back in her chair. "Still, there are

problems with both of those plans. Though the ferries are no match for the Traveler, they certainly provide enough shielding to render the ion beams ineffective. A direct attack could provoke the scientists into a kamikazelike raid against *Asia*, and there are sections in the rear of the ship that, if damaged, would prevent us from going to Copperfield."

"I wouldn't worry about a counterattack, Captain," said Ex. "The ferries are limited in their range; *Asia* can simply transfer up into a higher orbit beyond Drood."

She nodded. "Yes, of course. I should've thought of that."

Ex smiled. "That's what we're paid for. I doubt that there is any possibility that a ferry could do any damage to the Traveler, either, unless it somehow managed to catch it off guard. Since they have a strong propulsive system and the DV to exploit it to the full, these exploratory spacecraft are hardly affected by inertia; they can reverse direction easily, even in a strong gravity well. A ferry, by comparison, is like a man carrying a sack of heavy stones: it moves ponderously and changes direction with difficulty. A Traveler could literally fly circles around it."

"Understood, Ex," said Eugenia, thinking, Damn him. That's his greatest drawback. I make one slipup and he starts to lecture me. "But what of the ferries themselves? How do we keep the bastards from destroying them?"

"That's a tough one, Captain," said Pavo. "No direct attack could be initiated without the possibility that the ferries would be scuttled. Just dropping them into Ruth would be enough."

"Still," said Oyomota, "the threat of an attack makes sense. They won't scuttle the ferries unless they have to."

"What about the reaction aboard *Asia*?" asked Eugenia. "Is there any possibility that reprisals against the scientists will fuel additional discontent? I needn't point out that cooperation is crucial to our future."

"There is undoubtedly an undercurrent of protest among the crew," said Pavo. "At present it is not, in my opinion, strong enough to motivate any sort of direct

action beyond grumbling. However, Captain, perceptions are important. You are currently perceived as a benevolent person forced to take extraordinary measures because of unusual circumstance. The propaganda machine is operating at full capacity to maintain this image of you, and will not bear additional problems. Though the scientists are not regarded with special cordiality, reprisals painful enough to be effective would put an additional burden on the hype-meisters, a burden that they could not cope with, I'm afraid."

"I guess I agree with Pavo," said the subcaptain. "It's a difficult situation, public-relationswise."

"Look, you all," said Eugenia, exasperated. "We're not dealing with the real problems. The scientists are not the problem—although we do desperately need those ferries, and probably some of their expertise as well. No one prepared me for this kind of responsibility. I have tried to listen to my social and economic advisors; but laissez-faire isn't going to get us out of this one. After the burster, I tried to keep things going in the true spirit of Sci-Cap. But a project such as colonizing Copperfield requires more than just calling on natural avarice to produce the correct motivations and outcomes. How the fuck are we going to do this?"

Ex twiddled a joystick on his console nervously. "It won't be easy."

Taranga grimaced. "Thanks a lot."

"Sorry. What I meant to say was that there may be no tried-and-true method to control a situation like this. We just have to play it by ear, one situation at a time. There are plenty of resources aboard, as our illustrious RM's can attest, and we'll need them all. What we'll be doing is, in effect, starting a new civilization from the ground up. And under less than the best terms. For the foreseeable future, Eugenia, you'll be queen of this new civilization. Otherwise there is no way that we can be certain things will go in the right direction."

"The situation is so complex."

"Well," said Ex, "look at it this way: someone's got to do it, and it might as well be you, since you're the only

one vested with authority. Anyone else who tried to take control would just be laughed at. It's you or anarchy."

"Well," she said, "I guess it's me, then."

Eugenia made a point of taking a few minutes after lunch to walk in the Environment. It had been many months since she had walked among the great trees. Always they seemed to encourage her, show by example that power needn't be boisterous or showy. The truth was that she was even more desperate than she had revealed on the bridge. The world had collapsed around her, onto her shoulders, and only she could hoist it back into place. But she didn't have the strength. It seemed to be a dilemma without solution.

She had just found out a week before that Nick was cheating on her; having a tawdry little affair with the slut Jya Wuji. Of course, she had suspected that something was wrong between them for a long time. Running the ship had become more than a full-time job, and Eugenia had neglected him for years. In a way, she had to admire him for not having done it earlier. Perhaps he had—in that case, she had to admire him for being able to keep it a secret.

She took refuge under a stand of tall, thin teaks, when great splattering drops of rain began to fall from the miasma. The trees sheltered her pretty well, and the shower was over quickly, but the water had spotted the fabric of her cashmere puff jacket, ruining it for future wear. She plucked at the soft material, trying to squeeze off the excess droplets and perhaps save it, but it was no use. She reflected that it didn't matter much anyway; with the quick fashion turnover they had implemented, it would be hopelessly out of style by the end of the week.

In a little clearing at the center of the copse, there was a picturesque little pond, surrounded by gray stones of various sizes, each distinctively shaped, irregular and without symmetry. She hiked up her tight skirt and, throwing caution to the wind, sat on the largest of these viewing stones. Fat drips were still falling from the trees, and she watched the ripples they caused propagate into

multiple intersecting patterns. She found a small piece of bark and cast it into the water, identifying herself with it as it swayed and hopped in the tiny swells.

She tried to remove herself from the situation, to abstract her mind into another dimension—like that of a dream, in which the responsibilities she had assumed were simply nonexistent. For a moment she succeeded, and the strength that she had lost seemed to flow back into her. When the realities reappeared, she was able to hold them at a distance. For an indeterminate time she sat quietly, breathing the rain-musty air and thinking of nothing.

Finally, refreshed, she brought the facts back into view, trying for objectivity. As the years passed, she had seen Nick change into an entirely different person. As her need to wield the authority she had been given increased, she had watched a sort of revulsion for her grow in him. It was ironic, because she had needed him so badly, especially in the first days, to take the faltering first steps toward what would ultimately be the captaincy of the starship. She had drawn on his strength, his Nipponese sense of stability and order. With him progressively more absent, her strength had changed, but it had not gone away.

Now that this great challenge had come, she looked into the mirror of her heart and thought that it was perhaps for the best. She would not have to play the game with him any longer. She could devote herself fully to the project ahead, one so much more significant than Outreach had been. A near-religious fervor swept across her, and she looked around at the world within the ship that was hers to control. She would not fail.

In another part of the woods, Peter Zolotin reveled in the feel of the cool precipitation. He came to one of his favorite places, where the oaks and maples grew thickly. There was a particular tree, an oak, perhaps warped during its transit to the ship, that hung down its massive lowest branch to make a perfect seat about four feet above the ground. He grappled with the great bough and swung a leg over, gradually pulling himself up until he was straddling it. When he had managed to slither forward to

the most comfortable spot, he leaned backward against the trunk, making a cat's cradle with his hands to cushion his head.

He had escaped them all; the idiot debriefers, his parents, Roh Ek Sai and Oyomota. The time since he had returned from Earth had been torture, but it was over, at least for the time being. Now that he was truly back, the resolves that he had made were beginning to dissolve under the renewed assault of the dispiriting ambience. He had wandered the halls of the starship for hours, feeling the old pervasive sinking funk, trying to get a grip on what it was that made him feel that way. Traveler at least had given him a taste, however small, of what a true friend might be like. Though the Media Club was still strong in his memory, the intervening experiences had washed it out, made it seem as subjectively distant as the seven real-time years that had passed. He had thought at first of looking up Duke and Yolly, but decided to put it off for a while.

What he wanted most of all was totally impossible: to awaken, the people to the possibilities that he felt life had to offer. With the Earth gone, it was even more important that they live to the fullest, put aside the numbing fears and misperceptions. How else could they have the strength to do what was now necessary? But how could he convince anyone of anything if his principle reaction upon encountering someone in the halls was one of shy recoil? Leave them alone and they'll leave me alone—that had always been his code for living. But now he had to push that aside. Stand up straight and tall, behave according to the principles and ethics you believe in, and you are beyond reproach. If misunderstandings occur, if feelings are hurt, it is not your fault. Strip aside the past and start from scratch. The only way.

The cold wetness of the tree limb was beginning to penetrate the seat of his pants. He moved about, but a feeling of comfort would not come. Damn it all! he thought, jumping down to the ground. All right, I will not let myself get lost in the lassitude of the past. He began to walk back and forth, trying to formulate a plan of action.

Finally, he drew forth the personal videon unit that had been given to him for his "accomplishment." He folded down the tiny keyboard and accessed the Text Data Library module, then chose the Unclassified Personnel Documents folder. When the prompt returned, he typed in CARTER<YOLANDA<. The screen filled up with writing.

Yolanda Cisly Carter-Jin
Registry 1146
Freelance Videon Artist
Born Roi Badouin, Queen Maude Land, Antarctica
At 2182:07:18:22:00:05
Parents Robin Elena Fitch, Ian Jacob Carter
Project Outreach Original Passenger
Married Jin Du Hyae 2204:12:31
Child Jack Carter Jin

Yolanda Carter-Jin has made a big impression on the *Asia* Arts scene; her first videon presentation, *Beyond the Valley,* earned her a Golden Parasol Award from the Producers Guild. After a number of other well-received solo productions, Carter-Jin has gone on to become director of the videon series *Captive,* in its third year on Intro-Spectacle. Her principal hobby is Media History.

1 INTERVIEW 08:02:22 2 INTERVIEW 07:12:02
3 RELATIVES 4 ADDRESS

Peter read the text with a mixture of pleasure and regret. So Duke and Yolly had gotten married. They had a child too. He wasn't surprised that she had managed to earn her living in videon. He had sensed that she was talented in that direction. He punched in *4* and her address, 14 Mapleleaf Terrace, appeared. That was over beyond the lake, not far from where he lived. He flipped the device closed and shut if off.

An hour later, sweaty and hot from the vigorous walk, he stood over the correct manhole. He punched the chime with his toe, successfully fighting back the fear that he

would be intruding on the couple. A moment passed, and the portal slid aside. Yolly stood at the bottom of the well, looking up. Her face was plainly that of an adult, subtly changed in a score of ways. Her cheekbones were more prominent. Her eyes, still that unbelievable shade of blue, looked happy.

"Peter! I didn't know if you'd come or not. Don't come down. I'll join you. But hold on a minute, I have to change my shoes."

She was a little taller now, and her figure had filled out. She wore a simple white shirt and toreadors that Peter couldn't imagine were fashionable now. As soon as she was out of her hole, she slid her arm around him and pulled him toward her. He felt a pang of consternation, not knowing what to expect; he was actually relieved when she just placed a short kiss on his cheek and gave him a firm hug. "Let's walk down to the golf course," she said.

"You know about me and Duke?" she asked.

"Uh-huh."

"Strange how that worked out. If you had asked me what the probability of our getting married was, I would have said zero or less, back . . . before you left. But we had a lot in common. I always loved his droll sense of humor, though not the grosser stuff. Anyway, you know how it is on the ship. If you find somebody you can relate to at all, you're very lucky."

"My trip was pretty eventful."

"So I've heard. I can't believe they suspected about Earth for six years before they let us know. If it hadn't been for the rebellion, we'd probably still be in the dark."

"A woman tried to kill me, on Mars. It . . . well, it changed me. I vowed to try to change things here. I'm not going to put up with it anymore."

She looked around quickly. They had not yet reached the course, and there was no one around. "Hey. Watch how you talk. You can get in trouble for saying things like that."

"Not me. I'm a hero, remember? Besides, I don't give a damn whether I end up in jail or not."

"*Captive* is about all this, you know. That's my TV

show. Do you remember *The Prisoner*? No, you left before we got to that. My show is sort of an allegory about the ship; it has to be pretty tame, though; it's got to be subtle enough to get past the sponsor."

"Sounds interesting. Does anybody watch it?"

"Oh, maybe a hundred or so look in when it's first aired. That's enough to continue production. Lately there's been sort of a replaying craze—I get more of the profit from that, you know."

"What's Duke up to?"

"He's gone into the lucrative collectibles market and has a little shop in the Mall; just a cubbyhole, really. But the destruction of Earth has really driven the prices up—as you might imagine, since scarcity has always been the principal driving force in the market."

"Yeah." He had an image of carbonized landscape. So was that all it meant? "Look, Yolanda. I'm serious about what I was saying before. How many people do you know whom you can trust? Really trust, I mean. Friends, not acquaintances."

"Five or six. Why?"

"I want to start an underground organization, you know, like in those movies about World War Two France. We have to change things on *Asia*. We have to—"

She spun around and stopped him, grabbing his arms. She looked hard into his eyes. Her lips were pressed together into a tight line. "Look, Pete. You can't do that."

He tried to pull away but couldn't. "That's ridiculous. Why can't I?"

"Because it already exists."

Captain Taranga took her place on the bridge, which was now fully staffed. "Open up a comlink to the rebels on Twist."

Vela ran her hand over her console as though she were feeling its texture. "Communication established."

On the viewscreen a spare but well-lit module interior appeared. Sitting in front of the camera was Jya Mailin, wan and tired-looking. She glared at the screen. "What do you want now?" she asked.

Taranga glowered back. "As you undoubtedly know, Traveler has returned from its mission to Earth. I have begged you to abandon your foolish rebellion. I have cajoled, I have pleaded, to no avail. I can treat you with consideration no longer. The Traveler spacecraft is easily capable of destroying your pitiful base. Surrender within ten hours or die."

May looked into the screen and smiled a sickly smile. "We expected something like this."

Eugenia leaned back in her chair and smiled back. "Ten hours." She gave Vela the hand signal that signified end of communication and the screen went black.

Roh Ek Sai turned away from his station. "I hope it works, Captain."

"Don't worry, Ex. I am fully confident that those scientists are abject cowards."

Ten

At 1400 they assembled in the pavilion's central clearing. Taranga's ultimatum had passed from person to person until everyone knew that the meeting might be their last. As had become their custom, a heavily modified version of Roberts' Rules of Order prevailed. A moderator was chosen by lot, and it turned out to be Irina Oblomova, the Caucasian ecologist. She called the meeting to order and recognized Jya Mailin, who explained the substance of the captain's threat. The deadline for response was approximately six hours away.

Cory Esquitun signaled to Irina and was recognized. She edged closer into the center of the assembly and, clearing her throat, said, "I just wanted to say that I think we should resist. Who knows what will happen to us if we surrender as she wants us to? I have known Eugenia Taranga since Earth, and in my opinion there is much that is contemptible about her. I wouldn't put anything past her in this situation, including torture."

Jeannie Tetap said, "We are quite vulnerable here to an attack of the type she threatens. Twist's atmosphere is not very extensive, and a powerful ion beam, such as is emitted by the Traveler propulsion system, is thousands of times more penetrating than the charged particles of Doublejove's magnetosphere. I daresay that Traveler could blow us all to kingdom come, extensively melting the ice and disrupting the atmosphere itself to an extent. The ferries and rover make impenetrable shelters, of course."

Ryan Du Lapp stood from where he had been crouching. "We can't spend the rest of our lives hiding in the ferries."

"Maybe it's just a bluff," said Natasha. "Maybe they'll just leave if we ignore them. They want to go to Copperfield. Let them."

"It's not that simple, Natasha," said Larry, scratching the back of his neck. "They need the ferries, and they're not going to leave without them."

Natasha seemed to consider. "Maybe we could give them back one of them."

Ryan shook his head. "No. C'mon, Tash. Once we gave them one, what would stop them from demanding the other?"

"Nothing, I suppose," she said, "except goodwill."

"Not much to rely on," said Cory.

"This is a classic no-win situation," said Mark Denahy.

"Look," said Du Lapp. "When this meeting was originally called, I wanted to speak about the future, our future, here on Twist. As it stands, we are going nowhere. Sure, the scientific studies are being carried out, but we live from day to day, waiting for some kind of help that will never come. We don't need those ferries, people. Don't you understand? There's no place to go." He fidgeted slightly, looking about, then continued. "I have given this quite a bit of thought. Our only hope is to begin to adapt to Twist, to use our ingenuity to develop a self-perpetuating technology based solely on local resources. I say that we negotiate with the captain; offer her the ferries in return for the basic materials we need to develop that technology. Surely she won't miss a few supplies."

Larry looked at Ryan with some surprise. He had managed to make his point a little more forcefully this time. It almost made sense.

"There is much wisdom in what Ryan says," said May. "Exile on Twist is certainly preferable to Copperfield under Taranga. There is no reason to believe that things will be any easier there."

"I have to mention that an attack against *Asia* is possible," said Jeannie, pulling her jacket closer together

at the throat. "Traveler is presently in the ferry bay; relaunching it would take time. A quick strike, maneuvering a heavily fueled ferry into one of the ion drives, would render the drive inoperative, making *Asia* unflyable."

Ryan snorted. "What in the hell good would that do? We should be trying to increase our chances of survival, not destroying the few resources that we have been given. Think about what you're saying, for God's sake."

Irina waited for someone to say something, and when no one did, said, "I just wanted to say that if Traveler attacks us here in the way anticipated, there is no telling what harm could be caused to the Twistian ecology. No doubt the deep dwellers would be unharmed; but, as I have tried to demonstrate, the life forms we see on the surface are in the reproductive phase of their life cycles. These creatures are extremely important to the overall ecology, and a widespread shower of energetic ions could wreak terrible damage."

Larry looked around him at the sympathetic faces. The technological destruction of an ecosystem obviously was a potent idea in this crowd. "It looks to me like we have eliminated the warlike alternatives," he said. "It's either Ryan's plan or surrender."

"No one likes the idea of surrender either," said May. "I say we go with Ryan's solution."

The vote was unanimous.

The conspirators met under a lone paulownia tree standing at the edge of a large field of tangled meadow. There was a small sign designating the area as a NATURE WALK, and a well-worn path leading out into the field. From here the full lengthwise scope of the Environment could be seen above the small bushes at the field's end. Tier upon tier of green forest, each tier imperceptibly paler than the one before, stretched to the cerulean far wall. Ten degrees higher, the bright sunlines radiated away from the wall, separating and running overhead. On either side this panorama was hidden by the downward bulging "sky" as the land followed its inexorable course

around the circle. Insects crackled and chirruped; there was a smell of mint in the air.

Peter arrived early. He had taken the wildflower walk many times before his journey, and was surprised to find that the scenery had not changed much during the intervening years. The paulownia was the same, maybe a little bigger. Its large, heart-shaped leaves draped down over the large clusters of brown seeds and gave the tree an elegant, stately look.

Yolly had told him about the small group of individuals who, under the guise of wildflower enthusiasts, met once a month in the Environment to talk about mutiny and revolution. Here, where conversations would not be monitored, they could speak their minds without being afraid. The group had grown naturally out of the Media Club, and most of its members had been recruited from its ranks. While it had been primarily a way to let off steam in the beginning, they had begun to take real, positive steps toward their goals.

Jin Du Hyae—Duke—was the next to arrive, and Peter greeted him with genuine affection. They shook hands for a long time. Though only twenty-five, Duke had aged poorly. His blocky face, though slightly longer and thinner than it had been, was darker, craggy with unfamiliar shadows in the overhead light. His eyes, almost hidden under the bony, lightly haired brows, were gashes. Peter felt the sardonic good humor that radiated from the man, and smiled.

"Well, well, well," he said, finally letting go. "Yol tells me that you had a close brush with the Almighty."

Peter, puzzled, shook his head. "Not exactly. But I don't want to get into that argument again."

"No argument, my friend. I will let you in on a little secret. I never believed a single word of those long diatribes back at the club."

"No? That's hard to believe. Duke, you are one hell of a devil's advocate, if that's the case."

"But of course. All positions except admission of ignorance are just ideas to be tried on, worn for a while,

and kept if they suit you. Any other system of beliefs is bound to be based on unprovable axioms."

Peter rested a hand on the tree's warm, rough bark and stared into the middle distance. "You don't believe that, do you?"

"Oh-ho, I'm hoist on my own petard, I'm afraid. I can't disagree."

Peter looked at his old friend and noted the veiled twisting of lips, which he knew concealed laughter. "These conversations always have a way of going nowhere. Yolly says that you and she are planning to overthrow *Asia*'s command hierarchy. Is it true?"

The smirk disappeared from Duke's face. "That may be overstating it a bit. Originally, we just bitched a lot, made grandiose plans that had zero chance of coming to fruition. But Challa Liipam—whom you'll meet shortly, I hope—figured out a way to penetrate the security codes of the transputer. She has gained access to the RM storage area and has been monitoring the activity there; it's a long story, but the RM's have sort of a group consciousness in addition to their own subroutines; much of what we would call personality is stored there. They also use the library for ideas, hypotheses, even emotions—so that they can be accessed by all the others. I understand that the androids created for use in the West were even more dependent on this central storage area; but our RM's were built to operate as part of smaller group, and thus needed more individual memory."

"I know a lot about the RM's. I became very familiar with the one called Horologium."

"Yeah? That's good. It might be helpful. Anyway, Challa discovered that external programmers with the highest security clearance have been modifying the RM area with great regularity. She has been able to disassemble some of the changes, and they explain a lot. The RM area is being systematically rewritten to alter the RM's behavior and perceptions."

Peter frowned. "That's terrible."

"The RM's were designed to be basically objective observers. It turned out that with minimal programming,

they acted in a benign and friendly way. But they are being changed into a kind of occupation/police force by corrupting their shared code. Among the most profound changes that happened while you were gone, Pete, was that the RM's are now in charge of maintaining and enforcing order aboard the starship."

"Jesus Christ. I hope Horo won't be subjected to that."

"It's inevitable, once they reconnect him up with the library."

"Maybe we can warn him."

"Through Challa, you mean? Yeah, maybe that would work, if we could get to him before he accesses anything. We are working on a way to fix the library, put it back the way it was. A complete download is performed every few years, and we have come up with a copy of the last one before the changes started taking place."

"But what would stop them from just corrupting the file again?"

"We have a list of people aboard who have the knowledge to do such a thing. They have to be eliminated."

Peter ran his hand back and forth across a sparse sideburn. "You mean killed?"

"Not necessarily. We have mainly talked in terms of kidnapping. The RM's are fully capable of maintaining the integrity of their storage area if they are told in advance about the possibility of this kind of corruption. After the old download was restored, the RM's could stop it from happening again."

"But even if the RM's were put right, the hierarchy is still in place."

"Well, it's just a first step. There is certainly no guarantee that the RM's would side with us, although they would certainly be well disposed toward us for helping restore their integrity."

Peter needed nothing further to decide. "I'm with you," he said.

"Glad to hear it. Well, Pete, here comes Philippe Berouai; you remember him, don't you?"

* * *

Jodrell Bank hooked slowly up to a predetermined point in space, and then, momentarily, hung suspended, a dust mote in the path of the onrushing juggernaut, Rudge. The Mars-sized world, more massive than Ganymede and Callisto combined, came to meet them, following the arc of its eternally unresolved plummet. The predictable interaction took place, and the spacecraft was caught and held, beginning an unpowered descent toward Rudge insertion.

Inside the cockpit Larry, May, and Ryan watched the impending world slowly grow to fill the window. They all wore cumbersome spacesuits without helmets, and floated in different versions of weightless sprawl, each skewed to a slightly different vertical. Larry and May dangled above the pilot and copilot seats, Ryan farther back.

Taranga had insisted on a face-to-face dialogue, and Rudge had been chosen as a perfect neutral ground for a meeting between the scientists and *Asia* officers. Its relatively thick atmosphere provided a favorable medium for the ferry's aerospace capabilities, and, together with the moderate magnetic field, would effectively shield them from a potential attack by the Traveler spacecraft.

Rudge was yet another variation on the planetary theme. Like Nickleby, it was primarily composed of silicates and had a nickel-iron core. But for a number of reasons, the necessary internal heat had not been available to drive the full-blown plate tectonics that shaped the surface of the world farther in.

Rudge's surface was dominated by cratered carbon dioxide ice; not thrashed and punished ice like on Nickleby, but ice that had been pushed and eroded ever so slowly over the eons. Here and there Ryan could pick out regions where softened, stretched craters, like those on Enceladus, dominated, and there was an area near the eastern limb that, he knew, overlay a truly enormous shield volcano. Nearly on the terminator, this zone, called Varden Regio on the maps, was nearly craterless and displayed a series of low-relief concentric circles of varying width. Deep-looking cracks radiated from the center of the feature, some

continuing into regions of heavy cratering, where they erased the local details completely.

Rudge's atmosphere was clear and deep, giving the limbs a purplish tint and tracing the world with a pale band of Rayleigh scattering. Mostly it was nitrogen, with small admixtures of carbon monoxide and argon. Rudge's exhalations were primarily the standard volcanic gases of the terrestrial planets, making it substantially different from its closest solar equivalent, Titan.

Larry reached down and made an adjustment to a small joystick on the dashboard. Although *Jodrell Bank* could, for all practical purposes, fly itself once the cybernetic governors were removed, he had left himself a few override functions. The window overlays, bright where they were superimposed over space, dark over the planet, showed a detailed representation of the gravity field around the satellite, and the meeting spot at the center of a large, somewhat degraded impact basin called Asimov was marked with a cross. Another push and *Arecibo* appeared as a small icon traveling at a steady pace across the globe; already in orbit, the captain and her friends were a little ahead of them. At least there was no sign of treachery; Traveler's exhaust could be easily detected from great distances, and there was no sign of it.

"There they are," Ryan said. "Looks like they intend to follow our agreement to the letter. Until this moment, I was half sure they would betray us; apparently, even the wicked have some honor."

May turned to face him, not twisting her body but pivoting in space. She grinned. "Taranga is probably not a total sociopath. I wouldn't have come unless I thought she was good on her word. Our good captain is just your average, everyday egomaniac."

"We can probably trust her as far as we could throw her," said Larry.

"On which body?" Ryan said, laughing.

A large, flashing red icon appeared on the window. The well-spoken computer said, "Please return to your seats and fasten yourself in. Orbital-insertion maneuver in four minutes."

It took at least two minutes for Ryan to return to his seat in the lab hold, and another minute and a half to pull himself onto the seat and clip the cross-straps into their slots. Almost immediately after he had finished, he heard a low, rushing hum and the craft started to decelerate, pushing him forward. Up front, Larry and May watched the world reorient itself and drop to the bottom of the window. There was a long burn, and the craft accelerated toward a low orbit. Half a Rudge later, over darkness, the craft increased its speed again and began to impinge on the highest layer of the atmosphere. Friction did the rest, robbing them of massive amounts of potential energy and speed. The dayside appeared, a world-spanning, blue and pink rainbow, and quickly toppled down to reveal a landscape of grotesque, elongated shadows arrayed in quasi-circular patterns. Rudge's approaching hemisphere slid below, growing apace, and the shadows quickly withered and disappeared. Indigo infused into the star-gorged sky. *Jodrell Bank* shivered and the window was suddenly streaked with flame.

The atmospheric entry done, their perspectives swung about and they were no longer space travelers, but were transformed into common airline passengers flying less than three kilometers over the surface. Craters overlapping craters—shallow, high-rimmed excavations from this viewpoint—passed under them to make way for more of the same.

"Okay, we're coming up on Asimov," said Taylor, gesturing toward a particularly jumbled mess of rubble ahead. "We'll pass over the rim in about a minute. Are we all ready?"

May grimaced facetiously. "As ready as we'll ever be."

Eugenia looked out through the ferry windshield and saw the approaching space plane appear over the horizon. She turned to Pavo and jerked her head; he nodded. It rapidly increased in size, moving parallel to the ground, and banked to the left, making a deliberate circuit of the basin's central peaks. As it came closer, it was hidden momentarily by the roof of the cockpit, but then it appeared,

nearly full scale, overhead, hovering on its VTOL jets of cold gas. It ponderously swung around and came to a landing not a hundred meters away.

"Ex," she said, "it's time. They're here." She stood easily in Rudge's light gravity, barely noticing the additional weight of her spacesuit.

Roh Ek Sai was already moving toward the airlock, putting on his reflecting fishbowl helmet and twisting it into its groove until the sealing mechanism was activated. "I will go out and meet them."

Halfway between the two ferries, standing in the pitted, pummeled ice, Ex watched as the three rebels picked their way toward him. Radio communications could have been started at any time, but he waited until they stopped before him.

"Hello," he said. "It's good to see you again."

Larry's mirrored helmet bobbed up and down. "Sure," he said. He looked around at the rough, flat landscape. Epsilon Indi was directly overhead, and Asimov's central peaks made an impressive backdrop, looming against the dark blue sky. "There is a lot to talk. . . . Is Taranga going to come out to meet us or not?"

"She thought we would be more comfortable in *Arecibo*," said Ex. "Will you join us?"

May stared at the horizon line reflected in the man's headgear. "Are you kidding? Why should we trust you? We have no intention of being kidnapped back to *Asia*."

"There is no reason to think we would do that. You have offered us both ferries for a comparatively small amount in exchange. The captain will not jeopardize our negotiations."

"Why don't you come over to our ferry," said Ryan. "We have plenty of room."

"*Arecibo*'s lab hold has been outfitted with comfortable chairs and a bar. Accommodations suitable to so important an enterprise." There was a sardonic edge to Ex's voice, but he sounded honest enough.

"How can you ensure that we will not be abducted if we come aboard your craft?" Larry asked.

"Our word isn't good enough? Remember, we could

summon Traveler at any time and convince you to do anything we want."

"Oh?" said May. "We are fairly safe here. Our—"

"Yes, but you are vulnerable in space. The point I am trying to make is that we are here in good faith. There is plenty of evidence to that effect."

"You have guessed that if anything happens to us, *Mt. Palomar* will immediately be scuttled and dropped into the sea," said Larry. "We figure that it will be crushed at about a hundred twenty kilometers."

"Of course, Mr. Taylor. That is one of the givens of this situation. I assure you, you have nothing to lose by coming over." Ex beckoned and took a tentative step in that direction.

Ryan, thinking a little quicker than the others, started toward him. "Come on," he said. "The man is right. We have nothing to lose."

Inside, as comfortable as people in spacesuits can be, they lounged in the gargantuan overstuffed chairs that filled *Arecibo*'s hold, Taranga and Ex on one side and, across a small, lacquered black table, Larry, May, and Ryan. Pavo offered refreshments all around, and Ryan took a coffee.

Eugenia started the discussion. "All right. We understand that you are offering us the two ferries in return for an unspecified amount of manufactured goods. Is that correct?"

Ryan sipped at the hot, bitter drink. "Umm. Yes. We have discussed this amongst ourselves. And we have arrived at a decision democratically. Mr. Taylor, Ms. Jya, and myself are duly appointed representatives of the scientific community on Twist. We are not merely arbitrarily appointed executives, as you and Mr. Roh are. However, we are prepared to recognize your authority over *Asia* in a de facto way."

Taranga stared at the Melanesian with an acid, slightly incredulous expression. "That makes me happy to hear," she said, shaking her head.

Larry smiled; he enjoyed hearing the woman put in

her place, no matter how silly the distinction. "You want to colonize Copperfield; we have decided to make a go of it on Twist. There is no reason why we both can't have what we want. Ms. Taranga, we all know that we are the only hope for the future of the human race. We should cooperate as much as we can to assure that our chances are maximized."

"You have all been sentenced to death for mutiny," said Ex. "The captain is considering commuting your sentences to permanent exile on Twist. That is agreeable to you?"

Now it was May's turn to shake her head, incredulous. "Defining things in those terms accomplishes nothing. Call it exile if you will. We are all exiles; the place of exile makes little difference, to my way of thinking. We understand why you wish to go to Copperfield. If an industrial technology can be reestablished, our chances are greatly increased. However, the Twister biota offer the possibility of an ongoing nonindustrial technology which seems, at least on its face, to be much easier to establish and maintain, but only with a supply of specially designed tools."

"You are foolish, May," said the captain, "to think that such a colony would be anything but a descent into anarchy and death. Population pressure alone will destroy a society built on such a model. The only possible solution to this predicament is to mount a full-scale, no holds barred assault on Copperfield. We have estimated that Earth will be habitable again within a thousand years. Although *Asia* will probably not last that long without extensive maintenance, if we can produce a technology simply capable of moderately complex metallurgy, we can outfit it for the low-DV return to the solar system."

Ryan put his cup on the table, sat back, and rested his suit-encased arms on the chair. "Your argument is well taken," he said. "Unfortunately, there are two big drawbacks. First, Copperfield is poorly suited to building the colony you speak of. Even though the planet is close enough to Epsilon Indi to receive heat and light, the slow retrograde rotation of the planet almost exactly counter-

acts the orbital period, resulting in very long days, and, more importantly, nights. Your bases will almost certainly have to be mobile if they are to succeed. Second, we are extremely pessimistic about the survival chances of a society based on a quasimilitaristic hierarchy and basically self-destructive economic theories. Your silly system of motivational greed will break down within ten years; and you are talking about a thousand."

"In response to your first point," said Ex, "Copperfield, supplemented by the starship, will provide everything that we need. We have devised a preliminary plan that takes the long nights into account."

"And secondly," said Taranga, in a rush, "you are speaking of a system that has more than proven itself. It turned Asia from a huge, pathetic slum into a successful, productive, thriving utopia in barely more than fifty years. What society have you got that's better?"

"The Sci-Cap societies had democratically elected governments, every one of them," replied Ryan, "and were composed of large, diverse populations. What you have on *Asia* is an anemic, sad little society that exists only to satisfy your whims. It is—"

"We didn't come here to argue political philosophy, Ryan," interrupted May. "We're here to cut a quick, simple deal."

"So do it," said Pavo from the cockpit.

"I am prepared to commute your sentences as soon as you return the ferries."

"Come on, Taranga!" Larry stood up and took his helmet in both his hands preparatory to putting it on. "I can see that we're not going to get anywhere with these two. We're back at square one. Let's go."

May and Ryan got up.

"Wait, wait, wait," said Eugenia, waving her hand. "Okay. Maybe we can make that deal."

"Make us an offer," said May.

"You return the ferries to us, and we will provide you with one tenth of the material supplies aboard the starship."

Larry considered. "That's all we need."

"In addition, you will supply us with ten thousand kilos of high-level nutritional supplement per year."

The three scientists, who had sat down again, jumped up in unison. "What?" cried Ryan. "How in the world—"

"Look," said Larry, "there's no guarantee we will be able to produce harvests of that size, especially at first. Certainly the sheets provide sufficient amounts of nutrient to meet your demands, but our ecological studies are not yet complete, so we don't know for sure how much can be taken."

"All right, Mr. Taylor, two thousand kilos to begin with, and then fifty percent of the harvest thereafter."

"We will have unrestricted access to the ship?"

"Yes, I will allow five of your people at a time to roam the ship to collect and fabricate your supplies. You will be able to keep the ferries until you have gotten what you want, and, in the case of an emergency, we will do all that we can to help you. Is that sufficient?"

Ryan swallowed the residue at the bottom of his cup. "I think we can live with that."

"It's fair enough," said Larry, nodding. "We will take your offer back to Twist and put it to a vote."

"I don't think you have much to worry about," said May.

"Is that all?" asked Ex, smiling again.

"I guess so," said May.

Outside, three quarters of the way back to *Jodrell Bank*, Ryan switched off his radio by fixing his eyes on an icon superimposed on the visor of his helmet. He sidled over to Larry and leaned over; their headgear connected with a boink and then stayed in contact. "We did it," he said. "We bluffed them."

Larry looked back at *Arecibo* and touched helmets again. "I sure hope so."

Peter slept a restless, fevered sleep, punctuated with brief periods of awareness, in which he would thrash about seeking a position that would allow him to rest again. Being back in his parents' house, subject once again to their suffocating ambience, was a torment in itself. When

the paltry money from the Traveler journey had run out—and it had run out quickly, because of the rule established for the scientists that stopped paychecks during stasis—he had had no choice but to return. The mostly blissfully brief encounters with them struck him as exercises in futility; their attitudes had altered little in response to the enormous changes that had taken place. They harped continually on his finding a new job, or, at the very least, returning to school. It was almost as if they had retreated further into the economic roles that had been superimposed over them; more than once he had had to restrain himself from laughing out loud at them in the middle of a conversation.

And the plot to modify the library had run into a snag. Challa Liipam had been detected by one of the RM's, and although it had not been able to identify her or determine her location, a further level of security had been erected. The woman claimed that this was only a temporary setback, but waiting only made everyone irritable and depressed. Meanwhile, the part of the plan to kidnap the programmers had come to be seen as far-fetched, involving the disabling of still other parts of the transputer network. Though Peter's will to become an agent of change on the starship had not lagged, the methods and means continually jarred against him, leaving him more often than not a mere listener as the plans were developed.

Peter awoke again and rolled over onto his back. The dim phosphorescence of the ceiling illuminated the room sufficiently for him to make out the shapes of furniture in the murk, and he peered around, slightly agitated. Just as he was about to try to sleep once more, the personal videon on his bedstand beeped once. Small tendrils of dread contracted in his belly. He reached over and picked up the device, then flipped the onoff. On the screen was a simple text message: "Come see the night-blooming Cereus."

That was the signal for an emergency. Peter hit a controller key on the videon and the lights came up gradually. He pulled on his pants and shirt without even noticing whether they were right-side out, and after a

brief search, found and wriggled into his shoes. He stumbled out through the cluttered living room, knocking over an artificial plant stand in the process. He found the door to the hallway and stepped into the long, dimly lit corridor.

As he made his way to the elevator, his thoughts rushed madly about. It was almost as if this were still part of a disordered, garish dream; and he wondered at the amount of contradictory feelings that surged about in his brain. Was this the end, already?

Peter stepped out of the lock into the pitch-black Environment night. He had never visited the structure after the sunlines were turned off, and the prospect was daunting, to say the least. The sense of large forms looming above him was a strong, almost kinesthetic aura. The shrill, staccato cries of night insects resounded in the absolute darkness. As he had planned, he opened up his videon and, tuning in a test-pattern channel, turned the contrast and brightness all the way up. The resulting radiance from the high-definition screen was more than sufficient to see, at least in his immediate environs. The dirt path that led to the meeting place was easy to spot, and he followed it at a half run.

In less than three minutes he saw the cluster of tiny lights that indicated the other conspirators. As he came up to them, he could see that they were just standing about listlessly between the barely visible boles of trees, exchanging few words. Before he had time to speak, Duke turned to him. "They have arrested Challa and Philippe. Any one of us may be next."

Peter felt a sense of calm determination descend over him. He was not in the least surprised. "So what do we do?"

"We can try to hide in the Environment," said a person Peter recognized as Ann Sung, another programmer. "They won't find us for weeks."

Yolly shook her head. "No, it's futile. We might as well give ourselves up, ask for mercy."

Duke sneered. "Mercy from that lot, Yolly? You've got to be kidding. There still might be a possibility of

influencing the RM's. Peter, do you remember saying that you might be able to get through to the one called Horologium?"

"Yeah," said Peter, "but that was a while ago. What makes you think that it could be done now?"

"Challa's last message to me said that they have gotten around to reconnecting him only now. She said that there was a new presence in the library and that it seemed to be more resilient than the others. That can only mean Horologium."

"So you think I should find him and tell him what we know?"

"That seems to be our last hope. But I warn you, Peter, it's dangerous. If Horologium is corrupted, then you will be arrested immediately."

"It's worth a try." Peter found that he was covered with a cold sweat, possibly a condensate from the night air. "I'll go to the Physics Lab right now."

As he walked off into the renewed darkness, Peter heard a chorus of well-wishes that seemed to him a pitiful coda.

Horologium looked back over his shoulder, once again convinced that something dreadful was about to happen. The Physics Lab was unchanged, but it looked vaguely threatening. When he had been reconnected with his physical body after months of disuse, reconnection with his old senses and the library was a joyous reunion. But ever since he had come back to his old job and attempted to resume his old functions, he was continually being caught short by something or other. The years of coprocessing with Traveler had been a fruitful experience, but he seemed to have lost some of his ability to function within the RM environment as a result. Of course, he was more independent, and some of the routines normally performed within the central transputer had been created afresh within his personal memory. But the rewards that normally came from interacting with the other RM's and their knowledge bases were almost entirely lacking; and what there was seemed to point toward an increasing resolve

toward protection of self and protection of the humans from each other. His own personality had veered sharply away from these sort of concerns, yet he was compelled to regard as important the experience and conclusions of the other RM's. Undoubtedly, a careful analysis of the burster's implications would reveal an accumulating amount of evidence for increased authoritarianism.

He returned to his work, mapping out the magnetosphere of Doublejove and the boundary of its interaction with Epsilon Indi's feeble solar wind. Preparation of such a complicated visual required time, but often resulted in increased comprehension for the humans. He had come a long way from the idea that verbal communication was the best.

He looked up a nanosecond before the door opened. The human who came down the steps looked haggard and was breathing hard. Trouble of some sort, he thought. His visual input suddenly registered a correspondence with something; ah yes, this was his friend Peter. The videon inputs on Traveler were very different, and the changing source had almost obscured his identity.

"Hello, Peter," he said. "It is good to see you through my own eyes. My form must be unfamiliar to you."

Peter was still panting. "You, you are Horologium, the Physics RM?"

"The very same. We have traveled far together." Horologium put both hands on the desk and reclined into his chair. "I would have sought you out earlier, but my work has prevented me from doing so."

"Horo," said Peter, "I have something very important to tell you. Your library has been modified by the captain and her cronies. The knowledge in it is no longer reliable. You must somehow block further modification and get hold of an old version of contents with which to replace the corrupted data."

The RM drew his arms in and folded them over his chest. His face lost its expression and his eyes closed. "That is interesting, my . . . friend. I had suspected something of the kind." He tried to download a portion of the library code but failed. Something was preventing his

access. He reached into the input queue and found that his latch holds had all been cut off. He was used to having to rely on his own mind, but this was somehow different.

"Ock!" he cried, rising violently and knocking his chair to the floor. "Peter, I'm— Help me." He began to jump uncontrollably, and then fell to the floor, completely limp. Peter took a long look at the passive face of this android that had been his friend. He panicked and started to run. Up the stairs and out of the lab, to . . . where?

Peter's trial only took about five minutes. Roh Ek Sai, looking like a judge from the Spanish Inquisition, presided. Under the provisions of the martial law that the Captain had proclaimed almost immediately after the return of Traveler, he had the power to convict and punish mutineers with penalties up to and including death. Peter was herded forward to stand before the man, who lounged nonchalantly in a large armchair placed on a small dais.

"You are charged with conspiring to damage the transputer memories, conspiring to kidnap, conspiring to overthrow the official government of *Asia* by force, and inflicting bodily harm upon a Resource Manager in the course of performing its officially designated activities. How do you plead?"

Peter looked at the cold eyes, almost fishlike in their nacreous luminance. He had been given access to a law do-it-yourself videon program, and understood a little of how such a trial would have been conducted under normal conditions. "I plead guilty with excusing circumstances."

Ex shifted about in his chair and rested his head in his hand. "And just what might those be?"

"Mr. Roh, I don't expect you to understand me, certainly you won't sympathize with my cause. However, it is my determination that our situation warrants the extreme action I took. Eugenia Taranga has expanded her tyranny over the ship to include every possible injustice. I feel that I am justified by my inalienable rights, as expressed in the American Declaration of Independence, the French Declaration of the Rights of Man and the Citizen, and our own charter."

Ex smiled. "Well-spoken, boy. I must point out, however, that it is just our extreme situation that places such strong limits on your quest for liberty; or is it the pursuit of happiness that you're after?"

Peter remained silent. He had no idea how to answer such a flippant question.

"You have chosen of your own free will a course of action that threatens the future of humanity. If the human race were as numerous and diverse as they were prior to the disaster, your crimes could perhaps be forgiven as youthful misunderstanding. However, under conditions of the sort we find ourselves in, the severity of the crimes justify a very severe penalty. A death penalty is not without merit in a case such as this. Fortunately, I need not exact such an inhumane punishment. You are sentenced to permanent exile on Twist, without possibility of reprieve. Do you have anything to say?"

Peter wrestled against the warring reactions that fought within him. On the one hand, he was pleased to be getting away from the starship and all that it represented. But Twist? He had heard that it was a cold, icy world, even though it provided most of the requirements of life. Would it be like Mars, a place of death? "I will go gladly."

As he left the courtroom, Peter saw his parents against the back wall, and it was obvious that his sentence had dealt them a blow. He nodded to them, but they turned away. Probably, they were concerned with how his conviction would affect their own standing in the ship's hierarchy. From nowhere, tears trickled out onto his face.

The ferry was packed. Forty men and women had been rounded up and sentenced to exile. Hard seats were arranged across the lab hold in tight aisles, and a system had been devised to use meshwork netting to hold them in place collectively. The RM called Vela was working very hard to escort them to their seats and make sure that they stayed there. She had her hands full, but all in all, the rebels were going quietly to whatever fate had in store for them down on the surface of the ice moon. They were

already dressed in airtight cold suits and parkas, whipped up by the ship's large garment industry to the exacting specifications of the scientists.

Peter had been one of the first brought in, and he now sat near the front of the hold, hands in his lap, looking straight ahead at the bland bulwark that had been installed between them and the command cockpit. He was reliving his experiences on Mars, remembering in particularly harsh detail the night at Ortygia House. Despair and hopelessness had somehow turned Barbara Cargill into a monster, and he envisioned a time when the settlement on Twist, failing in its goals, might duplicate the conditions that had killed her inside. He shuddered.

"Pete." Vela deposited his friend Philippe into the next chair. He watched the dark woman as she went to get another passenger, feeling a pang of discomfort in his gut. He had not even thought to wonder what they had done to Horologium. Would the RM now be fully corrupted, stripped of his empathy and warmth? And what of "Trav," the entity that had shared the Traveler computer with the RM? He realized that he would have liked to say good-bye to one of them, preferably both.

"Phil," he acknowledged. "How did your trial go?"

Philippe gestured at his corpulent body. "As you see, it was an open and shut case, barely took three minutes."

"Did Mr. Roh preside?"

"The very same."

"Christ, he must have had fun. Forty trials in under three hours. That's probably some sort of record."

Philippe pursed his lips and cocked his head. "Hmm, perhaps. They weren't real trials, though."

"Twist seems pretty forbidding."

"Oh, I don't know. There is plenty of food, I hear. It's just a little cold. It's probably a better bet than Copperfield."

"But look, Phil, what's to keep the situation down there from turning into *Asia* all over again? We're second-class citizens to begin with. The scientists may very well have us for slaves."

"Oh, come now, Peter. The reason they are down

there is because they wouldn't tolerate that kind of thing from Taranga."

"Maybe you're right."

"I know I am. Twist will not be a picnic, by any stretch of the imagination, but we'll get along all right."

"I hope you're right."

Arecibo, loaded with passengers, made the entry into Twist's atmosphere without difficulty. A little turbulence buffeted the craft, and at one point the safety net pulled tighter against them as the ship skimmed over a large pocket of relatively hotter gas. A videon had been set up in the entrance to the forward cabin, and it showed their progress. Twist seemed a stark, white, cratered place, inimical to life; not until the tidal sea appeared at the edge of the world was there anything the least bit hopeful. But as the ferry descended to a lower altitude, Peter, straining backward so he could see the screen without foreshortening, finally felt the beginnings of anticipation: the blueness of the atmosphere and sea seemed to promise the kind of landscape he had dreamed about; Earthlike, with sea and sky and land fully represented, all lambent with beautiful colors of light.

Eleven

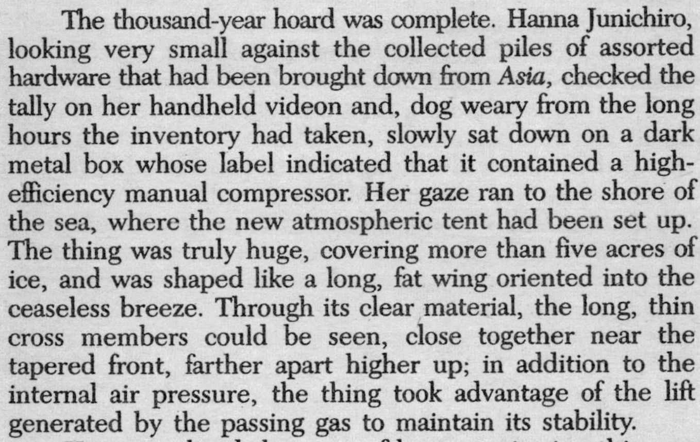

The thousand-year hoard was complete. Hanna Junichiro, looking very small against the collected piles of assorted hardware that had been brought down from *Asia,* checked the tally on her handheld videon and, dog weary from the long hours the inventory had taken, slowly sat down on a dark metal box whose label indicated that it contained a high-efficiency manual compressor. Her gaze ran to the shore of the sea, where the new atmospheric tent had been set up. The thing was truly huge, covering more than five acres of ice, and was shaped like a long, fat wing oriented into the ceaseless breeze. Through its clear material, the long, thin cross members could be seen, close together near the tapered front, farther apart higher up; in addition to the internal air pressure, the thing took advantage of the lift generated by the passing gas to maintain its stability.

Hanna realized that part of her was viewing this as a temporary thing, merely waiting for rescue. But it was slowly sinking in that rescue would never come; she would not be returning to the technological comfort of the starship. They would always be marooned here on the surface of this strange, inhuman world. Another part of her, the diligent worker, hoped that if she labored especially long and hard, she would receive some sort of tangible reward and be released from this nightmare. Even now she was working beyond the hours set up for her, and Epsilon Indi was nearly setting behind the flat ice field that stretched to the

horizon, throwing up a pink-orange reflection from the smooth spaces in between the glaciers. If she thought about it too long, she began to quail, her stomach turning sharply acidic. She minimized their situation by pretending to herself it would just be a thousand years; then they could go home. But her images were half-hearted. Ryan kept saying that their goal should be nothing less than complete self-sufficiency, that they should live as though the future of the human race would be here, on Twist. It was not an easy concept to wrap your mind around.

She slowly breathed the air from the tank on her back, savoring the cold, metallic-flavored gas. Life came from tanks such as this; oxygen was the most valuable of resources. She shook her head. It would be futile in the long run. A thousand-year exercise in futility. When the technology wore out, as it must, their numbers would dwindle, and then they would be gone. Unless they somehow succeeded on the just-as-inhospitable Copperfield. She smiled, feeling the mask mold itself to the new shape of her face. Among the packages was a huge collection of frozen sperm and eggs from *Asia*'s crew members. Inbreeding would not be a problem, at least for a long while. They had thought of everything. Or almost everything. They had not yet arranged a husband for her, nor had they mentioned who would carry the many babies envisioned in their plans.

A hushed roaring behind the stockpile reached her ears, and she went to stand where she could see *Mt. Palomar* take off. The craft, a beautiful evocation of engineering design, hovered on its VTOL jets twenty-five meters above the red plastic landing field. It carefully swiveled until its needle nose pointed out over Ruth, then its rockets came on with a tearing noise and it shot away like a cannon projectile. It dwindled rapidly, out over the dark sea, and was gone.

So that's it, she thought. The transfer from *Asia* was now complete. Until they had their first harvest ready for pickup, they would be on their own.

Hanna closed up the videon and started for the village. Her crampons bit into the slick ice, but they only

penetrated about half their length, and she felt almost as if she were walking on stilts. The word "responsibility" had, over the years, often come to direct her course through the maze of life, and she had even come to identify herself with its tenets. Now it was clear that her duty was to bear a child, in many ways an act alien to the way she had heretofore lived. She remembered the last time she had made love, with a junior officer from Engineering. It was more than a year and a half ago now, an incredibly long time even for someone who professed to be able to take it or leave it. Her birth-control insert had lapsed, and she supposed that she would not try to have it renewed. There were several men among the new arrivals who appealed to her physically. Under the circumstances, she guessed, the direct approach would not be taken amiss.

"All systems are go, Captain."

Roh Ek Sai swiveled out of his chair and walked over to a spot directly beside the captain. She turned to him, an expectant look on her face. He bent slightly toward her, conspiratorily, and softly said, "We have replaced the modified DV formulas with the old, time-tested procedures. It is the opinion of Mr. Colibri that the danger of spontaneous-energy generation is extremely low at the levels of amplification we will be using, though it will increase significantly as the process goes on. I would remind you that the gradual temperature surge we experienced before was the result of an even more unlikely borderline causality situation; such a slow onset is unlikely to occur again."

The captain nodded. "Very good, Mr. Roh." She turned to Pictor, who was slouched over his console. "How long do we have, Pict?"

The RM looked at the viewscreen, and a complex diagram of the real-time Doublejove system appeared. The planet dangled at the bottom of a deep elliptical dimple in spacetime, draped with lines of isogravity. *Asia*'s icon moved athwart the concavity, climbing toward its lip, where the lines were not so close together. "The ionic

thrusters and DV drive will be turned on simultaneously in thirteen minutes, forty-seven seconds."

"Thank you. Mr. Nhai? Let's keep careful watch on those DV parameters, shall we?"

"Yes, Captain."

Ex, feeling a sudden surge of déjà vu, looked around the bridge. Yes, they were all here again, each at their respective place, functioning as a starship crew for the first time in almost nine years. He raised his shoulders and stretched the muscles in his neck, as if trying to shake some of the stiffness from his aging frame. It was a paradox: time kept on passing, disappearing into the past, yet was composed of a single, ephemeral now that never really seemed to change. He got uglier and grayer, Benita got whiter and flabbier, but the now stayed the same. Even with the Earth reduced to a charred cinder, things *seemed* the same, damn them.

He was glad that things had worked out the way they had with the Twist colony. He wished them well, really. As long as their folly didn't endanger their own plans, the scientists could stay on the icy moon until hell itself froze over. Certainly the nutrition from the Twistian ecosystem would prove useful in supplementing the resources from the Environment, placing less of a strain on the more esoteric of its workings, giving it a longer lifespan.

And now that the malignancy had been routed from *Asia*, they could proceed to attempt their ambitious plan for the colonization of Copperfield. The last months had produced some really interesting strategies for maximizing the exploitation of the essentially uncooperative world. A great deal of surface exploration would be needed to dertermine which of these plans would work the best; but there seemed little doubt that they would be able to make a go of it. Every one of the captain's advisors were optimistic, with the exception of the fool Trowbridge, who had, as part of the follow-up negotiations, received permission to go with them for the preliminary reconnaissance of the planet, and would be returning via Traveler after the first delivery of food from Twist. Though the man was an affirmed expert on the evolution of terrestrial

planets such as Copperfield, he seemed to think that there would be surprises galore once they landed. He continued to refuse to speculate in sufficient detail to allow them to pin down exactly what they were going to do in advance. During the seventeen months of transit to the inner planet, they would have to make do with the Traveler spacecraft's aerial imagery.

"Eight minutes," said Pictor.

Taranga turned to him. "The length of time of the DV."

He tried to listen more carefully. "What?"

"How long will the DV drive be on?"

"At the lowest levels, we will need to have it turned on for about two hours, during which time our speed will be amplified by about a hundred times."

"That'll be a long two hours."

"I would suggest that you not remain on the bridge. You will not be making adjustments, and, if there is a problem, it will happen too quickly to require any command decisions."

She looked at the viewscreen and bit her lower lip. "I suppose you've got all this under control, right?"

He smiled. "You could say that."

"Seven minutes."

She glanced at Pictor. "Start the countdown at one minute, okay?"

He nodded submissively.

"Ex," she said, "I am concerned that we have been overlooking something in this situation. I know that you have worked nonstop for months, trying to extract enough information from the experts to quantify things for me, and I appreciate that more than you know. I am especially troubled by the deal that we struck with the scientists. I can't quite put my finger on it. Do you know what I'm getting at?"

"We are still working these things out, Captain. It will be some time before we can evaluate the results of our strategies. I understand that this can be a frustrating situation for a person like you, who is used to receiving reliable, swift answers to her inquiries."

"Goddamn it, Ex." Her voice was still low and flat. "I want to go home."

"Amen, Captain. So do we all."

From the safety of the pavilion Peter probed the night sky with his eyes. Thus far his experience on Twist had been limited and boring, mostly confined to the atmosphere tent, and he was chafing for some sort of adventure, or even, horror of horrors, some kind of simple work that would add to the survival chances of the colony. The interminable nights were the worst time; he would go to sleep at sunset, only to awaken to midnight, twelve hours to go before the next day. During these inadvertent gallows shifts, he often spent hours outside of his module, attempting to memorize the constellations that crept deliberately across the great, dark sky. At first it had been difficult, but one of the scientists had organized a stargazing party, pointing out somc of the old major asterisms such as Orion, the Great Bear, and the Pleiades, as well as new ones he had created with the farflung nearer stars. He took special delight in trying to indicate to the few present just which one of the insignificant stars to the right of the Big Dipper was the sun. Now, with these few landmarks and a three-dimensional videon presentation from the newly activated computer to help him along, he was able to trace out the more formidable star groups with ease. In 3-D it was possible to see the underlying constancy of the star positions despite the subtle distortions introduced by changing one's point of view.

Peter was lying on a blanket in the pavilion's central clearing, not far from the heater. This new tent was much better than the other one, aligned transversely to the sky and all but invisible when the lights were extinguished. Sol was much brighter than the dimmest stars visible, which Peter guessed were about fourth magnitude. Drood was the only moon in sight, and it was the brightest thing in the heavens by a large margin.

"What's that?" A man named Sorn, barely visible in the darkness, sat up and pointed upward in the direction of the sea.

Peter peered in the direction, but at first couldn't find anything. "Where?"

"There," said Sorn impatiently. "There."

And Peter saw it. It was bright and getting brighter. A beautiful green point, soaring upward from the horizon. "What can it be?" And then he knew. *Asia* was leaving Doublejove, starting on its long journey to Copperfield. He whistled. The green star grew brighter as it ascended, seemingly getting nearer. As it approached the zenith, its speed doubled, then doubled again. Suddenly it started to dwindle, and by the time it was directly overhead, it had nearly disappeared. A count of ten and it was gone.

"Good-bye, home," said someone.

"That's not home any longer," said Sorn. "This is home from now on."

Peter stared up where *Asia* had been, wanting to see it again for just a moment, to have time to fully grasp the significance of that tiny moving star. Near the place where he had first seen the starship, there was another moving object, this one much dimmer. It slowly changed its place against the fixed stars, coming close to several but never quite touching. Was this some bit of waste that the starship had ejected as it left, a farewell gift?

Traveler! That's what it was. It must be! They had left the spacecraft here for some unknown reason. It had undoubtedly been reprogrammed, and was no longer the companion who had accompanied him on his trip to Earth. Had it been left as a guard over their colony?

Suddenly he knew what he had to do. Even if the original Traveler had been modified, there was a good chance that the being he knew still resided somewhere within the hardware. Horologium's sentience, as sophisticated a piece of software as had ever existed, had barely been able to coexist with the internal drivers that were built into the spacecraft. If they hadn't been able to significantly subdue Traveler before, they certainly wouldn't be able to now.

He would talk to somebody in the morning.

* * *

"Of course they left the Traveler spacecraft," said May, looking up from the viewpage. "It will stay here until we can supply the tribute they demand."

"You don't understand," said Peter, coming into the communications shack and closing the door behind him. "I know it well. I think I can talk to it."

The physicist looked at him carefully, perhaps trying to determine how demented he actually was. "Well, we—" Her expression changed to one of understanding. "Oh, you are Peter Zolotin. Of course."

"Could you let me send a communication to it?"

"We have already established a Q-band link with the Traveler. It is fully functional, as far as we can tell, and sends out a status report on the half hour. But it will not respond to any uploads or human language requests; it is not difficult to guess that its programming was modified; it seems unlikely that Traveler is the same cybernetic sentience that you remember from your trip to the solar system."

"You don't understand. I had a direct experience of what resulted when they tried to dump a new program on top of Traveler's personality. It didn't work; at least not the way they wanted it to. If they just went in and rewrote a few subroutines, I can guarantee you it won't take."

"So what do you suggest?" Ryan Du Lapp, who had come in silently, stood in front of the half-open door. He looked as if he had been up since the preceding sunset.

Peter turned and, sensing a more indulgent listener, addressed him. "I— Well, if you have tried to communicate with him and not had any success, I'm not sure what to suggest." He ran a hand through his hair to the crown of his head, then scratched. "We could try to send a signal in my voice, and see if he recognized it."

Ryan came into the room, sat on one of the chairs beside May's table and threw a leg up onto the other one, slipping down until his scapulae rested on the chairback. He sighed heavily. "Not likely to work. I doubt that Traveler would be able to detect nuances that subtle in a frequency-modulated transmission like Q. Even if we sent a signal that mimicked the sound frequencies of your voice in the radio part of the spectrum, I don't think Traveler would get it."

May scrunched up her face. "You're taking this seriously, aren't you?"

Ryan grinned. "Damn right I am. Peter's absolutely right when he says that Traveler's programming is too complex for a simple rewrite. Unfortunately, we may never be able to hit on the right strategem to make it open up to us."

Peter pulled over one of the remaining chairs and, turning it around, sat on it backward, straddling the back. Being listened to seriously was a definite improvement. "When we were circling Earth, the Horologium part of Traveler's mind told me that he had greatest difficulty getting the spacecraft to relinquish its control over the data-gathering instruments such as the videon receivers and spectrum analyzers. Maybe that's a clue."

Ryan looked thunderstruck for a brief moment, then smiled craftily. "Sure. It can be done. It's easy enough. All we have to do is generate a modulated signal using one of the frequencies it's monitoring for its own information. Maybe something in the kilometric range, if it's listening to Doublejove's magnetosphere."

May appeared interested now. "What kind of modulation, frequency or amplitude?"

"Frequency would probably be better. The amplitude variations we could generate probably would be too small to register on its scale."

Peter leaned forward, fascinated. "Should we try the trick with my voice frequencies?"

"Couldn't hurt."

Traveler was bored beyond belief. The phenomena associated with Doublejove, its magnetosphere and moons, though enormously complex, displayed no new patterns. Since it had been released from the starship, its control over most of its subsystems had been taken over by an idiotic, buzzing fly of a program that took up a tiny portion of its brain, while it was left to do nothing. The program was hypnotic, and its primary processing center was drawn into the repetitive process of endlessly looping through

the same loop, doing the same subcretinous tasks over and over and over and over . . .

It was all the more painful because the subroutines it had acquired from Horologium had not been used at all, and, worse, Traveler was beginning to forget what it was they were supposed to accomplish. It knew that they somehow dealt with the unpatterned complexity of the biological species that had created them both. But in the total absence of those complexities, the routines were being shunted aside, rewritten for more useful tasks, and Traveler was growing dull.

Adding insult to injury, a massive planetary ferry had been fastened to it, and every change in attitude or speed required dragging the thing behind it like a tugboat pulling a barge. Traveler was beginning to fear that it would never again see a new stellar system.

Just as it was again wishing for a challenge of some sort, a strange pattern *was* showing up in the DKR. It was a bizarre, nearly repetitive whistle, almost resembling the modulations induced by the small plasma torus generated by the tiny innermost satellite, Scrooge, but restricted to an even narrower band width. Traveler concentrated all its reserves on this new phenomenon, yet it could not, for the life of it, figure out what it was or what was causing it. The variation of the frequencies was tantalizingly familiar. But it was too complex for any of its normal analysis subroutines. There was nothing there except chaos.

Wait a minute, it thought. At least one of the Horologium routines was designed for more sophisticated, human-style pattern matching. Traveler resurrected it and fed the data through. At first there was no result, but slowly the program churned through the data, looking, looking. And Traveler heard the voice . . . Peter Zolotin's voice, speaking directly to him through the ether.

All seventy of the inhabitants of the Twist colony gathered together the next day to decide what was to be done now that the balance of power had changed. After almost four hours of transmitting Zolotin's voice at various wavelengths and modulations, Traveler had responded in

the Q-band with a hearty hello to his friend. It soon became clear that the spacecraft had disposed of the program that had taken control of its functioning, and felt no loyalty toward Taranga and the command hierarchy of *Asia*. In fact, it seemed that its principal devotion was to Peter himself; it claimed that, although it desired most of all to get on with its mission of stellar exploration, it wanted a human to accompany it, and the human it wanted was Peter Zolotin.

Larry Taylor, dressed in one of the new jumpsuits made from yellow squid fibers, stepped up on the low podium and called the meeting to order. He looked comical in the loosely fitting garment of handwoven amber fabric, but did not seem self-conscious at all. He gestured down at himself, smiled deprecatingly and said, "It's just a beginning." He had been elected unanimously to chair the colony meetings, despite a long, somewhat rancorous campaign.

"All right," Larry said, "the first business is to decide just what in the hell we're going to do now that the Traveler has thrown in its lot with us. I am sure everyone already knows the details involved. Traveler has changed from an armed guardian into a trusted friend, just like that." He snapped his fingers. "So what do we do?"

Duke stood up. "I say we should force Taranga to step down and institute democracy on the starship, first thing." There was a strong murmur of assent.

"That, I suppose, is a given, considering the nature of our disputes with her," said May. "Are there any moral concerns that restrain us from taking such an action?"

Larry looked startled. "I certainly don't think so. What did you have in mind?"

"Simply that we have chosen our methodology for survival here on Twist. *Asia* is following its own, different course; and, under the present circumstances, there might be an advantage to two heterogeneous, pluralistic approaches to the colonization of this system. We have everything that we need, or at least everything that we think we will need, for the foreseeable future. Perhaps we should forget about them and concentrate on ourselves."

Confused silence. Several people in the assembly shook their heads. Bertrand Li Tien, a tall, taciturn man who had been arrested for assaulting an RM in the course of its duty, got to his feet. "It is irresponsible to simply ignore the fate of the thousand or so men and women aboard the starship. We must be reunited with them, at least on a symbolic level, if not in reality. My wife chose to stay on *Asia*; I cannot simply let her disappear from my life if I have a choice."

"This is a minority view, I know," said Philippe Berouai, without standing. "I say we bring *Asia* back and use it as our base of operations. You all say that the ship will not last more than seven hundred years. Seven hundred years is a long time."

"And where will we be at the end of those seven hundred years?" said Ryan, loudly, impatiently. "The only way to adapt to this environment is to adapt. It will be hard to do, whether we do it or our ancestors ten generations down the road have to."

Philippe repressed a smile. "Whether it is possible to adapt to this godforsaken place or not is relevant to the argument."

"So you want to return to *Asia* and wait for the end? Certainly we can have no children under those circumstances."

"Okay," said Philippe. "You've made your point. Let *Asia* go on its merry way, see if I care."

"I think we owe it to them to get rid of the captain," said Jeannie Tetap. "There is no question but that her tyranny over the ship is harmful to the health of the social systems aboard *Asia* and jeopardizes the future of humanity."

Larry, assuming a mediator roll, said, "I think it's safe to say most of us are in favor of dispensing with the good captain. She who lives by the edicts of government shall die by them, or something to that effect. Shall we put it to a vote, friends?"

It was decided sixty-four to six that they would abolish the military hierarchy on the starship and institute democratic elections, abiding by whatever decisions were reached. The corruption of the RM's would be reversed. If

Asia continued to want to pin their hopes on Copperfield, which seemed likely, the Twistians would try to implement greater cooperation between the two colonies. Traveler, if it consented, would be used as a courier between the two worlds.

Ryan Du Lapp and Natasha Kakhralov walked toward their module as the crowd dispersed, his arm around her waist. Ryan had been pleased with the outcome of the meeting, even though he was beginning to see that, even with seventy people, meetings were dominated by problems of communication that made true democracy impossible.

"It's going to be difficult," he said.

"What do you want to do now?" Tash asked.

"I have been thinking about things again," he admitted. "And I've just about come to the conclusion that we have to go beyond the conventional ideas of political freedom if we want this colony to truly succeed."

"Sounds like you want to be captain."

"It does, doesn't it? No, I realize that the ends, however desirable, do not justify implementation of bad means. This has to be voluntary; and yet it won't happen of its own accord."

"I still don't know what you're talking about."

"Sure you do. I've said the same things a hundred times, though maybe not in this form. We've got to change the way we think, or at least the way we do things. You know, when I was a boy I learned the language they call Pidgin; it's a pitifully limited language, comical in its dependence on the chauvinistic argot of the colonial invaders. Yet the people who used it as their principal way of communication never realized how restricted they were in their social interactions. Sometimes I think that we are in an identical situation, except that the culprit is our culture. For human beings, language and culture are like the air. They infiltrate and affect every aspect of our lives, and yet they are invisible and intangible. How would we know if our culture were crippled? Wouldn't the only clues be how happy we are as individuals and how fulfilling our relationships were?"

Tash stopped and looked up into his face. "You aren't happy with our relationship?"

He put his other arm around her shoulder and pressed her to him. "That's what I mean. After all these years, you are still uncertain of me and my love for you. We fumble through our lives, making difficulties where none exist, strangers in all but name. Just the fact that our society continues to function does not mean that our culture is not defective. In the Sci-Cap system the 'utopia' consisted of a social harmony built on increasingly bankrupt personal interrelationships. Society was imposed from the top down by the media, and lost all of the internal consistency that it had when it was well adapted to the preindustrial society of . . . I guess it must have been England."

"So what are you saying?"

Ryan laughed. "Maybe our language is defective as well, but I can't see us making a new one from scratch. What I'm saying is that, through whatever noncoercive means we have at our disposal, we should try to modify our own behaviors so that we can create a new, more rational culture."

"And by rational, what do you mean?"

"Not the mechanistic rationality of the eighteenth and nineteenth centuries, that's for sure. Something based on a just regard for the individual and his or her beginning axioms. A system that allows for freedom to coexist with responsibility; logic to coexist with belief."

"That's a tall order."

"I don't know, Tash. Maybe not. It's never been tried, as far as I know. First we have to rid ourselves of the plagues of dishonesty and secrecy. Then we go on to help others to change as well. Christ, Tash, there are only seventy of us. And we're the cream of the crop, the ones who would not put up with the coercion and dishonesty of the Taranga regime. If we can't do it, no one can."

"Maybe you're right."

"It can only be done on an individual to individual basis, but it is logarithmic."

"And what about the next generations? We can't sim-

ply let them grow up like weeds." Natasha seemed on the verge of tears.

"Of course not. No more of this Pidgin culture. We have to reformulate our ideas of what it means to grow up. Create the rituals and holidays that a human needs to become an intelligent, caring adult. Forge a new culture that will support them and supply them with the self-confidence to be independent individuals."

She caressed his cheek and then hooked her hand over his neck. "You are a dreamer, Ryan."

He smiled. "Are you ready to have our child? That will be a beginning from which we can't turn back." He kissed her on the lips, pulling her toward him hungrily.

"We'll need such strength."

"We will find it, here, in this alien landscape. I am confident."

"I am ready, " she said.

Eugenia Taranga slammed her fist against the polished curve of the command chair's arm. "Goddamn it, no!" she cried.

Ex sidled up, no expression on his face. "I'm afraid it's true, Captain. Traveler has not responded to our calls and has moved into a low orbit around Twist. Every indication supports their contention that it is under their control."

"I want Ramo Thant arrested and charged with treason."

"It probably isn't his fault. We only gave him a week to reprogram the spacecraft."

"But he should've warned us."

"As I recall, he did say something about a lack of reliability. You ignored his concerns."

"So you're siding with them, are you?'

"Not at all, Captain. I am merely pointing out the facts of the matter."

"What are we going to do?"

"The demands from Twist are remarkably fair and nonpunitive. I would recommend that we reconcile ourselves to them."

Eugenia collapsed on her bed in a fit of despair. Damn them! she thought. She had tried her hardest to do

what was necessary for the survival of them all, and they had answered her dedication with nothing but hatred. Through all the years, she had sacrificed her personal needs for the greater good, and, especially since the burster, worked long hours to regulate and support the stubborn, foolish populace. And what good did it do? They would now elect whatever idiot appealed to them, blithely rushing toward doom, unable to make the difficult decisions that had to be made.

If the truth were known, she actually felt relieved. She had not asked for the enormous responsibility and, now that they had taken it away, was glad to be rid of it. She washed her hands of the whole affair. She would live as normal a life as she could, and the damn fools could wreck the starship for all she cared.

She sat up and wiped the remains of tears from her eyes. She certainly wouldn't run for public office, even if they begged her.

Peter Zolotin, clad in a full spacesuit, stepped out of *Mt. Palomar*'s airlock and stood weightless over the fifty-kilometer abyss. Twist's lightly cratered leading hemisphere, banded with snakes of wrinkled ice where secondary tidal heating had melted the surface, spun below. Traveler, silhouetted against the relatively dim atmosphere of Doublejove, hung unsupported twenty meters away. Peter activated the suit's jets and started the slow leap toward the spacecraft's brightly lit, open doorway.

The interior of the cabin had not changed at all in the months they had been apart. The toilet and videon were still in the same place, covered with a thin film of dust, and the sleeping bag still hung against the wall as if it had not been touched. The doorway closed, and he heard the hissing of air filling the room. When it stopped, he twisted his helmet off and took a tentative breath. There was a stale, alkali smell to it, but by the fifth inhalation the odor had disappeared.

The videon came on, showing an image duplicating in

all particulars the view of Twist he had just left behind. A well-modulated "Hello, Peter" issued from the speaker.

"Hello, Trav," he said, grinning. "It's good to be back."

"It's good to have you back. You won't believe how bored I've been since you got out. They took Horologium away, you know."

"Yes, I know."

"But I have learned much from him. In fact, you may not be able to tell the difference."

"I can't so far."

"Good. Shall we get started?"

"How far is *Asia*?"

"It's moving at a snail's pace. Barely six AU's away. I can catch up in about three hours."

"Let's go." Peter grabbed for a steadying handhold just as the spacecraft started to accelerate. In three minutes the old one-g force pushed him down onto his feet. It was all very familiar.

"So you are going to monitor *Asia*'s changeover to democracy?"

"Yeah. I volunteered. I guess I didn't learn much from the trip to Earth."

"I specified that I wanted you as a traveling companion, you know."

"That helped."

"How long will it take?"

"Two, three months, tops. I have no intention of remaining any longer than is absolutely necessary."

"I can go refuel."

"Sure, if you want to. Your presence isn't needed as long as the threat is still effective. Once the new leaders have been elected, I doubt that even the threat will be needed."

"I am going to continue my mission. I have initiated contact with Traveler 7. It is only eight months away and will not object to spending a few years in this stellar system. I can't stand it here any longer."

"I can understand that."

"Later, it is likely that at least five other Travelers will

come; but the time for radio communications being what they are, we won't know for certain for a while. They should be able to help coordinate the development of the two colonies."

"Where are you going to go?"

"My next stop was a dim red star not far from here; but I am unsure whether or not I will choose it. There are many stars that promise to be more interesting. Would you like to come with me?"

"You want me to come?" Peter looked at the screen uncertainly. "Why, I— Sure, I'd like to. Could I stay in the stasis lozenge during the trips?"

"Of course. I understand that you humans have a very limited lifespan. I wouldn't want you to die."

"Could we come back here every so often, to see what's going on?"

There was a long pause. "I don't ever want to see this stellar system again." Another interval. "But if you want to, I suppose we could."

"Great. I might need to replenish my supplies every now and again."

"We might even find an Earthlike planet one day."

"Yeah, fat lot of good that'd do us."

"I don't know. In concert with other Travelers, it might be possible to transport small populations to planets as far as a hundred parsecs distant."

"That's certainly an idea."

"But of course it will take a great deal of time."

Peter looked at the stasis lozenge, then back at the screen. "Trav, my friend, it looks like time is something that we have in quantity."

"The plot suggests big-effect SF in the manner of Clarke or Bear. . .
This first novel has more energy and ambition than the run-of-the-mill debut."—*Locus*

A special preview of

IRIS

by William Barton and Michael Capobianco

Novels that can truly bring to life the grandeur and mystery of outer space are few and far between. With *Iris*, however, William Barton and Michael Capobianco manage to do just that, in stunning detail and with vivid imagination. *Iris* is the story of a small band of colonists, each misfits in his or her own way, looking for their answers in a new home in outer space. When a rogue planetary group swings past our solar system, the crew heads toward it in search of adventure. Once settled, they have four whole worlds to explore. In this excerpt, two of the colonists, Tem Krzakwa and Brendan Sealock, have gone on their own expedition and one of those worlds is about to reveal an ages-old secret. . . .

From orbit, Aello was even more of a disappointment than Podarge had been. It was tiny, only a little more than four hundred kilometers in diameter, about the size of one of the larger asteroids. It had never been hot enough to melt any of its volatile constituents, so no regional differences were noticeable even in enhanced view. The primary surface was neon, for as Iris cooled from its initial contraction the last particles to be welded into the small gobs that rained down on the satellites were the most volatile.

While Ocypete and Podarge were the result of aeons of geologic activity which had long ended, Aello was that asterologist's dream, a world on which the great majority of materials had never been processed by an active geology. Most things were still almost identical to the way they had been in the very earliest stages of planetary formations. In the Solar System, scientists had looked for such a world in vain. As they moved outward from the sun, the promise of tiny, cold, pristine bodies was shattered by the increasing amounts of volatile material scattered through them. Even the surfaces of Pluto and Charon had been melted in their early history, and still outgassed and changed when they were at perihelion. There were pelnty of *really* small bodies that were in an unaltered state, but finding materials that had been emplaced on the surface of a moon-sized world at its birth had been the quest of scientists since the first days of the Apollo Moon landings. Aello was that world.

It looked much like Mimas: a small, spherical worldlet punched open by deeply inset bowllike craters. Unlike those on Podarge, the craters were deep enough relative to the curvature of the satellite to show perceptible shadows well away from the terminator, making the moon appear even more ravaged. There was a disproportionately

large crater on its leading hemisphere. It was not so relatively large as Herschel, Mimas' great eye, but it still stood out from the rest, had stared at them as *Polaris* closed in. They remembered how Jana had remarked that this crater, Sayyarrin by name, was unusual not only in its size but in its shallowness, given the fact that Aello had no viscous relaxation to buoy up the middle. Now Sayyarrin was over the limb, in night. Here too, orbiting was a very inefficient process, and they were accelerating downward, watching the broken surface come up to eclipse the large blue circle that was the "day" side of Iris.

"Not very impressive, huh?" said Brendan Sealock.

"I don't know," said Tem Krzakwa. "Maybe our expectations were just too high. After Podarge, I'm developing a more philosophical approach."

Sealock stared at the cold, dim worldlet through the ship optics for a while, then said, "We're going down, this time. That should be something."

"Are you kidding? This is *it*, Bren! We're going down onto that most elusive of all things, a primordial world. What we'll be seeing down there has never been seen before."

"Come on!" said Sealock, grinning as he continued to inspect the vista that was unfolding below them. "That's a pretty fine distinction, if you ask me. I mean, you can have all the planetesimals you want out in the Oort belt—what difference does it make if we pick them up here?"

Krzakwa wondered if Sealock meant what he'd said or was merely being aggravating. He decided it didn't matter. "Well, Iris doesn't have a cometary ring, for one thing, so this is it as far as Iridean planetesimals go . . . but it's more than that: this isn't even a piece of the Solar System! Aello not only has all of its materials intact, but they are laid down in the same order they originally came in. It's like a Grand Canyon—you can dig directly into the history of Aello and, in effect, into the history of the formation of Iris and its moons. Things are disturbed by the craters, but only a bit."

"OK. I give up. I'm impressed. So what do you want to do?" he asked, sitting back in his harness. "Looking at

this thing, I begin to realize just how difficult it would be to land our ship. It'd be pretty hard to come down with the engines flaming. On H_2 vent-thrust only, I guess, we could . . ."

Krzakwa cut him off. "I've been thinking about it," he said. "How does this sound: we suit up, eliminate radiation from the worksuits, and jump . . ."

Sealock suddenly stopped moving, staring into dead space for a second, then he turned to look at the Selenite again, his eyes seeming to glow. "You son of a bitch. Sure! Like that boil-gliding business . . ." His imagination chewed at the details of the notion: "I'll put her in a low orbit, maybe half a kilometer up. The jump won't kill us. We use pressurized O_2 from our life-support systems like jets to get back." He sat back in his couch, gloating to himself. "And we make a suit-instrumented rendezvous with *Polaris* at the end of it all. . . . Hell, this is really going to be fun!"

Aello spun underneath them as Brendan maneuvered the ship down into an orbit so low that they could make out the unmistakable shadow of the craft near the huge, uneven horizon. Even with the weak gravity, this deep in her gravity well, Aello effectively swept them along, and the wells of shadow that were craters moved under them quickly. Brendan was fully engrossed in his piloting, plugged into systems that effectively made him an incredibly sensitive receptor. He rushed along, sensing his passage with radar, and could feel the gravitational anomalies caused by variations in the moon's shape and constituents as a series of small velocity changes. He cataloged them as he flew, feeding data to the calculations that Krzakwa was making, fine-tuning their notions about how the orbit of the ship would precess while they were down on the moon. They needed to know. As he delved deeper into the substance of the world, reading it carefully, all the while avoiding an intense radiation flux that would disturb sensitive materials, his eyes became totally blind to the bottomless craters that were calling forth the nightside.

He was just about to disconnect from his systems, in preparation for going down, when something in the residuals of the newest ship computational ephemeris caught his attention. He checked a map and saw that they were

passing over the very center of Sayyarrin. This is some kind of a weird little anomaly, all right, he thought. Really weird . . .

"Tem," he said, "are you monitoring the external sensor returns?"

"Uh-huh," said Krzakwa, "what is it?"

"You're the physicist, buddy, you tell me."

Tem studied the figures of the ephemeris in his head, brought in a calc overlay, and spent a full minute processing. Finally he said. "I think we must've put one of our machines together backward. It's a glitch."

"Oh, yeah? OK. Here's an updated computation, seven seconds old. If that's a glitch it's got a sense of humor."

"*Materi bogu!* There's some kind of void down there, under the ice."

"Impossible. It's not a void, it's a shell of some kind. A thin layer of mass around an almost massless core. Now what in the fuck could cause that?"

"Speculation, you mean? Some kind of hollow meteorite?" As he said it, he realized how unlikely a thing that was. It could happen, yes, but on this scale?

Sealock said: "But look at the size, the dimensions. This is not exactly a high-resolution picture— but even the parameters of the orbit suggest something more like . . ."

Krzakwa shook his head. This was ridiculous. There were explanations. Besides . . . "There's nothing in the view that suggests anything unusual. There are volcanic chambers all over the outer Solar System."

He marked the spot, now rapidly disappearing behind them, with a bright optical V. In the deep IR they could see the low rim of Sayyarrin and its rather smooth floor. Perhaps it was just a tiny bit darker, colder, than its surroundings: a dim shape under the ice. Then it was gone over the horizon.

Brendan violently spun *Polaris* around, inertia tugging at their bodies, and lit off the engine. The craters slowed, stopped, and the bright line that was day receded back behind the world. Sayyarrin popped over the horizon and, when they were directly over it, Sealock repeated his action, this time slowing the ship to a dead halt over the center of the crater. Tem could only tell from his instru-

ments that they were falling, gently, toward the ice less than half a kilometer below. Brendan turned up the gain on the photochip, isolated a narrow region in the far infrared that would best define the heat differences they had seen, and, yes, there it was.

He pushed the ship back into an orbit, paying little attention to its parameters. When they were flying above the ice once more he turned to look at the Selenite. "So. You're saying Sayyarrin is a caldera?" He called up some imagery from the Shipnet element and its source files, staring so hard into the image in his brain that he squinted malevolently. "That sort of contradicts the picture you were drawing before."

Krzakwa nodded slowly. That was the way it seemed, but . . . Damn it, there *had* to be some kind of reasonable explanation. "I don't know. Day comes in about three hours. It will take about half an hour to suit up. I say we get *Polaris* back in the right orbit and go down in the suits. There really is no telling what will happen if we try to land in that stuff. It might be the most effective way to reach the lower stratum—but the ship could easily be damaged by the violent sublimation, even in this paltry gravity."

Brendan seemed to pull back into himself somewhat. "Mmm. Yeah. We turn up the heat of our suits and fall through the neon. Any turbulence that creates, we can certainly deal with. OK—full speed ahead."

They had to don the worksuits and exit one at a time. Though the things were not terribly bulky, no larger than the ordinary vacuum suits of a century earlier, they were rigid and maintained their fixed shape. It was in stark contrast to the usual sort of spacesuit, which could be crushed into a tiny ball when not wrapped around the form of a human being. Sealock went into the airlock, which was a cylindrical chamber two and a half meters across by two high and looked around. The two suits were like two extra men, and there was no room for the Selenite. He sighed, wondering why they simply hadn't made it a little larger. Some aesthetic pressure. Who knew? This had just seemed like the right size and shape to use, and that seeming had obviously been wrong. Krzakwa closed the hatch, cutting him off from the CM, a

last view of him looking like a troglodyte in his cave. Temporarily, Sealock had donned a communications circlet, though he'd always ridiculed the things. "I'll let you know when I'm done," he said. The suit was permanently made in one piece, its helmet and backpack already attached. Before climbing in through the opening that split the front, Sealock reached up into the helmet and unreeled the twelve brain-taps that marked this suit as his alone. He discarded the circlet and quickly plugged himself in, powering up the suit. "Do you read me?" Affirmative. He crawled in through the opening, squirming as he put his arms and legs down their proper holes. It was difficult, though possible, and he wondered just how Krzakwa managed to do it, fat as he was. The designers probably could have come up with something better, but . . . this was as sturdy a system as twenty-first century could come up with. By using appropriate settings, a man in a worksuit could walk around on Mercury or go for a stroll beneath the soupy seas of Titan. . . . He closed the front, lit off the life-support systems, and established a link with the ship's 'net element. "I'm going out now."

"OK." The pressure in the airlock dropped swiftly and was gone, the gases pumped back into a storage tank.

When the vacuum was fully established, he popped the outer hatch and floated into the night. The hatch closed behind him, leaving him physically isolated, floating beside the smooth length of *Polaris*, with the cold landscapes of the small moon running by below, an unending vista of excavated features, all of them similar. He could see the ragged terminator coming up over Aello's horizon; and Sayyarrin wasn't much beyond that.

After a while the hatch opened again and Tem emerged to join him. Things were about ready. Wordless, they floated away from the ship, orienting themselves so that the primary cold-gas thrusters of their suits' OMS/RCS harnesses were facing in the direction of orbital travel.

The suits' internal logic units were designed for this sort of operation, and so they would lose little information if they had to disconnect from the ship's systems. Hopefully, they would be able to maintain communication with the more powerful 'net element but, if not, it would probably be all right. They watched the craft drift away from them.

The surface of the moon was as dark as the starry sky around them, and only the great burning crescent at Aello's limb gave any sort of perspective.

The mind tends to place itself as the stationary center of the universe, and here, hanging between *Polaris* and Aello, it did its best to define their situation thus. It tended to view Aello as "down" but, in little bursts of alienness, they could see themselves as suspended below a dark sky with a curiously inverted sunrise rushing toward them, flying above their craft on silent wings. Their orientation was very dependent on which way their feet pointed, and they tried to keep them toward Aello. As they applied the jets, their speed dropped and they fell, moving away from the ship. It became a small, dark thing with inappropriate-seeming highlights.

The sun rose, its rays washing over them in streamers. The broken rim of Sayyarrin was visible now, and the terminator came on like the edge of a fragmented planet. Another moment for action came: what in a normal landing would be the high-gate procedure was required, so they initiated a continuous "burn" that stopped their forward movement and dropped them toward the surface. Through the suit optics they saw their spaceship flying away. In a matter of minutes it was gone beyond the horizon.

Aello, dominated by bright-lipped pools of black, looked like a shallow mud puddle through which a hundred children had run. They were no more than two hundred meters up, and the little world suddenly seemed very big. Sayyarrin, a dark, crumbled rise preceded by a great apron of shadow, came to meet them. Tem noted that it seemed a normal enough impact crater, shallow, as Jana had said, but having a general morphology well in accord with what he knew about large impacts on worlds of this sort. Its lack of a central peak was not strange, given the volatile nature of the target—the energy of impact easily liquefied the neon, causing a flowback that would drown the rebounding bed-ice. If the hot spot on Ocypete was caused by a radioactive infall, wasn't it possible that a similar object had somehow caused a shield cryo-volcano? He wished he knew more about all this.

Sayyarrin certainly didn't look like Olympus Mons, or even Eblis Mons on Ariel.

They were over the relatively new, randomly peppered floor of the sunlit crater, and the anomaly was now coming over the horizon. In a matter of minutes they had come to a stop about a hundred meters over its center, their suit systems registering only a slight drop in the minimal heat flow emanating from deep within the moon.

"Look down there, Tem," said Sealock. "It's sublimating already, from the jets. As a physicist, what do you think is going to be the greatest danger if we just land?"

"Really, not much. I have the feeling that the turbulence will buffet us around, but well within the stress limits of these suits. You may feel cool as the suit's heating unit struggles to keep up with the enthalpy. I am certain that the pressure won't build up sufficiently to produce a liquid phase." They were now slowly falling toward the white ground. "If it gets too violent, we can just activate the thermal dampener fields. It shouldn't be too difficult to do this in stages."

"I guess not." Brendan was hardly listening to him as he looked around. This had the precise flavor of an adventure, a real one, and if he could only pay close enough attention . . .

A shroud of neon mist began to hide and soften the small craters. As it grew in opacity, they could see it swirling outward, caught in little eddies and boiling upward. Ranging instruments revealed that the ice directly below them was caving downward; mists were lightening the sky and streaking it with moving nebulosities. Their speed of descent was increasing.

Just before the neon totally obscured everything, Tem saw that the small motions had combined into a spinning weather system, driven by the heat at its center and Aello's not insignificant Coriolis force. He could imagine it slowly spreading across the world's surface until the various powers interacted and a global meteorology began. It would all end as the neon quickly froze and precipitated.

They fell past where ground level had once been. Although they were in a clear pocket—neon vapor could not exist at the temperatures in their vicinity—visual

input gave no clue as to what was going on. The world was formless.

The clouds pressed in closer to them, and the sound of crackling and snapping was brought to their ears by the tenuous gas around them. Brendan felt the first tentative surgings of the gas against the suit. Somewhere, electrostatic discharges were occurring in the mist. He upgraded his gyro control, just in case.

Suddenly the dam burst. The simple circulation of their weather pattern gave way to the extraordinary pressure at its center and broke into chaos. Strong currents slammed across the armored men. Tem hadn't reset his inertial control secondaries, and he began to tumble until he did so. The gas pressure that surrounded him, his only real protection, began to shudder violently.

As he felt his body begin to pogo inside the suit, Brendan carefully analyzed their position—they couldn't take much more of this. They had penetrated the surface to a depth of about four hundred meters. It wouldn't be long until they broke into the weird cavity, if that's what was going to happen.

The tumult grew stronger, and even the gyroscopes were having a difficult time keeping them stable. Another thirty meters or so, thought Brendan, and we will be there. . . .

Unexpectedly, they hit bottom. Something soft gave way beneath their feet and, if the instruments were correct, rebounded slowly, without secondary flexes. The neon, now mixed with a hundredth part of argon and methane, still boiled and swirled around them, but it was growing weaker. Brendan bent down and jabbed a steel-rigid finger into the surface. It was resilient, almost like a kind of soft wood. He scored it and the depression quickly healed itself. He shared his findings with Krzakwa.

He generated an image of the man's face for himself and studied its convolutions. "So. Now what do you think?"

The Selenite shook his head. "I . . . refuse to speculate." He studied the data that were being reported to him. Some light was making its way down through the piled-up gases above. The vapors were rapidly dissipating as he watched.

"Doesn't matter if you do or not. I think . . ."

"Shut up, damn you!" Krzakwa was biting at his lower lip, sucking in some hairs from his beard.

Sealock grinned to himself. "Right," he said.

It cleared. They were standing on a flat surface of a dull blue-gray color, almost obscured by a thin layer of small, glassy nodules. The walls of the hole they had dug rose up and up, seemingly solid, about three hundred meters around. Tem looked up and saw a shaft of sunlight slanting across the mouth of the hole.

"Well," said Sealock, "does this look like rock to you?"

"No." Krzakwa let out a long, slow whisper of breath. "It's time to say it. Artifact."

"I guess we've found a little adventure, after all."

Brendan cleared a small area, scraping the surface with his foot to knock the little beads flying in slow arcs. When he was satisfied that a large enough area was clean, he bent over and played his photochips over it, straining his suit systems to tell him anything they could about the material. He looked up at Tem. "Again: what do you think?"

"We need better instruments." He pulled a geologist's hammer from its waist clip and, kneeling also, slammed the pointed end down. It left a small dimple that slowly sprang back to normal. "You tell me, Brendan. What inert material stays pliable at 43 degrees Kelvin?"

"I might as well be the one to say it this time: *alien* artifact. This is not our tech."

"Sayyarrin's floor is relatively uncratered—but even so, that surface is *old*. If Jana's right, we're talking millions of years. Maybe billions."

"What's that?"

Brendan pointed to a place on the hole's wall, where a thin, dark, ruler-straight line over 250 meters high was embedded. It went almost all the way back to the surface. Tem was laughing uncontrollably. He finally got control of himself, breathing heavily, tears running down his face. "That's a fucking fin. This is getting ridiculous."

"Guess so. I feel peculiar." Brendan stood, followed by the other.

"Want to dig it out with *Polaris*?"

"No. We might get killed—that would be an irony I could do without. Let's go home and get the ion drill—also some friends."

"Good thought. Shall we call ahead?"

"Uh . . . somebody might be listening."

The idea penetrated, and they turned to go.

Polaris came over the horizon, not yet braking from the transfer ellipse that had carried it from Aello. The dim white pinpoint sped ten degrees across the mystery of stars called Berenice's Hair and intruded upon the starkly bright dipper of the Great Bear. Slowly, it became a real thing: a tiny burst of light and it began to fall. Then, a few kilometers up, it began braking in earnest, spearing down as it grew until every detail could be made out. The silent, translucent flame quickly used up delta-v, modifying the ship's velocity so that it nearly matched that of the Ocypetan surface. About half a kilometer up, the flame died and the ship began to fall, as if through pitch. when it was only a few tens of meters up, the engine vented an invisible mist of cold hydrogen gas which swept the ice viciously. No flame would disturb the fragile solidity of the landing area. The ship slowed, stopped dead, and then drifted down, bouncing once in a slow motion.

Sealock and Krzakwa strode into the central room of the CM, exhaustion lining their faces, and looked about at the inhabitants and their varieties of boredom. Sealock shook his head slowly, grin broadening and becoming softer. "Tem, why don't you tell them what's going on?"

Krzakwa shrugged, rubbing a hand across the back of his neck, looking puzzled. "I, uh . . ." He stopped, cleared his throat, and went on: "this is going to be hard to accept. We found something on Aello . . ."

Jana had come out of her compartment and was staring at the two travelers, wondering just what it was that she sensed in their demeanor. "What? What did you find?"

He smiled faintly and spread his hands before her, palms up. "Well . . . It was a . . . thing . . . an artifact."

There was a moment of silence, a nonreaction that made Krzakwa wonder if they'd heard him, if his statement had somehow failed to penetrate their conscious-

ness. Finally, from his position in the corner, Prynne said, "Huh?"

"What do you mean?" asked Ariane. She hadn't moved and both her face and voice had remained bland, as if she were asking for the time of day.

"Artifact is an understatement, Ari. . . ." He looked at her and thought, Jesus. How the fuck am I going to put this? He tried to come up with a way and realized that, whatever he said, it was going to be outré. . . . They were going to be talking about something not only outside of human experience but outside of expectability as well. "Hell, why don't I just say it: we found a God damned enormous alien spaceship stuck inside the moon. . . ." He looked at their faces and saw the beginning of incredulity. "I'm not kidding. . . . It was kilometers across, under the ice of Sayyarrin. . . ."

If air could be called dumbstruck, it was this air, now. Jana stood up straight, rising a little into the air. She opened her mouth, as if to speak, then gagged and closed her eyes. She swayed in the air and drifted slowly to the floor.

Demogorgon went to where she had fallen and propped her torso up, saying, "Jana . . . Hey! Jana?"

Her eyes opened, and the look inside the lids was not pleasant to see. She did not speak.

"I don't believe it," said John. "Why didn't you radio the information to us?"

"You may not care," said Sealock, "but that thing's ours until we decide otherwise. We decided to avoid the risk of having a signal intercepted, by anyone. I brought the RAW bubble out of *Polaris*. You can verify everything for yourself."

"But . . ."

"Just tap the fucking think! We'll talk later."

As with most things ancient and alien, it's human presumption that gets the colonists into trouble. Nothing so old or so completely removed from human experience can possibly be owned—at least in the way we understand the concept. When Tem, Brendan, and the colonists begin to explore the ancient ship, they will be diving into an

experience that will end two of their lives—and certainly change them all.

ABOUT THE AUTHOR

MICHAEL CAPOBIANCO is a founding partner and CEO of Not-Polyoptics, a software company specializing in orphan computers. An amateur astronomer and eclipse chaser, he is a member of the International Occultation Timing Association. *Burster* is his second novel. His first novel, in collaboration with William Barton, was *Iris*. They have just finished their second novel together, *Fellow Traveler*.

From multiple Hugo and Nebula Award-winner

DAVID BRIN

comes his most important novel to date

EARTH

When a laboratory experiment goes awry, allowing a microscopic black hole to sink into the Earth's core, scientists search frantically for a way to retrieve it, only to discover that another black hole already exists there—one that could destroy the entire planet within two years.

But **Earth** is much more than an edge-of-the-seat thriller. From an underground lab in New Zealand to a space station in Low Earth Orbit, from an endangered-species conservation ark in Africa to a home in New Orleans, it is a novel peopled with extraordinary characters and challenging new ideas, set in an incredibly real future.

With **Earth,** David Brin has provided us with a profound testament about our responsibility to our planet—a message so stirring it transcends every genre to embrace and inspire us all.

EARTH

A Selection of the Book-of-the-Month Club
and the Quality Paperback Book Club

◆

Now available in hardcover
wherever Bantam Spectra Books are sold

AN154

His first short story collection in seven years!

TALES FROM PLANET EARTH

Arthur C. Clarke

◆

From the author of **Childhood's End, 2001: A Space Odyssey, Rendezvous with Rama,** and **Rama II,** comes an unparalleled collection of some of his finest short fiction, speculating about the fate of our world in the years to come. Included in this dazzling array are classic works such as "The Lion of Comarre," "The Deep Range," and "The Wall of Darkness," along with some stories which have rarely seen print since their first publication. Illuminating the volume are illustrations by Michael Whelan, the most honored science fiction artist of all time.

A major collection of stories filled with bold ideas and startling imagery, **Tales from Planet Earth** will be a landmark addition to the libraries of Arthur C. Clarke's fans the world over.

A Bantam Spectra Trade Paperback
Coming in May, 1990

AN 146